Cameron Lost

When Found Is Different Than We Believe

Craig Matthews

Published by

Craig Matthews Media, L.L.C.

Cameron Lost

Permissions for quotations or use may be sent to:

Craig Matthews Media
P.O. Box 611235
Port Huron, Michigan 48061-1235

This book is a work of fiction and in no way describes any particular person living or dead.

Cover by: Mark Coon
Editing by: Larry Giroux
Formatting: Nancy Kuykendall
Proofreading: Tracy Jones
Bruce Daney – medical and firearms consultant
Greg May – firefighting consultant

Visit www.CraigMatthewsMedia.com for news and information on this and other exciting titles.

THE UNVEILED SERIES
Book #2

Endorsements

"Cameron Lost" is a book that – from the opening pages to the very end— I did not want to set down. Every reader, especially those that have spent time in Michigan, will connect with the characters and the places they pass through. The story is about Cameron, his life journey and the demons that hound him. It is also a story about the people we encounter along our own journeys and the impact that they have on our lives. And maybe life just isn't as random as we might think. Cameron Lost is a book that will stay on my shelf, both to be loaned out and re-read somewhere down the trail."

Dean Smith, Michigan

"Craig Matthews has touched upon pure humanity in his book, **"Cameron Lost"**. Every reader will see a piece of him or herself within the pages of the story. Readers will likely recognize others they know as well. We all have demons to some degree at some point in time. When we least expect it, or even recognize it, devine help may by our side. Reading **"Cameron Lost"** may help each reader help themselves sooner than later."

Nancy Kuykendall – Author – Inspirational Nonfiction and Fiction

"Compelling characters wrestle with their beasts, their demons, even while attempting to forgive and encourage others. Cameron does something unspeakable to his family, knowing it can never be forgiven—by God, by anyone. His journey through his misery takes him on a real one, hiking and hiding in Michigan's Upper Peninsula. Known by his trail name as Caveman, this miserable misfit meets Butter, also a trail name, who runs a place called the Oasis. Theirs is such a compelling friendship, deeper than that. Cameron Lost takes the reader on a journey through rich UP vistas while sharing in Cameron's losses and terrible choices and misery to eventual redemption".

Joy Neal Kidney – Author of the Leora's Letters Book Series

"Craig Matthews coaxes his readers onto a tightrope, offering a seemingly innocuous choice between simply enjoying his artful prose and peering into the abyss of the central character's world. Amazingly, both choices reveal the restorative power of faith."

Dobie Mcarthur – Author of the Civil War book series

One

Cameron Lost

— Section One —

"The End of the Beginning"

"He is no fool who gives what he cannot keep
to gain what he cannot lose."
Jim Elliot

Spin

"Help me!"

The room was spinning again.

"Help me! Please!"

Whoosh. Whoosh. Whoosh. As he forced his eyes to stay open, the sliding glass door streaked past, dragging the drab wall behind it. Blinds tilting against centrifugal forces, dashing round. Whoosh. Pictures on the wall followed suit, twisting against the pull. Grabbing for the rails on his bed, he tried to steady himself and force the ride to a stop through the strength of his will, straining for a break lever in each clinched fist.

"Why can't I make this stop?" he asked through gritted teeth as his head leaned into the phantom wind. A few more harrowing moments and he gave in to the uncertainty, closing his eyes again, and the powerful push from the left stopped driving. The darkness allowed him to coast.

"Breathe. Just breathe," he thought and steadied himself.

Gliding in a distant canoe, spinning in an eddy, like he had done a hundred times. Those river memories ushered in the trees in full bloom just above his head. As if he had come through the intense power of the rapids, to the place where gravity's surging was swallowed by the sudden depth of the river. Everything slowed. His boat turned, not out of control, or frightening. After a deep, invigorating breath, he relaxed, resting his trusty wooden oar across his lap. Above him, in his mind's eye, the maples and oaks were gliding by like row after row of maidens in a glorious ballroom. The illusive peace settled in like a damp morning fog, so long as he could manage to keep his eyes shut.

This was a sweet spot, coasting in a virtual canoe while the volume of nature was turned up with each gentle spin, like an inquisitive child twisting a knob on a dusty phonograph in a bygone era. One thing he knew for certain was hearing the sounds of nature soothed him and brought his whirling world under control. As long as he could keep his eyes closed, the pull slowed and life returned to the canoe on the river, to a seat on the edge of a precipice overlooking a lush valley or majestic sea.

From a bush, desperately clinging to the sandy riverbank, a gentle chirp, chirp, chirp. A content goldfinch welcoming the morning. Across the stream came the response from several of his comrades, as they danced among the thistles. *"They call them a charm of goldfinch,"* he thought and smiled, puzzled as to where he picked that up. Gliding, he recognized the familiar "pureep pureep, pureep," of a robin calling from high up in the maple canopy, and he pointed to the bird, as if showing a friend.

The sudden shift of his arm caused the oar to clunk on the edge of the fiberglass craft, sending a deep note rippling across the surface of the water, pausing nature's symphony. The squirrels, birds, and frogs stopped to take notice, frozen in place, becoming quiet, seeking to identify the sound and its source.

"It's okay, it's just me," he said to his audience, smiling as they continued their joyous songs.

"Hey!" a voice thundered above him, intruding on his peace while grabbing his arm tipping him out of his boat. The oar on his lap and the cushion beneath his butt were ejected as he splashed face down into cold reality. The canoe surged away while his arms and legs were flailing, thrashing, grabbing for something, anything— to get him out of the depths.

"I can't breathe! I can't breathe!" He screamed as his head broke through the surface of the deep. Sheer panic enveloped his mind as his heart slammed against his chest, while his arms and legs were caught in some sort of net.

"How?" he asked, while pulling, fighting, and tugging, being drawn deeper.

"Where?" Bubbles shot from his mouth and nose. He yanked harder, unable to move past a fixed point. This was a desperate moment, as fear ripped his heart and soul.

Forcing his eyes wide open, the water and the boat flashed into beige walls, draining through the floor, as the carousel commenced its damnable spin. As reality replaced fantasy, he thought he could hear music from the center of the ride, just past the flashing lights and gentle beeps. He threw his head back to catch a glimpse of the middle. Slowly at first, but there was no ignoring the powerful thrust driving him down, pulling him around.

Without notice or hesitation the poles flipped in his bed and his head, his dizzy head, was pushed to the outside. He knew from a lifetime of experience these type of rides were the worst for him, feeling as if the floor were about to drop out of his personal Graviton. He struggled to lift his head as a desperate and demonic anxiety began flowing from his feet, like a dye in his blood.

"I want to go back to my river!" He screamed through clenched teeth.

"I want to go back to my river!" he said again. The veins on his neck and forehead bulged with a sudden hatred flashing across his eyes. His back arched against the pull at his feet and legs, while fresh tears stained his cheeks running down toward his ears.

"I want to go back!" He flashed his yellowed teeth in vicious anger.

The yelling caused no change on the face of the woman who was touching his arm. He grabbed for her but his limbs were weighed down, failing to listen fully to his commands.

"Why am I stuck?" he asked the insolent woman standing next to him. She smiled but ignored his question as the room sped up. She was spinning with him in time but didn't seem to be affected as walls and windows flashed by her. Faster now. "I know you. Why won't you answer me? I am stuck on this ride and you refuse to help me!" His bright blue eyes blazed with a confused rage at the strangely familiar face. She was smiling at him swiping at his hair and yet, was unwilling to help. Her mouth was moving but no clear sound was reaching his ears. Muffled grunts and groans accompanied the incessant grins from the ineffectual woman. She took pleasure from his entrapment, mocking him by not communicating in a way he could understand.

Dizziness fully invaded his skull and his empty stomach flip-flopped pushing upward against his lungs. He felt like retching and immediately began his controlled breathing exercises. In his mind the ultimate humiliation was puking your guts out in front of a stranger, familiar or not.

This silent woman had been hanging around a lot recently, she never seemed more than a few paces away. Touching his face, stroking his arm, caressing the inside of his hand, these things he could feel most of the time and it was both soothing and confusing. Every now and again she would lay the back of her warm hand across his forehead, like she was feeling for a fever or something. She checked his pulse and looked at her watch.

"Did she think I was sick?" he wondered.

"Was that pity in her eyes?" he thought he recognized it. *"Or tears?"* he questioned.

Speaking of sick, the dizzy won. He reached over the side of his bed and vomited across her blue jeans. The second spurt landed on her bare feet. The Lamaze breathing techniques he had learned long ago failed him, as the carousel wrung his guts out again and again.

"Maybe you should answer me the next time," he thought and even smirked while he laid back, searching for his canoe again. She wiped the yellow bile from his face while sleep beckoned and won.

Pause

How much time? He was not sure, as his brain was still foggy, but he did recognize the sun was on his side of the house. The carousel lights blinked and the rhythmic notes still sang, but they were now behind his head. Morning had retreated into the past along with an apparent rain shower as the trees outside the French doors hung heavy with moisture. The blinds had been pulled open, revealing the scene over the top of his feet.

Drops from the gutter break their bonds and splash somewhere out of sight. Glistening gold from the light of the sun behind them, refracting the brightness into a multi-colored hue, like a rainbow was melting and dropping off one glowing piece at a time, altered on this side of his nap, elongated. The water drops from the gutters edge become streaks of light, still testifying to the unending draw of gravity. They slow their bond breaking process with the forest green gutter, giving way to the relentless pull. Like a passing meteorite, they flash toward the ground, out of sight.

"Everything must come down," he remembered. *"The end of all meet on barren ground, gathered to a place without distinction of sight or sound. Whether its writhing in pain or passing in sleep, everyone goes down, down so deep. Fight it as you may, scuffle and swear, but dirt was our beginning and dirt is the final coat we wear."* His foggy head rolled from side to side as the old words teased at his consciousness.

Even though the spinning had stopped he gazed through dulled eyes and longed to return to the river he had rediscovered that morning. His river. The peace of nature had always soothed him like soaking in a hot tub, relieving tensions, centering, and grounding him.

"Walking would be better," he thought, while feeling like a prisoner in his bed, glancing toward his feet. Then he realized, he could close his eyes and find his freedom. It called him out of his body as the fresh scent of rich earth teased at his nostrils.

Rising and leaving the canoe on the sandy shore, his familiar hiking boots grab the ground as he steps away from his captors, leaving his bed and the silent but vigilant woman behind, hopefully for good. His favorite walking stick appears, shimmering in his right hand. He eyes it with a familiar smile.

He had embedded it with his sweat and grease from his years on the trail, sealing his trusty companion against weather and wind. It was coated and soaked with his personal linseed oil, bathed from the sweat of miles of strenuous pulls against time and gravity. The distance they had traveled together, the rivers and mountains they had crossed, the innumerable places they witnessed had bonded them. They had walked into displays of glorious beauty and had fought off inquisitive beasts, experiencing nature in its perfection, along with its actual terrors, and in all of those moments, he had his trusty stick to lean on. He had spent years carving the maple branch. Stripping its bark and notching a trench for each of his fingers and thumb to wrap around. The corners he carefully rounded after splitting his forehead open with a stumble. He sharpened the bottom end to a point, hardening it patiently with a campfire and grinding it in the sand.

He remembered a particular campsite. On the shores of Superior, in the middle of a solo hike many years ago, far enough away from the fire to be comfortable while watching God's magnificent end of the day display, he rested. Whimsical clouds had become the canvas for all the colors to be painted on the sky. He never tired of these memories, and often yearned for their comfort, when saddled with the ordinaries of life. Sunsets and sunrises seemed to be the confirmation he looked for, the proverbial cherry on the top of the ice cream sundae. It was reassuring to rest at the end of a struggle against the trail, watching God paint his sky.

It was there that he met him. It was not a cordial greeting. He barely noticed him at all while grinding the smoldering end of his walking stick, spinning it back and forth between the palms of his hands to a finished point. While inspecting his work he noticed a distant sound. Distinct in its nature and tone but unfamiliar. As he paused to listen, it was gone. Moments later it returned. One beat. Then two. He glanced away from the sunset spectacle over each of his shoulders. Noticing nothing, he returned to his task of firing, grinding, and watching the sky.

While in his tent after witnessing the glory of the night sky, he heard it again. Straining to listen, it sounded like footfalls through the wilderness. Not the careless type of walking in the woods when branches and limbs are snapping, beneath the weight of careless feet. No. More like the walking of a tremendous beast through a pine forest. Muffled, yet powerful. This would have to be a bear, he first guessed. There was more to the sound than an ordinary animal foraging. Almost as if one of its legs were wounded and being dragged. Thump, grind then there was no sound for hours.

This is where he met the dragging feet, the one who stalked him the latter half of his adult life. The relentless trail beast who never rests. He avoided direct attacks, but not the terror.

The Beast, or better said, his Beast, chased him over wooded hills and through grassy fields. Hounded his walks through forest and along the shores of the thousands of miles he hiked.

"Where can I run?" he asked in a thick sweat.

His opened eyes brought him back to reality and there she stood like the guard at the tomb of the unknown soldier. Was his heart fluttering with anger or residual fear from his Beast? Then the hidden terror gripped at him, nudging him while he lay defenseless.

"Will this woman standing over me, offer me up as a sacrifice while I am strapped to this infernal bed?" he worried.

"I am dead since I cannot run any longer. Maybe its another test, or just a ruse used to stir me to fear and cripple my thinking? But he, he is so close, I can feel his hot, rancid breath on my shoulder and his only desire is to consume my life. I must hide. I must run. Flee to the other side of life itself." His eyes closed with the thought and a warm wave splashed paralysis through his veins and sleep returned.

This is it

"Is this all I am? Has my life been boiled down to a slurry of concentrated pain? Like all of the pressure of the gathered moments are pressing down upon my chest in some sort of sadistic inverted pyramid. Trapped on this bed, shackled, and imprisoned by memories and fear is all I know. Finding solace in dreams of worlds gone by or days consumed by the relentless machine called time. My allotment has expired in dread. Who am I? What am I doing here? Is there a lesson? Am I supposed to look for God in all of this? My mind is bent and twisted with pain and uncertainty as I thrash against my final foe. My life has been wrung out like a twisted garment after being ground on the washboard. I am waiting for the snap of my neck at the end of time's rope. I am saddened by all of the loss as my years are unfurled and pinned to a line for every passerby to examine. I have many stains and spots grimed into my soul as relentless eyes gaze and judge me. I am not whole, in fact I'm filled with holes, torn as the fabric of my backless gown. I try to cover and hide, but I can only dance so fast to distract the stares of my judges." Warm veins return, ushering in another burst of smooth blackness.

Nightmare

"Fire!"

"There's a house on fire!" He uses the bottom of his fist to pound on the front door of the bungalow across the street. It is obvious that no one is home, but he is alone and the pressurized fog of the moment distorts his thinking. The glass in the long window next to the door jumps as he rapidly pounds the steel entry. He glances back over his shoulders to see new brighter flames inside what must be the front living room, dance up the curtains. This causes fear to surge and violence to explode from his hands. Now both hands hammered the beige steel door. Nothing inside the house gives any clue that anyone could hear his pummeling. He presses his face into the glass, cupping one hand next to his face.

"There's nobody home!" With the realization he turns and runs toward the house on fire. He grabs for his cell phone as he sprints, searching his pockets for the telltale sign.

"Where is it?" It was not with him.

He looks up toward the front window again and instinctively knows that he is out of time. He is certain that he must act or the people inside are going to die. He bolts for the porch hoping his earlier failed efforts to open the front door were because of the heat. *"Maybe the door was swollen,"* he hopes.

Arriving he slams his fists, which unbeknownst to him were already showing signs of bruising. He screams at the top of his lungs and dances toward the edge of the concrete porch to get a look inside the window. The curtains are turning into flaming cinders falling to the floor and across the couch which had its back to the window. He steps down behind the holly bushes and uses the flat of his left hand to smack the glass. The ring on his hand sends a high pitched ting echoing through the neighborhood and into the home. He can see flames inside the house, through an archway into the kitchen, where the fire is more intense. This realization causes him to shout louder over his shoulder, but his shouting, banging, and tinging all fall on deaf ears. He needs to act. He has to get inside and rescue the sleeping people.

Behind him is a low retaining wall built from precast concrete blocks. He stands behind the bushes inside of the flower bed next to the window. He pushes through the holly's and scratches his arms on the shrubs, stepping down he tries to pick up a solid block but it won't budge. Forgetting that when those stones are set in place a couple of beads of construction adhesive keep the wall solid. He had torn down these walls in his past and knew the adhesive sometimes didn't budge even when being beat on with a sledge hammer. He bends over and begins to frantically test each block until, on the ninth attempt, he finds a loose one. He snatches it up and circles back to the front porch while the flames in the front window explode as the couch fabric ignites.

The block smashes through the window in the front door, crashing onto the hardwood floor with a spray of broken glass and with it a wind whistles past his ears like the fire itself is inhaling, filling its gigantic lungs with needed oxygen. Two upstairs windows blow out, sending glass fragments onto the lawn and a tongue of fire back out the front door. The intruder covers his face with crossed arms as the fire mercilessly shoots toward him.

All of the hair on his arms and exposed parts of his face are singed and the skin on the bottom of his forearms blister with the fiery greeting.

"Ahhh!" he screams as he is thrown off of the porch. The fire recedes into the house, acting like a gigantic chimney, drawing in the oxygen rich outside air, burning it inside the firebox which used to be the living room and spewing the thick black smoke through the blown out windows.

Standing up ready to charge inside, he wails into the inferno. "Get out! You have to get out!"

His eyes open and he was still on his bed, pulling against his restraints. The woman was stroking at his face to comfort him as he thrashed.

"He must of had another nightmare," she thought.

For him, it was getting harder to distinguish between dreams and reality. When he could focus his eyes, the sun was pushing against the horizon and beginning to sink into the earth again while his head was still trying to pull out of the stupor of the other world. It seemed so real, so vivid. He felt his arms and realized that his hair was still in place, not singed by fire. He was able to relax a bit, but the skin on his forearms was tender to the touch. As he turned his palms up toward the ceiling, blisters and boils appeared on his bright red skin and he fell back in sudden pain and shock.

"What the hell?" he attempted to say, but she heard a muffled scream.

"Hey have a look at this," the woman called out to the visiting nurse typing on a lap top. The dining room table had been pushed off to the side to make room for the medical bed and equipment.

"Wow! What is that?" the nurse asked.

"It looks like blisters from a burn."

"It does. Did you put anything on his arms?" She hurried over to inspect the man's arms.

"Like what?"

"Lotion or some kind of soap, maybe?"

"No. I haven't put anything on his skin since the chap stick on his lips this morning."

"That wouldn't caused this," she said while looking at his burns. "I'm gonna have to treat and get a wrap on it."

What?

"My arms are free," he touched his bearded face. It seemed forever since he felt his own face. *"I think I want to take a..."* He couldn't recall the word for the place you go stand and warm water pours down over your bare skin.

"What is it's name?" he whispered.

He longed to feel warmth and wash the greasy feeling off of his skin. His hands were touching his face trying to remember what he looked like. He dug into the corner of each eye and freed a crusty adhesion which stuck to his fingertips. It was green like it had come from his nose. His mother's smiling face danced into his vision. Her lips were moving, he knew she was telling him what the things he pulled out of his eyes were, but there was no volume to the memory. *"Had she lost her voice?"* he wondered and his growing sense of frustration began to put pressure on his chest, but he couldn't remember the word for that either.

He stared blankly at the green lesions on his index fingers and wondered if he was losing his mind. *"A man brought them. Or was it a song? Maybe it was the man gave him a song about his dreams?"* he thought.

It was then that he noticed the wraps on his arms. They were... he didn't like the way they made him feel and an image of a growling dog came to mind. A black dog who was baring its teeth and the fur on the scruff of its neck was standing up, trying to make himself appear larger than he already was. He decided that's what he felt like, a growling dog. His whole life was beginning to feel like that mad animal who couldn't remember the right words to say or think. He flicked the object from his finger and returned to probing his face, picking at the things on his cheek. Digging at the itchy places. Wiping the sweat and grease. Wondering where it all had come from.

She returns. Her face is different. He knows the form, but cannot explain. "What is the word for that?" he bellows out the sentence but it is received as a growl. His arm is held down again and he cannot touch his face. The towel she is pressing against his face returns to her with crimson blotches that she restores with a glob of grease.

"She is the giver of the grease," he thinks and his inner dog growls with more intensity. The warmness invade his veins, the dog lies down and resigns himself to a nap. Before sleep drags him away, he thinks, "shower."

Two

Cameron Lost

— Section Two —

"Burned"

"I stand amid the dust o' the mounded years—
My mangled youth lies dead beneath the heap.
My days have crackled and gone up in smoke,
Have puffed and burst as sun-starts on a stream.
Yea, faileth now even dream."
Francis Thompson

* Mirror Lake *

"Would you look at that!"

"Sure, is somethin'."

Two men, two very different men, sat side-by-side on the edge of a five-hundred-foot cliff overlooking a lake to the south. A few white pillowed clouds passed between them and the forest canopy below. The clouds, along with the shadows they cast, marched across their view from west to east as light winds pushed them along. The hikers munched on a snack while taking in the iconic Lake of the Clouds in Michigan's Upper Peninsula.

The lake below looked like it may have been round at one time but God's fingers pulled and stretched it out like a piece of pristine deep blue taffy. The backcountry area offered no access for power boats, cars, or off-road vehicles. People wanting to experience the undefiled waters of the lake below could hike to it into the middle of the sixty thousand acres of old growth forest. The only access to the lake was a trail at each end and the only camping area was a single camper cabin which lay tucked back in the woods, away from the rocky shoreline, near its southwest corner.

Sweat rings had enveloped the backpackers arm pits and backs from the hike up to the escarpment. Their ancient and outdated packs were sitting thirty feet behind them, leaning against a three- foot-high stone wall. That buffer was the boundary for the viewing area, which both of the men figured was their duty to ignore. Life felt much more real to the old friends to live on the edge of the cliff than to be contained by an artificial barrier erected to keep brainless sheep people from falling over the precipice.

Both men were comfortable with silence, more than just comfortable, they enjoyed it. Their friendship didn't require words. In each other's company they were secure enough to allow time to pass with nothing but a breeze and the sounds of nature, along with a few tourist snapping pictures.

They also knew each other well enough to sense when something was bothering the other. They could feel when life was out of kilter. It was this intuition which motivated Cam to invite Butter on a week-long hike through the Porcupine Mountains in the first place.

"Thanks, man."

"For what?" Cam replied.

"For this," Butter opened his hand to point at the valley and the view.

"I didn't create this," he said as a goofy grin crept across his face.

"No, you didn't. You're good, but not that good," Butter said while watching another cloud come into view to his right. "But you did think enough about me to see that I needed this getaway."

"It seemed like you were up to your neck in all the pressure that comes with helping other people."

"In quicksand," Butter thought.

"But why did you come this time? It's not like I haven't asked you to come out with me on the trail before," Cam asked.

"You know, this is the first time I've strapped on a backpack for an overnight since I toppled over into that snow bank?"

"That's over twenty-five years ago. The question remains, Butter. Why now, with me?"

"For real?"

"Yeah."

"I was more than ready for a getaway before I fell over into a different kind of pile. I'm a slow learner, but when I noticed an emptiness in your eyes I had never seen before, Cam, then I wanted to spend some time with you," Butter said and tossed another cashew into his mouth.

"Oh?"

"I don't know if those guys stealing your boots flipped a switch inside of you that I can't wrap my fingers around, or if it's somethin' else."

"How so?"

"It's just a feeling in my gut that says you ain't right, and I needed to intervene."

"That's been true my whole life, Butter," Cam began to laugh with a shortened version of his outrageous cackle.

"No, I'm not talking about your general weirdness," Butter started winding up his deep belly laugh like a steam locomotive.

"Right on."

"I've known you for a long time Cam. You're one of the most thoughtful people I've ever met, and I know somethin' is off in here," Butter said while pointing to his own chest.

"Yeah, maybe. But I actually think I've been managing it pretty well."

"You do? Hiding out here in the woods, for how long?" Butter followed with a one syllable laugh.

"Well, it may be hard to believe and I know it takes a lot of effort, but yeah, I think I am."

"You're not."

Those words echoed off the stone-cold walls inside Cam's heart and made him pause. "*He can see me,*" he thought, but tried to shut the idea down. His arm flickered in his vision, like it had been doing for the last few weeks. It was as if his arms became transparent right in front of his eyes. He could not see them, or better, he could see right through them. With a flicker, fear surged inside his chest. He gulped it back down with some water. He would not be sharing those visions with anyone.

"Managin' ain't really livin', Capt'n."

"How so?"

"To start, you are admitting a real issue exists. I know there is a problem. Giggles and Beamer know there's a problem. People who camp by you know somethin' ain't right, Cam. Obviously, your abandoned family knows you've disconnected from 'em. It seems like everyone who gets close to you lately knows you're going through it. Everyone except, Cam that is. That's why I knew I had to come out hiking with you, brother."

Butter decided to let those words soak in for a while and went back to picking out individual cashews from the plastic zippered bag, tossing them into his mouth, and admiring the clouds rolling on by below them. The forest canopy was showing signs of fall with a few trees already making the color change. The speckles of yellow from the aspens, along with red and orange from the maples, dotted the landscape all the way out to the horizon. It was a perfect day in terms of the weather in an area known for a finicky climate, especially during the first half of September. Upper seventy's and sunny was a gift from God when it could just as easily be a miserable forty with a driving rain.

Cam was stewing on what his friend had said. He decided to crack open the door with his friend. "This despicable beast has been really hounding me, but."

"Don't tell him!" the voice whispered inside his head. *"He'll never believe you!"* His left arm flickered again.

"How so?"

"Everywhere I turn it seems to be there with its dragging foot, pacing me. Stalking me. It's not just every once in while anymore. Even my dreams are agonizing, like I'm being tortured for a different crime every couple of days."

"What does it want, Cam?" Butter asked. With Cam's ever-present sunglasses perched on top of his head Butter took notice of the dark circles around his friend's eyes. He looked exhausted.

"I haven't asked that!" Cam snapped.

"He thinks you're crazy," the voice thundered inside his head. His right arm disappeared from his vision. To him it appeared the canteen he was holding was floating in the air.

"What?" Butter asked.

"Don't talk about him like that, he can hear you!" the voice said.

Cam hesitated by pulling in a long breath and fought back against the illusion. He wondered how much he should reveal. Insecurity pounded at his head and his veins. He was not sure how Butter would respond to this obvious weakness. Deep inside he knew this was the right path, but he needed to walk down it cautiously.

"I know it wants to destroy me. It seeks to end my life. Or at least make me miserable," Cam said.

"How do you know?" Butter asked.

"You're a fool!" the voice said.

"It's always wanted to destroy me, to ruin everything."

"Just cause someone is chasing you doesn't automatically mean they want to kill you, Cam."

"How can you know?" Cam's eyes lit up with anger at the mere suggestion that the beast was anything other than a personalized evil.

"I think we can know because it's been chasing but hasn't caught you yet."

"He's going to hear you," the voice warned again.

"I've managed to keep a step ahead," Cam said and his arm came back into view.

"Didn't you tell me that you are being punished for breaking some kind of laws?"

"Kinda."

"To be brutally honest, Cam, that sounds crazy. Beyond that, if this beast can know your offenses, why can't it catch you?"

"SHUT UP!" The voice screamed inside his head.

"Because I have learned over the last few years how to deal with it! How to outsmart it," Cam said.

"But you just said it has been hounding you more."

"Yeah?"

"So, you aren't controlling it."

"I know if I can put out of my mind anything to do with it, then it tends to leave me alone."

"Your sayin' it knows when you're thinking about it?" Butter asked.

"Yeah, like it gets a hold of the electrical activity in my brain when the wavelengths are fixed on thinking about him."

"Now you have gone too far," the voice warned.

"You could wear a tinfoil hat and block out those cosmic wavelengths," Butter used his hands, one on each side of his head with fingers extended, to give a physical picture of the wavelengths bombarding his thoughts, and laughed.

"Funny, but maybe."

"He thinks you're an idiot," the voice said.

"You just said you know how to control it but, apparently that's no longer working."

Cam sat in silence thinking about what Butter had just asked him.

"I know he thinks you're an idiot now," the voice whispered.

"I don't think you're managing this beast, but it sure is controlling you," Butter said.

"I told you!" the voice said.

"You must think I've gone insane! Did you come out here to put me away?"

"No, not insane, Cam. Oppressed, but not crazy," Butter said in as calm, serious, and steady of a voice as he could muster.

"Here I was thinking I was helping you and you came out thinking you were helping me?" Cam asked while staring into the man's dark brown eyes, trying to calm himself down as his arms stopped flickering.

"Relax man. I'm on your side." Butter touched his shoulder.

Cam lowered his eyes and took in a long breath.

"Kinda how this life thing happens, I guess. Don't forget, I walked a long trail away from everything at one point in my life, too," Butter said.

The pair touched water bottles in recognition and appreciation for each other's concern. The nagging voice went back into its room inside Cam's heart and slammed the door like an angry teenager.

"Hey mom! Why are they sitting out there on the edge of the cliff?" The five-year-old boy was wearing a baseball cap and pointing from the behind the wall on the overlook deck, as Cam and Butter just sent a smile back in his direction. His mother did not appreciate the fact that two grown men would so blatantly disregard the clear rules written on a sign mounted on the wall the men had stepped over.

"No, it's dangerous," she said louder than necessary while nodding at the sign.

"I wanna go out there and look down!"

"No, you'd fall off the cliff."

"They're not falling, I'll just sit down like them," the boy said pointing again.

"No. They're breaking the rules. We don't break the rules that are in place to keep you safe."

Both Cam and Butter turned away from the woman who was trying to impose her will on the resting men and just smiled to themselves, allowing her complaint to waft away on the gentle breeze.

Half an hour later the two men were on the trail, slowly descending from the escarpment, while their knees objected to the steep incline and the weight on their backs. Walking poles helped alleviate the discomfort, but nothing could replace some of the cartilage in their knees that had been worn through the countless miles spent hiking. Neither complained with words but both understood the other's pain. This was why they had scheduled to hike just a few miles each day in the interior of the park. Their Mirror Lake campsite was only another four miles south where they would be staying in a cabin.

* Fancy Campin' *

As soon as Butter saw the log cabin accommodations, he declared the whole scene to be "fancy campin'" and was overjoyed with the elaborate back woods shelter. Other than staying dry, they would not have to put up the tent and sleep on the lumpy ground because there were wooden bunk beds built into the walls. Both men were carrying the extra weight of a self-inflating sleeping pad, which allowed them to sleep through the night without their hips and back waking them in protest, except for, like all old men, the need to pee. The picnic tables, one inside and one just off the porch, were a nice touch since the only thing to sit on in most backcountry sites was the cold ground. The cabin was not equipped with indoor plumbing and the latrine was forty feet into the woods behind the rental.

Upon waking the view from the front porch was stunning. Looking east over the pristine waters of Mirror Lake there were a couple ancient white pine trees to see past to catch the glimmering sunrise. Branches on those pines had been trimmed up ten feet to enable the view from the Adirondack chairs on the low deck.

Butter made his way out to the fire ring near the picnic table to stoke the fire he had sat by the evening before. Cam had claimed to be too tired to hang out so Butter spent his alone time staring into the dancing flames and watching the shooting stars jet past, leaving florescence streaks of light that reflected off the still waters. He figured the lake must have gotten its name from the fact that it was as calm as a mirror, being protected by the surrounding hills and the old growth forest.

Gently blowing air into last night's hidden coals forced smoke to begin rising up from the ashes. A couple more breaths and a tiny flame jumped up and caressed the new stack of twigs above it. Within minutes Butter was adding larger broken up pieces of dead branches and the fire was resurrected. He placed his covered titanium water pot on the edge of the fire to bring the lake water to a boil as the fire grew. Sitting back down onto one of the four upright logs that were used for seats around the fire, Butter reached up toward the sky as a yawn consumed his face, while several vertebrae snapped and popped up his spine.

"Oh, that was a good one," he smiled.

The screen door spring squealed against pressure as Cam exited the cabin with his goofy smile plastered all over his face. The grin was as if he knew something important and was going to share it with you whether you wanted him to or not. Butter knew it was coming as Cap't made his way off the porch while keeping his eyes on the lake in all of its morning splendor.

"Mornin'," Butter said over his shoulder.

"Hey."

"Sleep alright?"

"Yeah, for the most part," Cam was standing behind Butter and running his fingers through his mop of hair with one hand while holding his hat in the other.

"What does that mean?"

"I had to pee in the middle of the night and was going to go back to the outhouse but I didn't bring my flashlight, after wandering around for a couple minutes I just went behind a tree." Cam was talking louder than what the situation called for, like he was announcing to the world that he had lived through the night.

"You mean like every other man in the woods?"

"Right." Butter poked at the fire with a stick.

"Want me to go ask a park ranger for a rake?"

"Rake?"

"You know, for that mess on your head."

"I know, at least I got hair, buddy," Cam cackled so loud all the birds in the area stopped singing.

"I got hairs."

"Not much left on the top of your head these days."

"So, are we staying here tonight too?" Butter asked.

"Yeah, we are supposed to hike around the lake, up to Government Peak then back."

"My knees are killing me this morning. I'm taking a zero."

"That's fine we can hang out here." Cam replied.

"You can go explore if you'd like,"

"Naa, I'm tired. I'll take a zero and hang out here by the lake."

"Sounds like a plan." Cam was sitting behind Butter at the picnic table instead of on a log nearer to the fire. Those seats, Butter officially called hillbilly chairs. Four of them spread around the fire ring in a semi-circle. Cam was gently rubbing his forearms while looking away from the flames. Butter was not sure if he was going to cross into that subject first thing in the morning or not. The men were quiet for a long stretch, lost in their own thoughts.

Birds distracted the men as the hyper creatures returned to their squawking and singing while the early morning sun's rays reflected off the lake. The men were mesmerized by the scene while nursing warm drinks. Dragonflies were dancing on the shore, waking from their long night while mosquitoes hunted for blood, buzzing around Cam's face and nest of hair.

"I gotta ask you about the arm thing," Butter said, unable to wait any longer.

"Arm thing?"

"Yeah. Whenever you are by a fire, not that you ever get close to them, you actually do everything you can to stay away from them. Not only that, you've got this thing where you caress yourself when you are near one."

"Yeah," Cam said and his head sank.

"Yeah, what?"

Cam thought for a few moments about how to describe another one of his afflictions to his friend.

"It's like I'm allergic to the flames or the heat," he finally said.

"I've never heard of such a thing."

"Don't mean it ain't true, Butter."

"Alright. Alright. Good to know."

Staring off into nature interrupted their conversation and Butter was not sure how to proceed. He knew something was wrong but knew he couldn't force his friend to talk about it. A slight shift in the gentle breeze pushed smoke up into Butter's face and he fanned at the intrusion.

Cam, on the other hand had been trying to avoid this conversation for a very long time. He had used every technique available to him to dance around, change direction, bury, avoid, ignore, and deny its existence. Now the red blisters forming on his forearms couldn't be hidden any longer. Just the mention of the problem had brought the reaction on his skin. He felt naked while sitting in his shorts and stretched out wife beater t-shirt. On the inside he was planning on offering a partial explanation, figuring it would satisfy Butter's curiosity. That is what he was hoping for, but he was a long-time friend who knew him so well.

"Come on, Cam. I'm not going anywhere. You're not going anywhere. What do you have to lose?" Butter had turned his back to the fire, rotating a half turn on his hillbilly chair to face him.

"I can't lose this fight with him," Cam said surprised at his own sudden confession. He glanced away, then looked down as a surge of emotion welled up inside of him. Tears bubbled at the corners of his eyes, threatening to spill out and onto his beard. His blistered arms suddenly flickered in and out of eyesight.

"But we both know you can't win this all by yourself."

"We all have our own battles."

"But we're not supposed to fight alone, we need each other, Cam."

"I own this. This is my struggle to win."

"What? What do you own? For the life of me I can't figure this out." Butter was beginning to show some of the frustration he had been feeling.

"I have to figure it out Butter! It's my journey, my cross I have to bear."

A pair of hikers walked past trying not to interrupt their intense discussion. Neither of the men noticed them until they watched their backsides walking away.

"Tell me this, Cam. How did this all start?"

Cam remained quiet while staring past the flames and caressing his blistered arms. He winced at some hidden pain, searching for a way to verbalize the unspeakable.

"What is going on with your arms?"

"Happens around fire," Cam admitted.

"Looks like blisters!"

"Feels like them, too."

"How do you explain that?" Butter demanded.

"I don't. I hide it from everyone. I wear long sleeve shirts to cover them up. You're the first person to ask about them. You may even be the only one who has ever seen them."

"Not Caleb or Curtis?"

"No."

"Why?"

"I guess I'm too embarrassed, ashamed." Cam's head hung low.

"What's up with you and fire?"

"I have nightmares after I sit by the fire."

"How do you make it out here? We have to make fires all the time."

"Yeah. It's part of the price I have to pay to live where I want."

"That'd make me want to go back to civilization," Butter said.

Cam didn't reply, but he had thought about returning to live in a community many times. He just didn't know how he'd do it. How could he face them? What would he say?

Butter saw the man shut down right in front of his eyes. The blisters on his arms were bright red and looking like they wanted to burst and ooze.

"The water is done boiling. I can put the fire out if you want," he said after grabbing the pot with his fire gloves and setting it on the picnic table.

* Sinner *

The men spent the day resting and laughing, while occupying the real chairs on the front porch of the cabin. Butter noticed Cam change right before his eyes once he was away from the fire, he switched back into a more typical version of himself and the blisters on his forearms vanished with the move. Butter wanted to get him comfortable enough to be able to talk about what was going on without having him turn into an emotional mess and shut down. He waited and watched for an opportune time in the conversation while keeping an eye on his friend's arms. The fire was dying a slow death, down to a single, thin line of smoke rising up and disappearing through the canopy of trees.

The conversation turned theological in nature. It was one of their favorite subjects. They had spent hours discussing major threads of the Christian faith over the years. Agreeing on much, but disagreeing on a few significant things like Sacraments and the security of one's salvation. It was their disagreement that usually drove more of the discussions these days. There was a great amount of respect for the other man's position, even when they argued.

"But we're all sinners saved by grace, Butter."

"Yes, we are, but that's not our true identity. Our calling is to live as the sons we truly are."

"I fall short and miss the mark every day," Cam said.

"We all do and at the same time we can't use it as an excuse to keep on running after a life which is contrary to who we are called to be."

"But the reality is like Paul said in Romans seven, the "things I don't want to do, I keep on doing.""

"Well Cam, if you're going to Romans don't stop at chapter seven, you gotta read chapter eight too."

"And what's your argument?"

"It's not my argument. Paul talks about setting our minds on the flesh which is death, but we are called to set our minds on the things of the Spirit, which is life and peace."

"Doesn't he start out the chapter, which follows right after seven and doing the thing he doesn't want to do, with, there is now no condemnation for those who are in Christ Jesus?" Cam asked.

"Sure, he does. Which is great news for all of us who believe in Jesus."

"So, when I sin it is not I who is doing it, but sin who lives inside of me?"

"You're not responsible for your actions? Didn't you just say we're all sinners?" Butter said.

"Yes, we are," Cam replied.

"I know I am. I own my stuff. Nobody else does."

"My stuff is covered by the blood of Jesus," Cam pressed. "It's my only hope."

"That's where I live, too. But you can't just turn away from what the rest of the Word says, Cam."

"I'm not. No one can say they aren't a sinner in need of God's forgiveness."

"You're right, we all are."

"Okay." Butter thought the conversation was over.

"But that's not the end of the story."

"Sure, it is."

Butter sat back in his chair and tried to gather his thoughts but his stomach was getting in the way of him being rational. Neither man had bothered to take a break from their discussion to eat dinner, now Butter's stomach was beginning to protest in earnest.

"Let's eat somethin'"

"Right on," Cam said.

Within ten minutes Butter brought his pan of boiled water to the porch. The men poured some into their dehydrated packages. The smell of basil, oregano and Parmesan cheese puffed up into their faces as they stirred the hot liquid into their dusty 'lasagna' entree. Then, according to the instructions, they resealed them to wait the eight to ten minutes for the magic to happen.

"So, eating is kinda a picture of God's grace," Cam said while shoveling the food into his face.

"What 'choo mean?"

"We need food every day or we die."

"Yeah."

"Like we need his forgiveness every day."

"And his grace, in this case food, enables us to live."

"Yes!" Cam said.

"Cam are we humans the crown of his creation?"

"Of course."

"We are made in his image and get to co-create things here on the earth?" Butter asked.

"Kinda of ironic the Creator of all things made creatures with the ability to create," Cam said.

"Do you think that there are things we can do to separate us from God?" Butter asked.

"Yeah, it's called sin."

"So why does Paul talk about fleeing sin and that some people won't inherit the Kingdom if they are acting out in certain sinful ways. The whole "that is what some of you were" passage in Corinthians, "But you were washed, you were sanctified." Plus, the countless exhortations to live such different lives among the pagans that they will want to know what makes you different?"

"We will never be perfect. We always need the grace of God. It's what I am counting on." Cam was getting more confident.

"But when someone is living contrary to God's calling are they relying on God's grace or are they coping the way they want and hoping it will all work out?" Butter was not swayed.

"Coping and hoping?"

"It's pain avoidance, living in a fantasy land, just pretending to follow Jesus on Sunday's, but doing what they want the rest of the week."

"Is that what I am doing because I am well aware of my need for grace?"

"Is it?" Butter was looking right at Cam not wanting to back away from what he thought was his key point.

Cam sat in silence, mulling over what Butter had said.

"When our coping mechanism is more important than anything else it has become the god we are clinging to," Butter said.

"But he won't help me beat this beast. He has left it up to me. Like it's my cross to bear."

"God has given you this thing to defeat and he won't help you?"

"It seems that way to me." Cam's eye twitched at the sound of his own words.

* Front Porch *

After eating the pair had walked down to the still waters of the lake to watch and listen to nature. Then the mosquitoes found them and chased them back to their backpacks for spray and to their seats on the porch.

"Having chairs makes all the difference!" Butter exclaimed while settling back into his seat.

"I hear that," Cam replied as both men let out a long satisfying sigh. They sat in silence, taking it all in. The sky grew dark with evening while a pair of bats fluttered about, filling up on buzzing prey.

"This is a good reminder for me, Cam."

"Helps ground you?"

"Yeah, for certain."

"Listen, I'm no expert on psychology but I know if you care about people and listen to their stories it makes a big difference."

"That's exactly how Butter's Famous Oasis has become such a big draw in the middle of nowhere," Cam said.

"No, that's all the power of my Grammy's fried chicken!"

"It's good Butter, but not that good. You're the reason. You care about those hikers."

"People like to be heard. They do lots of listening out on the trail and by the time they walk up to me they've all got somethin' to say. What about you, Cam? You got somethin' to say to me, yet? All this isolation with no outlet isn't good, my friend."

Cam turned to look at the man's big brown eyes as they burrowed into his soul and then his confession just stepped out of his mouth on its own. All the years of hiding his most grievous of sin and he finally named it to another person.

"I set my own house on fire," he said and more tears bulged at the corners of his eyes, threatening to drop on his reddened face.

"What do you mean?" Butter asked and sat forward turning his body toward him. Their body language had appeared to be talking to the lake, sharing without the need to see each other's face, but with Cam's admission Butter wanted to catch everything his friend was saying out loud. And not just his words but the way he expressed them.

Cam, with his eyes burrowing into the dirty wooden deck, arms on his lap full of the ripe blisters, and slumped shoulders, drew in a deep breath to continue.

"I piled up kindling against the outer walls. I gathered dead branches from a lifetime of picking them up in the yard and poured lighter fluid all over the brush. When I ran out of lighter fluid, I dumped all the gasoline I could find. From the garage and shed, even the cans themselves, then I sat and waited. The fumes got thick enough to make me cough. I tried not to do it, Butter. I prayed to God not to go through with it!" Now thick tears and snot flowed from the man's face and both his arms phased in and out of his vision. Cam's whole head became bright red and the veins stuck out on his neck while the blisters pulsed all over his arms, looking as if they would burst.

"Tell me you didn't go through with it, Cam. Tell me you didn't light that brush." Butter was almost begging his friend. Emotionally he was breathing in the fumes with him, coughing and hacking against the burning sensation that the story was bringing out in him, too. Then, like he had been exposed to poison ivy, a deep- seated itch began burning in his arms too.

"I took the matches in and out of my pocket a hundred times trying not to do it. I looked at them and smelled their sulfur's sting— then I looked back at the house. I knew I was at a crossroad. I understood that I would never be allowed to take back this decision. But the pain of the old life had grown like a cancer inside of me and this, this escape, was the only way out. This was my way out. Like she was a sumptuous woman calling to me to come out from behind my pain. The agony I had buried over the years had compounded like interest on a shady credit card. And there she stood, naked in front of me."

"No, Cam." Everything except the sound of Cam's breathing went silent in anticipation of the next few words. Butter's universe paused, skipped a beat, just to hear this confession.

"It was then I remembered the old poem, like I had just learned it," Cam said while leaning in his chair now looking up to the porch overhang, and back into the past at the same time. Tears streaked his face.

"Alack, thou knowest not

How little worthy of any love thou art!

Whom wilt thou find to love ignoble thee?"

"And I lit the whole book of matches at once." Cam threw himself to his knees in a high pitch wail as all the pain, failure, and hiding was released in that very moment. Butter enveloped the man in his arms as they both swam in a suffocating lake filled with a fiery solution. Cam's arms snapped back into sight, after being transparent for the final time.

Three

Cameron Lost

— Section Three —

"Butter"

"Thousands of tired, nerve-shaken,

over-civilized people are beginning to find out

that going to the mountains is going home;

that wildness is a necessity."

John Muir

* Tripwire Alley *

Intertwined cedars and white pines swayed and whispered in the stiff lake breeze. The narrow trail snaked away from the water's edge and was filled with slippery roots covering sandy soil. The heavy boots on the moist fingers that stretched across the ground sounded hollow and were a dead giveaway that hikers approached. Occasional curses and crashes punctuated the difficulty of this section of the North Country Trail. Backpackers dealt with hiking through thick beach sand, which was like walking through molasses, as the trail ground away all leg stamina.

A mental reprieve from the beach takes place as the trail turns south, away from Lake Superior. The relief from the endless sand was short-lived as exposed roots from the cedars and pines intersect the trail at every angle imaginable. On the way up inclines and hills the multi-faceted roots acted as steps and stairs, almost choosing the path. Sometimes they were two or three feet apart. The tree anchors were like walking on narrow railroad ties that had been mixed in a blender or a tornado. Twenty-five or forty pounds of house on the back, with the roots, and the fight to remain upright was constant.

A few moments of broken concentration can send even the most avid of hikers to the ground and off of the trail for weeks with a broken ankle, torn ligaments, or high ankle sprain. It is the reason this section of the NCT has become known in local quarters as "Tripwire Alley," or just "The Tripwire."

"Make it through the Tripwire uninjured at the end of a long day of trudging through twelve miles of sand and you can say you accomplished something," was an official newspaper quote in a yellowed article, clipped and nailed to a log wall in a restaurant. The accompanying picture was of a smiling Billy Cantrell, who at the time, was one of the only black men living in Alger County, Michigan.

How Billy Cantrell came to live in Michigan's Upper Peninsula is a story unto itself. Twenty-eight years before the article, Billy was an avowed city dweller, clinging to his meticulous home in the Motor City, like a lighthouse in tumultuous seas. By the mid-eighties the block where his house sat had more condemned properties than occupied. Gangs, drug runners, and crackheads, were constantly moving through the neighborhood, bringing with them the disease of destruction.

The city was falling apart at the seams, said the news pundits. What they failed to see, what they always failed to see, was the intact families surviving among the wreckage of modern urban life. Reporters never did stories on the stubborn pioneers who fought to stay on their claim and fight for their homestead in the middle of the carnage. Those were the people they should have focused on, but blood and guts, doom and gloom, sells more papers and retains more viewers. "If it bleeds, it leads," is the journalistic idiom that is echoed off of newsroom walls all around the country, which excludes much of the population.

* Go Get'em Tiger *

Billy loved all the local professional sports franchises in Detroit, but baseball was his game. He worked downtown and occasionally snuck in an afternoon game at The Corner. That would be Tiger Stadium, at *the corner* of Michigan and Trumbull, in the heart of Detroit's Corktown. This section of the city held one of the oldest neighborhoods in Detroit, settled by a massive influx of Irish immigrants during the famine years of the 1840's. Its name derived from the largest county in Ireland, Cork. Professional baseball had been played on the site for over a hundred years. Tiger Stadium was considered to be a genuine *fan park,* as most of the seats were close to the action, unless you were a bleacher creature in center field with its wall being 440 feet away from home plate. The bleacher fans got into the game for a buck and a half.

The Cantrell season tickets went back a couple generations, even before the hallowed grounds was known as Tiger Stadium. Billy's grand Pap and dad had owned the seats in what was known as Briggs Stadium as far back as he could remember. They were on the first base side of the field, which is where the visiting dugout was located right along the wall that separated the fans from the field. The bullpen was so close you could almost touch the pitcher's hat as they warmed up. Billy's favorite pastime, while watching his favorite game, was eating peanuts and messing with any pitcher who was warming up. His mission was to screw with their heads so much he'd rattle their confidence. Over the years he had become quite adept at getting under the skin of opposing players and was an unofficial leader of section 130, training all of the season ticket holders to step up their efforts of the psychological war. That was the name his father had given the practice of pestering opposing players.

Baseball was literally in Billy's genes. He was conceived the night the Detroit Tigers won the 1945 World Series against the hated Chicago Cubs. Hammering Hank Greenberg, Hal Newhouser, Virgil Trucks and Dizzy Trout lead the Tigers that season. Billy, the fourth son, after his brothers Hank, Hal, and Virgil would have been called Dizzy if not for the right-eous anger of his mother who saved him from wearing the moniker of a crazy man. She had signed the birth certificate while her husband was out celebrating at the bar. His dad was the only one to ever call young Billy, Dizzy.

William Wallace Cantrell grew up the youngest in family of nine kids on Detroit's east side. Unbeknownst to his siblings, who had always called him Billy, he had the same name as a white, part-time, race car driver from California. That driver only drove in five professional races over a twelve-year period and won less than $1,500 his entire career, but he was a somebody with the same name. Eddie, Billy's best buddy from elementary school, said he should be proud to have the same name as a race car driver, even if he was white.

"You're almost famous!" he said out on the playground. From that day forward Billy Cantrell wore his name like a badge of honor and next to his first love of baseball, he developed an unusual affinity for NASCAR racing.

As life turned out, Billy was the only one in his family to go to college, while two of his brothers managed to finish a five to ten year stint in Jackson Penitentiary on assault and battery charges. Billy graduated from Wayne State University and went to work in the auto industry for almost 25 years, putting his mechanical engineering degree to work designing truck frames for Chrysler. That same year he married the quiet, cute girl from down the street, Charlotte. They had their daughter Tonya ten months later and moved into actual adulthood, watching the '68 Tigers comeback to win the World Series after being down three games to one. Like the city of Detroit rising from the ashes of the '67 riots, the Tigers fought back and won. It was a win for everyone. Those were the good years, "the golden years," as Billy still calls them. Everything ahead was bright and their future held endless possibilities for the three of them.

Tragedy struck one sunny April morning and Billy Cantrell embraced an affinity for alcohol that same afternoon. Both his parents were killed in a car accident on their way home from church in 1984. If that wasn't hard enough, one by one, like a row of domino's, his siblings passed away and he grew distant from his wife. The only bright spot was his beloved Tigers won the World Series after winning thirty-five of their first forty games.

That baseball team and alcohol proved to be his favorite escape from the pain of life.

A few years later, when their daughter moved away for college in Colorado, Charlotte left him for good, choosing to shack up with a carpet salesman from the other side of town. They left for Florida after the divorce was final and Billy was lost, alone, and drunk. It was so bad he let the Cantrell season tickets go while he fell backwards into the abyss.

* Nature's Gravity *

Billy had always been attracted to nature and during this most painful of seasons in his life he found himself spending a great deal of time in parks to soothe his broken soul. Much of the time he spent outside during these days he was drunk, lying in the grass, and staring up at the clouds on Belle Isle. Then things went from bad, to worse. He was arrested one September day when he got into a fight with two cops and wound-up spending four months locked up in Wayne County jail.

His thinking cleared when he got out, or at least he thought it did, because he was sober and determined to remain that way. In jail he had a cell mate who shared his middle name of Wallace. He swore by the challenges of backpacking through the wilderness to get your mind right. So, before he was released, Billy simply decided to go hiking to get some clarity. He sold his house, took an early retirement, and bought some used backpacking gear at a garage sale.

He didn't start off slow, not Billy Cantrell, he squeezed his eyes shut and swung for the fences like he had done in little league so many times. He sold his truck right after closing on his home in Detroit and bought a bus ticket for Atlanta, Georgia. From Atlanta he hiked and hitched north seventy-five miles and found a engraved marker which said; "Georgia to Maine— a footpath for those who seek fellowship with the wilderness." Then he stepped through the stone archway and into his new life.

Ready or not, Billy Cantrell in March of 1992, was going to walk the Appalachian Trail from the beginning to the end, or die trying. His first genuine blessing was the mild spring as he began pounding out mile after mile— like a man possessed. Up and over mountain peaks, rarely pausing for meals or pictures, he blazed through Georgia. Word spread through the trail community that a black man from up north was on an unstoppable mission, like a man possessed. Many fellow through-hikers had caught a glimpse of the man flash through campsites or power past them on the trail, but rare was the person who ever held a conversation with Billy Cantrell. The mystery surrounding his story grew. Some said he was a bank robber on the run from the feds, while others guessed that he was a recluse millionaire wanting to escape the pressure of life, but the story that seemed to be most accepted was that Billy was a famous athlete trying to outrun the paparazzi after a nasty divorce.

Somewhere in the Smoky Mountains he was bequeathed his trail name but was not present for the blessing. They called him *The Hurricane*, which Billy appreciated when it caught up to him through the grape vine later that spring around a campfire somewhere in southern Virginia. The issue was that the name was not meant as a compliment, more of a warning, from the senior hikers on the trail. His hurry was gonna get him a cane. Meaning, if he failed to take care of himself and plan in a few zero days, he was going to injure himself. More than likely by blowing out a knee or ankle and then he would need a cane to finish the hike.

The Hurricane refused to heed the warning and he did not slow down. He was bound and determined, like he had never been before, to make it to the end. He believed Mt. Katahdin, the terminus in Maine, was not only calling to him, it was also wanting to give him a gift which would only come if he made the entire trip. Billy figured as long as he kept moving, somewhere along the way he would find what he was looking for, so forward he pressed himself. By the time he got to the Shenandoah Valley in Northern Virginia he was hiking well over twenty miles a day. A week later he ran into the boulders in Pennsylvania and took a pounding trying to keep up the miles. After a couple of days his thighs wanted to explode from hoping up and down hundreds of boulders. He knew he needed to average sixteen miles a day to get to Katahdin by July 15th. It was noon on the fifteenth when he got to the northern terminus, standing on Mt Katahdin in Maine almost 2200 miles completed in just 137 days.

Tears filled Billy's eyes and mixed with the sweat rolling off his head as he sat down next to the famous sign on the peak of Maine's highest mountain. He was happy to have made the entire trip, but he felt like little had changed deep inside of him. He had expected an avalanche moment, where he could look back and point to as the event that changed his life forever. The gift he had longed for proved to be elusive. He sat for the whole day with his back to the northern terminus sign, waiting. It was not the northern mountain that had been calling to him, whispering his name to press on, it was the trail itself.

Billy was addicted. He needed the answers the trail was holding back from him. So, he flip-flopped through the Maine wilderness— through the Blue Mountains into the rugged back country of New Hampshire and spilled out into the Green Mountains of Vermont. Hiking 500 miles to a small town in Vermont, then north for two days to the Eastern Terminus of the North Country Trail. The N.C.T. was the longest hiking trail in North America covering over 4,800 miles from Vermont to North Dakota and Billy believed it offered his next hope for discovering his purpose.

It was in the midst of a new challenge when The Hurricane of Appalachian Trail lore morphed into another being, with the name "Miles." He marched across the peaks of Vermont and New Hampshire. Pushed through the Adirondacks of upstate New York, through the north west corner of the Keystone State and then around the border region of Ohio and up into Michigan. He walked until a winter snow storm stopped him cold in Michigan's upper peninsula, near Grand Marais. In ten months, Billy Cantrell hiked over 4,500 miles, averaging better than fifteen miles a day. When he got to Grand Marais it was in the middle of a lake-effect blizzard and he came to his end, spent. His knees and hips ached and his feet were so swollen he could barely tie his boots. Miles had lost over a hundred pounds while transforming his skinny chicken legs into tree trunks. He destroyed four pairs of hiking boots and was carrying his third backpack, when he collapsed unconscious in a snowbank.

He was found in a pile at the side of the road by an elderly couple walking their dog the next morning. They managed to get him on a sled and dragged him home with a snow machine. They took care of him for several days before he could even speak. Once out of his stupor he began telling Tim and Kathy his story. He droned on for hours, needing no prodding. His life simply fell out of his mouth and lay at their feet. As it turned out Tim was a retired Pastor from Michigan's lower peninsula. They were not even supposed to be at their summer cabin, but a mild heart attack a couple of months earlier had halted their annual escape to Florida and the need for exercise put them out walking on the road that morning to find him. Kathy credited the encounter to a miracle from Jesus himself and was more than eager to serve the wandering soul. She cooked a mean stew and baked first class bread, most of those skills had been abandoned after Tim's heart attack, for the low sodium, low fat diet he required. Now, since Jesus had dropped Miles into their laps, she was eager to cook both.

He was unconvinced of her faith conclusions: The long buried engineering brain had little space for divine intervention, considering who he was and what he had done for ten months. Tim, on the other hand was also a logical thinker, he had trained as a scientist, but after investigating the claims of Jesus for a couple of years had become convinced that Jesus of Nazareth was indeed the Messiah of the world, like he had proclaimed. He responded by dedicating his life to following Jesus. He went to Seminary in St. Louis and served three churches over the next thirty-five years.

"I thought I could find the answer to my pain out on the trail," Billy confessed to the both of them ten days later, while sitting in the flickering light of their fireplace.

"We all go on that search, Billy."

"Yeah, well I almost walked myself right into my grave to find it, Tim."

"But you didn't." Tim sipped at his steamy mug of green tea and made a face.

"What's wrong with the tea?" Kathy asked.

"Nothing. It always tastes like warm grass to me."

Billy's mind was still back on the trail.

"You didn't walk yourself into oblivion," Tim said, to the crackling fire.

"You wanna know what I think?" Kathy asked while giving Tim a spoonful of honey.

"Sure," Billy said.

"I think when you said you believed that Mt. Katahdin was going to give you an answer, then, when you hadn't heard anything sitting on top of that peak, even with tears running down your face, you were determined to press on to get your answers. Even Jesus said if you seek him, you will find him."

"And where did that get me, 'cept broken down in a pile of snow?"

"It brought you here. Right now. You are here."

"I don't think I can honestly say that I was searchin' for Jesus."

"You were searching for the truth so hard you were willing to walk thousands of miles to find it."

"More like runnin'. You know how many people I've hurt to get here? I haven't spoken to my little girl in a year. She's got to be thinkin' that her daddy is dead! My ex-wife, too."

"We can change that with a simple phone call or two." Kathy grabbed for his hand to encourage him.

Billy Cantrell broke down and cried like a little boy who had lost his favorite puppy. He had never felt so lost after coming so far, which was the opposite of what he expected the adventure to give him. For ten months on the trail he was convinced he would be in a better place at the end of it all. Now the only thing that felt right was to cry at the death of a dream. He was not ready to call his Toyna or Charlotte.

"I am sorry that you are suffering," Kathy said, handing him a box of tissues while offering up silent petitions on his behalf.

Around the first of the year he found a part time job shoveling snow and stocking shelves at the only grocery store in town. A close friend of Tim and Kathy who owned the only Real Estate office in Grand Marais rented Billy an old cabin down the road a piece. He hunkered down in a tiny one room hunting shack with a wood stove, a twin bed, and a chair with a bad leg. There was a broken down bench next to the lone window which looked out front at a waiting pile of logs, right next to the weathered outhouse. The previous owner had recently keeled over looking out the same window and being found a few days later, frozen to the floor, by his only child. A witness to the unmistakable pull of nature and gravity.

* The Oasis *

As providence would have it, the rickety cabin was on five acres, only a couple hundred feet off of the North Country Trail, hugging a creek to the west. He dipped into his retirement savings and bought it for $4,000 the same month. Everyone thought he had lost his mind, everyone except the daughter of the deceased.

Billy Hurricane Miles Cantrell then took a year of zero days, limping and milling around his new property. Occasionally doing odd jobs for folks in and around Grand Marais. He shoveled a ton of snow that winter. If the cold wind was whistling out of the west over the relatively warm water of Lake Superior, the town of Grand Marais got snow. When the wind screamed out of the north, Grand Marais got a lot of snow. When the wind charged from the northeast out of Canada, the people of Grand Marais prepared for a blizzard. The aging store owners were more than happy that Billy was available to shovel off the front of the store and the loading dock each morning, and they paid him in groceries, most of the time.

Then one morning while shoveling an idea struck him like lightning from a summer squall and he decided right there on the loading dock that he was going to open up a small store for hikers. He could stock it initially through his shoveling gig. He would use his personal knowledge of trail life to outfit his place for hikers and his engineering skills to build it. He stocked up with some essentials and a few extravagant items, like chocolate and cold pop.

A few months later Billy placed a home cut sign on the trails edge and an arrow pointing the way to *The Oasis*. He smiled at himself when he hung that sign. The irony of being in a wilderness and opening an oasis made him laugh a deep hearty laugh and a wave of peace rushed through his big old heart.

By the second year he had cleared out some space for tents to camp and hung up a black solar water bag behind a tarp for showers. For the camping and showers, he took a donation bucket, never bothering to check what anyone put in, if anything at all. That same spring, he began maintaining the twenty-mile section of trail from his spot on Baker Creek just east of town, all the way back to Muskallonge Lake, within a quarter-mile of the State park, and a stone's throw from Lake Superior. He hung up small flyers advertising *The Oasis* on the community bulletin board in the state park and in a few stores at each end of his section of the trail.

This went on for the next few years while he continued to add to the amenities he had to offer at the Oasis. He built a pavilion, then walled it in the next year so folks could get themselves out of the blowing rain. The following spring, he began cooking meals for weary hikers. He loved watching the life creep back into his exhausted visitors. More than any other amenity, it was his fried chicken dish that put him over the top. He smeared it with garlic butter and parsley, served with smashed potatoes and fresh corn on the cob, when he could get it. This is how Billy Hurricane Miles Cantrell got his final trail name and "Butter" was born, again.

Folks from far and wide came to love his little oasis on the trail. They paid him good money for his kindness, hospitality, and chicken. Travelers donated a buck to carve their trail names along with the year they had visited, on his picnic tables and all over the log walls. "Chum-lee '97" was next to "Drake '99," which was by the crooked "Fox-Tail '06," and across from an upside down "Grunt '11." The money went to N.C.T. trail maintenance and expansion.

Not long after, the normal people, those non-hiking types, from Grand Marias, Munising, Newberry, and many scattered towns across the Upper Peninsula began to turn up at *Butter's Famous Oasis* on a regular basis. It became an annual pilgrimage for many and beginning in '06, food service was extended through the winter snow machine season as well.

Butter's waistline re-expanded from the comfort of living in his calling. One thing he had not expected was the joy that snuck up on him in the middle of his simple living. He was a self-confessed happy fat man, working out his stumbled-upon dream, smack dab in the middle of nowhere important— unless, you are an exhausted through-hiker stumbling over Tripwire Alley on the North Country Trail, in Michigan's Upper Peninsula.

On many cool nights sitting around a campfire, he retold his story of conquest to anyone who would listen. He was not motivated from a braggadocios spirit, but shared it as a warning. "On your way to finding yourself, you can rush right by all the beauty God has surrounded you with. Lift your head up and walk with gratitude. Take a few zero days and recharge your depleted soul," he would often say.

Butter had become an avid reader over the years and left the used books laying all over his oasis. He encouraged everyone to read as they made their way through the wilderness and offered personal discussions after they were done with the books.

"Butter, you have the knack to ask the right questions at the perfect time." "Bunny '05" wrote on the wall of the Oasis and was his favorite compliment.

Looking back in time while over-looking his new kingdom, Butter was filled with gratitude over what God had done inside of him. How Tim and Kathy were still some of his most vocal supporters, even volunteering to help during the busy summer months. He would have never guessed how God was going to use him and his outlandish journey to help everyday folks walk through life, even in the middle of the wilderness.

Four

Cameron Lost

— Section Four —

"Cam"

"No man knows how bad he is till he has tried very hard to be good. A silly idea is current that good people do not know what temptation means. This is an obvious lie."

C. S. Lewis

* School Play *

"Bye, K!"

"See ya, Cam."

"Have a good day, honey."

"Thanks, Mom."

Caleb was off, new shoes clapping down the familiar sidewalk toward his first day of school, while his three-year old brother smiled and waved at his back from the front porch. The September sun warmed the morning air as the five-year old walked away, smiling and hurrying to meet up with a few friends from down the block. Caleb's mom beamed as she watched her oldest son march off in his blue plaid short-sleeve shirt and tan pants. Smiling, she wiped at a lone tear as it streaked her cheek, while touching the head of her youngest boy.

"Are you sad?" Cam asked, using one hand to block the morning rays.

"No, honey," she said...thinking, *I was just holding him in my arms, yesterday.*

"Mom, is K gonna stay at school?"

"No, your brother still lives here, silly." Caressing her youngest child's thick blonde hair, she knew he would need a haircut soon or the curls would set.

"Oh?" Cam was confused by this new reality.

"This year he will go to school for half a day."

"Huh?"

"Last year we walked him down the street to the Presbyterian Church two days a week," she held up two fingers. "Now he's going to be gone five days a week."

She could see his brain spinning around the new information.

"K will come home around lunch time. Don't you worry," she said kissing his head.

"But he stays 'dere 'til wunch time?"

"Yes, dear."

"I'm gonna go play!" His eyes flashed with excitement.

"Okay, Buster," she said, a bit confused by his change in countenance.

Gina waved from two doors down as the group of kids marched off.

"Hey, Toots," Mags called, using one hand to amplify her voice.

Gina made her way over, white-knuckling a handkerchief.

"This is supposed to get easier," Gina said and dabbed.

"It's your little girl, Gina."

"I know... It's a big day for you too! Look at Caleb. Aw, he looks so grown up, Mags." They reached for each other and shared a few more tears while following the group of kids with their eyes. Then they were off talking about life as another sidewalk meeting was called to order. Words and hands went flying, wrapped with hopes and dreams, as more neighborhood kids feeling the pull of school hurried past. The pair only knew each other for a couple of years, but connected right from the start. Mags had always thought Gina was a pretty woman, but learned to admire her even more as her inner beauty became more evident.

"Oh look at him!" Gina pointed to the front storm door.

"What are you doing, Buster?" Cam had his nose smashed against the glass, with hands cupping his eyes like he was using binoculars. He turned and ran as his mother broke away from her friend.

"The little stinker is up to something," she said.

"He's got the look. Talk to you later," Gina said and laughed.

"Hey, I was going to tell you."

"Yeah?"

"Cam says he's going to Gene-downs to get some more tookies."

"Cookies? Oh, the frosted chocolate ones from last week?"

"Yeah, he loved them. I'll have to get the recipe."

"They are easy to make. I'll write it down for 'ya when I get back," Gina said.

"Thanks." They were off to their days filled with managing their households and herding kids.

"Cameron, what are you up to?" Mags called while stepping through the front door into the entryway and then up one small step to her right and into the living room. She paused at the turquoise couch and picked up the laundry basket filled with folded clothes.

"Cam, where are you?" Listening for an answer she stepped into the hallway and then a quick left into her bedroom to put the clean whites in the dresser drawers. Walking down the hallway humming MacNamara's Band, she passed the opening on her right into the dining room which connected with the kitchen. Caleb's room hiding behind the closed door, to the left. Straight ahead was the lone bathroom, the linen closet was on the right where she stored the rest of the laundry and the basket. Cameron's bedroom was across the hall, just to the left of the lavatory. She walked into an empty room.

"Cameron?"

Silence.

"Cam where are you?" she said with a more commanding voice.

"Playing," came the muffled voice from behind the door to Caleb's room.

"Why are you playing in here?" She pushed the door open and noticed the guilty look on the boy's face.

"I wike K's cars!"

"You have some of the same toys, Buster."

"K has more good better cars."

"Okay, but you're going to pick them all up before nap."

"Okay, mom."

"Cameron, all of them, okay?"

"All of 'dem."

"Before your nap."

"B'fore nap."

"Otherwise, you won't be able to play in here anymore."

* My Stuff *

"Mom, he's doing it again!"

"What's going on Caleb?"

"Cam is always is playing with my stuff."

"Is he breaking your toys?"

"No. But I don't understand why he uses my cars all the time, when he has his own."

"If he's not hurting them, what's the problem?"

"Whenever I go to play with his cars he hides them and screams like crazy."

"I know his screeching is hard to listen to, believe me, but you're the older brother, and older brothers have to show their siblings how to behave."

"Why does he get to keep all his stuff like new and mine always gets wrecked?"

"That's just the way he is," she pulled him close with her right arm. Mag's, a shortened version of her grandmother Margaret's name, was sitting at the dinner table leafing through her Betty Crocker's cookbook looking for a recipe.

"So, we always have to use my cars to play and Cam's stuff stays in his case?"

"He's not hurting anything, Caleb."

"It's not fair!"

"Life isn't fair, honey. What if I told you that you were gonna start sharing a room with Cam?"

"Why would I do that? I like having my own room." Caleb loved his mother's hugs and pressed in close, melting in her warmth.

"It will be fun."

"But why, mom? Why do we have to share a room?"

"We weren't going to tell you until next week at Cam's birthday party."

"Tell me what?"

She whispered in his ear, "Can you keep a secret?"

He looked up into her blue eyes and nodded, as his own eyes grew wide.

"Your going to be a big brother."

"Huh?"

"You are going to be a big brother— again."

"How?"

"We're gonna have a baby," Mags leaned back in her chair and rubbed her belly.

"Really?"

"Yes. Your dad and I are very happy."

"Does this mean I have to share my toys more?"

"Well not for a long time, but eventually yes. That's part of being the oldest."

"So, are we getting a baby brother or sister?"

"I don't know, it's a surprise."

"What a s-pise?" Cameron asked as he walked wide-eyed into the dinning room, wanting to know the secret.

"Your gonna be a big brother, Cam," Caleb said, immediately forgetting about keeping a secret as being a part of the conversation.

"Really?"

"Mom's havin' a ba-by!" Caleb said. Both the boys danced and yipped in a circle.

"Ba-by, ba-by, ba-by!"

"Now both of us are gonna be big brothers so we'll both have to share our toys!" Caleb said to Cameron in the best big brother voice he could muster.

Cameron stopped jumping and thought about what his brother had said.

"We'll share all your toys, K."

"We're gonna share all of them, it's what big brothers do, right mom?"

"No! You be 'da big brother, I don't wanna!" Cameron ran off to his bedroom in protest. To protect his stuff from the new baby's arrival he stood in front of his closet with his arms spread wide to block the door.

* Sand Pile *

"Cam, have you seen the baby's blanket?"

"Huh?"

"The baby's blanket?"

He shrugged, keeping his back to his mother.

"Cameron come here." She gave him the serious mom voice without saying it too loudly to stir the baby boy resting in her arms.

"What mom?"

"Over here." She pointed to the floor in front of the couch.

"Mom!" Caleb dashed past Cameron into the room.

She shot him her 'be quiet I've got the baby' eyes.

"Sorry. Can I go play with Bobby and Steve?" Caleb whispered.

"Did you finish your homework?"

"Yes it's all done."

"What did you have to do?"

"I had to read a story and answer four questions."

"Put it on the table so I can read it."

"I did."

"Where are you going?"

"To ride bikes."

"Don't go far, dinner is in an hour."

"We wanted to ride down to Catalpa."

"No, they are doing all that road construction down there."

"But there are piles of sand and big machines, mom. We just want to check them out."

"Caleb, don't go down there. You remember what your father said? You can ride your bike between Bobby's house and here."

"But, mom!"

"End of discussion."

"Okay." Caleb stomped out of the room headed for the garage and his bike. He did not like his bicycle even though he loved the color his dad had painted it. It was a girl's bike with the double center bar lowered instead of straight across. It had belonged to his cousin Sarah and the older kids teased him when he road past. Outside, he paused to look into the open garage. The bike was leaning against the back wall, but Caleb decided against taking it. He sulked down the block to find his friends, content to watch them ride back and forth.

"Cameron. I want you to come over here, right now."

Cam thought twice, but then got up, rolled his eyes, and wandered over to the couch. He stared at his younger brother swaddled in his mother's arms as she was sitting on the couch.

"Hey baby Curtis," he said to divert attention.

"I asked you a question, Mr."

"What question?"

"Do you know where Curtis' blanket is?"

"I didn't know you asked me that question. I thought you asked me a different one."

"Do you know where his blanket is?"

"I don't fink so."

"I know when you are not telling me the truth, remember I have motherly intuition, plus the eyes in the back of my head."

With that statement Cameron's own eyes grew wide and he wanted to see beneath his mother's thick black hair. The last time he had hugged her in the rocking chair, before bed, he had searched for her hidden eyes but couldn't find them before falling to sleep.

"I don't know where it is."

"Listen, I know you are lying to me right now and I won't stand for it."

"You're sitting down, Mom."

She grabbed his face and made him look into her eyes, but he kept averting direct eye contact, which, in his case was the dead giveaway. She knew it was the clearest signal he was lying, again.

"Your father is not going to be happy about you lying to me, is he?"

"Well, maybe I should go wook for Curtis' blanket?"

"You better go get it right now."

Cameron shuffled out of the room and down the hallway. He was back in less than a minute dragging his nine-month-old brother's soft white blanket.

"Do you have anything to say?"

"Curtis, I found your blanket!" Cameron held it up then leaned in and kissed his brother's thick, curly black hair.

"I was thinking more along the line that you were sorry for taking it."

"Sorry. Can I go play now?"

"Sure, but no more hiding things from the baby."

Cameron made a beeline for his bedroom, knowing that his brother's newest set of cars were lined up on the dresser in front of their window. He studied them to remember the order in which they were placed in a line. Then he grabbed them off and began driving them on an imaginary road on the floor. The blue '57 Chevy got into an accident on the freeway with the green Ford pickup truck and both flipped over in dramatic fashion. The red '58 Corvette screeched its tires and steered around the pileup, but the poor black '55 Ford couldn't stop fast enough and ran into the truck. The cars then became people yelling at each other for not driving right and being stupid. The firetruck came and put out the fire, after rescuing the people in both vehicles.

This was the scene when Caleb arrived.

"Cam, why are you playing with my new cars?"

"I dunno, cause they are cool!"

"Hey do you want come play with me?"

"I dunno. I thought you were riding bikes with Bobby and Steve?"

"They had to go in for dinner. Don't tell mom but we could go down to see what the construction guys are doing."

"Yay!" Cameron was a bit too willing for Caleb's liking.

K grabbed Cam's arm. "Shh. We can't tell."

"Okay. Let's go!"

Caleb picked up his cars and lined them up on the dresser in the "right" order. The pair tiptoed out of their bedroom, across the hallway and into the kitchen. Cam went to get his shoes off the landing at the back of the kitchen.

"Mom, Cam and I are going out to play."

"Okay," came her muted response from the front living room.

"Caleb."

"Yeah?"

"Stay close, dinner is gonna be ready soon."

"Okay."

"Watch your brother."

"I will," he sprinted for the back door. Cameron was pulling on his last shoe on the bottom steps. The painted metal milk door was to the right and Cam always had to check it for new bottles of milk.

"The milkman doesn't come today, silly," Caleb reminded him.

"Oh yeah, let's go!"

They shot out of the screen door leaving it to slam behind them, through the open gate, and down the concrete driveway. They ran for the sidewalk out front. The sun was bright and a couple of cicadas made their buzz high up in the neighbor's maple trees. Caleb glanced back to see if mom was watching from the living room window. The pair made the turn and hurried down the block, out of eye sight of the lady with four peering eyes. Off in the distance was parked a gigantic construction loader surrounded by mountains of glorious golden sand.

"Hurry, Cam, I don't think the guys are working on the road."

"I'm gonna climb that big hill."

"Not that one, mom might see us. We have to go around the corner to play."

"Okay."

"Look, Ernie is out playing in the sand on the wrong pile!" Caleb said and pointed at the neighbor boy.

* Pay Up *

The afternoon sun was gleaming off of the hood of the Catalina. The paint was shinny because Marty had waxed it the day before. The top was down and the rushing wind buffeted his thinning red hair. Marty loved his new car. He had not even been in the market for a vehicle when he fell in love with its sleek lines and stacked headlights. He traded in his '61 Impala, a car he also loved, to buy the '63 Catalina the day after the test drive in the spring of 1964.

The throaty dual exhaust from the 389 V8 motor hummed and pushed him west on Twelve Mile Road, where he wheeled into Jake Levi's gas station. The frail gas jockey was sitting on his trusty stool out near the three tall pumps. The bell on the side of the building rang twice as the Catalina rolled over the air hose, then came to a stop.

"Marty, she is sure a pretty thing!" The old man exclaimed as Marty turned the motor off at the last pump.

"Thanks. Give me two dollars of the premium, Jake."

"Check the oil?"

"Na, I just changed it last week."

"Tires all look good but do you want me to put a pressure gauge on them?"

"Took care of that last week, too."

"Looks like you've done all my work for me. I guess only one question remains, Marty."

"What's that?"

"What kind of jam do you want?"

"Got any strawberry left?"

"Sure do. Let me grab that for ya."

"Thanks." Marty loved the idea that Jake offered free items when you spent a couple of bucks on premium gas. For the last couple months, it had been eight-ounce jars of homemade jams and the strawberry was top notch.

The trip home from Jake's was less than five minutes and only two left turns. Marty's stomach was rumbling with hunger while he put on his signal to turn into his driveway. As the gravel crunched under his tires he happened to glance south toward Catalpa and noticed two young boys turning the corner just in front of the sand piles. Marty stopped the car just beyond the sidewalk on the concrete part of the driveway, but still in front of the house, and shook his head knowing he had to act. Anger and disappointment welled as he walked down the street. He knew he could not let this outright betrayal stand when he had specifically told them not to play in the construction area. They were old enough to know better.

Three minutes later, when he turned the corner, both boys were on their hands and knees grabbing at the forbidden sand letting it fall through their fingers like they were pirates watching a new heist of golden coins drop into a treasure chest while they laughed.

"Hey! Boys! We're going home!"

Caleb and Cameron momentarily froze and then threw the sand down.

"I told you K, that we shouldn't come down here," Cameron said and pointed. "He made me do it!"

"We're leaving, now!" Dad said.

The march home was not a happy time for the four- and six-year-olds, both were hanging their heads in defeat while their hearts filled with the dread of anticipation. Each step toward their house brought the impending punishment closer as the drying sand fell from their knees, arms, and hands. By the time they walked past the gleaming sky-blue car, the fear was biting at their heels and gnawing at their hearts.

"Both of you go downstairs," Marty said as they approached the back gate.

Caleb gulped, not ever remembering hearing the command before. He knew his father was not a man you wanted to mess with, so he walked straight for the back door. As the two boys walked through Marty closed the gate so the dog would not wander out of the yard.

"Bonnie, outside." The black Scottish terrier bolted off her rug on the landing and out of the door.

"Marty, what's wrong?" Mags asked her husband who was sporting a stern face.

"I caught them down the street playing at the construction site."

"Oh, really? I told them to stay close! I just told Caleb not to go down there."

"This needs to happen," he said and Mags agreed with lowered eyes.

Downstairs the dread was hanging over the boys like a pall.

"Go over to the table and drop your drawers."

Tears welled up in Caleb's eyes as he unbuckled his pants and let them fall to the floor. Cameron was about to speak but thought better of it. The table they were supposed to hang onto was the homemade dinner table Marty had constructed for when company visited to share a meal. In between those gatherings it became a landing zone for every abandoned item in the basement.

"Grab onto the table and don't let go." The boys' eyes got as big as dinner plates when they saw their dad remove his thin leather belt.

"I told you both not to go down around the corner and play in the sand, didn't I? We told you it could be dangerous."

"Ye-yes," Caleb said.

Cameron nodded in agreement but Marty didn't notice.

"I told you Cameron, right?"

"Caleb made me go, dad."

"That doesn't matter, you still went. I know he didn't drag you down there because I saw both of you walking down the sidewalk."

"Oh."

"I told you Cameron not to go, right?"

"Right."

"Turn your heads around and look forward." There was not a second between the command and the first strike of the black leather across the Caleb's rear end, followed immediately by the yelp from the boy due to the sting of the strap. Cameron's cry rung through the basement with his crack. Each boy received two.

"You will listen when your mother or I tell you something." Marty was not enjoying the discipline, wishing his boys would have made better choices.

"Do you understand?" He bent down to ask the question face to face.

"Sorry, dad," Caleb managed through the tears, while grabbing at his butt.

"Yes," Cameron said.

"Alright, pull up your pants, clean up the sand on the floor, and get washed up for dinner." Marty walked away lacing his belt back through the loops on his pants, he was convinced the boys had learned their lesson.

As Cameron pulled up his pants over his stinging butt, tears dripped off of his reddened cheeks, he was thinking that he should have done a better job of hiding, then he wouldn't have gotten in so much trouble. The life lesson he took away from the experience as a four year old was to figure out how to better conceal things from his father and not get caught.

* Three Sons *

"All right boys, get in the car," Marty said.

"Where are we going?" Cameron asked.

"Cam, just get in the car."

"It's a surprise," Mags said to her three boys.

"Surprise?" Caleb said and climbed in the back seat smiling a toothy grin.

"Keep your shoes off the seats," Marty said, like he did every time they got in.

The '65 Oldsmobile Starfire came equipped with white leather interior which offset the forest green metallic paint perfectly. Marty had worked all winter to keep the interior pristine even with three young kids climbing in and out of the car. Curtis, the two-year-old, had the hardest time keeping his feet off the backs of the front seats, so dad inspected his shoes before he got into the vehicle.

"Mom, where are we going?" Cam asked.

"Well, you're just going to have to be patient and wait to see."

"Sit back, Cam," Marty insisted as he closed the driver's door.

"Is it far away? The surprise I mean."

"Not too far," mom said.

"We'll get there when we get there, now sit back and keep quiet." Marty was trying to head off the thousand questions from Cam about every conceivable situation between here and their destination. He was beginning to wonder if the kid was going to grow up to be a lawyer.

"Your father has had a hard week at work and wants to spend the day relaxing, so you boys had better mind your manners. You'll just have to wait until we get to Mt. Clemens to see."

"Okay, mom," Caleb said. Cameron sat and glared at his perfect brother while baby Curtis dropped his security blanket on the floor. Reaching for the shrinking rag the toddler almost tipped over on his head onto the carpet, but Caleb caught him on the way over.

"I got it, Curt," Caleb said.

Curtis clutched the still soft but yellowing blanket against his face as he had done since the earliest days of his life, using it to caress himself. He leaned over against his brother's leg and Caleb let the little guy snuggle in for a nap. At two-and-a-half he was worn out from a hard morning of playing. Cameron was watching the pair in the seat next to them, to make sure Curt kept his feet off of the white seat. Otherwise, he would have to inform his parents of the infraction.

As the car rumbled away from their house, Cam did not want to be disturbed while he read his new book, Magic Made Easy. Magic was Cam's newest thrill and he was trying to become the best magician since Harry Houdini. Mr. and Mrs. Sebastian had bought Cameron the book as a gift for his seventh birthday and Julius teased the boys relentlessly for sport. The Sebastian's had no children of their own but were always invited to Christmas and all the holidays, along with birthday parties for the boys. They were kind and generous people— old friends of Marty and Mags. They met them right after they were married and had gone to check out an apartment for rent. Julius and Helen owned the bungalow on the shady street in the cozy Detroit suburb. They were seeking to rent their upstairs apartment for the extra cash, and so Helen wouldn't feel so alone when Julius traveled for work. The two couples hit it off right away and would become life-long friends after Marty and Mags lived there for only a year.

Now, thirteen years later, with a house of their own and three boys, Julius and Helen were regular visitors. Julius loved to needle the boys, he would amaze them with tricks and sleight of hand moves meant to confuse their young minds into thinking the impossible had just taken place right in front of their eyes with another abracadabra. Mr. Jake, as the boy's called him, would often make up stories about going to Vietnam and talking with his old pal Charlie. He wanted to know which of the boys were willing to go with him and meet him. One Christmas he was telling the trio an exotic story about Australia and how he was going to vacation there so he could ride a kangaroo everyday into the supermarket, putting his groceries in its pouch, then he would ride her home like an old mule. The kids howled at Mr. Jake's stories and antics.

Part of the camaraderie between the couples stemmed from the fact that Jake was from Italy and Helen was of Scottish descent, exactly like Mags parents. Julius enjoyed smoking his pipe and cigars. He would joke that he had to go see his buddy Fidel Castro and pick up a few more Cuban cigars to smoke because he was running out and the communists were running out of money, like always. Helen loved her Virginia slims by the carton. Her gold soft-sided carrying case seemed to never empty of those mile-long thin cigarettes. Before lighting up she would connect each of them to her white filter extension— adding a few more inches, which made them feel like they could reach across the table, smoldering under your nose while she smoked, and she always smoked. Add to the smoky haze a steady flow of martinis with two olives, and you begin to understand why Helen was the life of any celebration.

"Are we going to Mr. Jake's," Cam asked, looking up from his book.

"No, honey. Now read your book," Mags answered. "Mr. Jake will like that you're reading the book he got you."

"He calls me Harry now," Cameron said with all the seriousness of an accountant.

"I know, why?"

"Cause of the greatest magician ever, Harry Houdini."

"That's funny."

"It's why I'm reading this book again so I can do the best tricks ever!" Cam said.

"Mr. Jake will love it."

"When are we gonna see them again?"

"Next weekend," She said and Cam reentered the world of magic.

Fifteen minutes later the green car holding the family rolled into Romex Marina on the north side of the Clinton River a mile east of downtown Mt Clemens. As they piled out of the car, the smell of water and gasoline greeted them in the rocky parking lot. Grabbing a bag and a cooler out of the trunk Marty told the gang to follow him down an ancient wooden dock. The boards creaked and groaned with each step as the family passed by rows of boats lined up on each side of perpendicular boardwalks. The rows intersected the main walkway every hundred feet or so, stretching out into the dark river. At the fourth intersection, Marty went right to the sixth boat on the left. It was a brand-new Owens cabin cruiser and he walked to the back of the boat, set the cooler and bag down, then waited for everyone to catch up. He pointed to the letters on the mahogany stern— 'Three Sons' and waited for the meaning to sink in. Caleb's eyes grew wide when the realization hit him. Cam was lost in thought as to what the name meant, and young Curtis, still groggy from his nap, buried his head in his mother's neck to escape the blinding sun.

"Dad, is this our boat?" Caleb asked.

"Why would you say that?"

"It says Three Sons, and you have three sons."

"Are you sure?"

"Yes. Me, Cam, and Curt."

"It's our new boat," Marty beamed.

It was this moment that the light went on in Cam's head and he too, was overcome with excitement.

"Come on boys your gonna have to learn how to be sailors now," Marty said and smiled.

"Permission to come aboard, Captain?" Cam asked, which drew uproarious laughter from his mother.

"Permission granted, sailor!" which was followed by a salute from all three boys.

* Red Rivers *

"Caleb, throw the anchor," Marty said from the bridge a little annoyed. Caleb was perched on the bow holding onto the stainless-steel railing with one hand and trying to pick up the anchor with the other.

"You're gonna have to use both your hands," dad said.

Caleb, after a slight hesitation, let go of the rail and reached down to pick up the anchor which was connected to the boat by a long, coiled spool of white rope. His right leg pressed into the railing to steady his balance against the gentle rolling waves.

"There you go, just like you practiced," Marty said.

"Throw it!" yelled Cam. He was watching his bother from behind the windshield in the co-pilot seat. Caleb tossed the anchor overboard, with a grunt.

"Now pull it taunt around the cleat, around the end, over top, around the other end and under. Good. Hang on, buddy."

Marty put the cruiser into reverse to slowly set the anchor in the lake bottom and when he felt it grab, he took it out of gear and shut the motor off.

"Good job honey!" Mags said.

Cam and Curt clapped for their brother who offered a coy smile in return.

"What a beautiful day," Mags rubbed Marty's shoulder in a sign of appreciation for taking the time out on the boat after a busy stretch of life. The plan was to spend the evening tucked away in a cove near the eastern shore of Lake St. Clair.

"Is this Canada?" Cam asked.

"Yes. You can see their flag over in Mitchell's Bay," Marty said while pointing.

"I thought we lived in the United States of 'merica?" Curtis was confused.

"We do, but we are visiting Canada," Mags said.

"Oh. Okay." The four-and-a-half-year-old seemed satisfied and continued to roll his toy car across the mahogany deck.

"Mom, can we swim?"

"Sure, for a bit. Then were gonna have dinner." She turned to Marty, "Do you want a beer?"

"Yes!"

"I put the Stroh's on ice."

"You're the best!"

"Do you want to swim Curtis?" Marty asked.

"Naw, not right now."

"What do you have there?"

"A car. You know, like what you build at work."

"Let me see that one."

He gave up his new favorite toy car for examination.

"Ah this is a '65 Pontiac GTO. See the headlights are stacked on top of each other instead of side by side."

"It's my favorite car, for now," Curtis said.

"I like it too," Marty offered it back to his youngest son. He used his finger to rub upwards on the side of the boy's head. "And I like your haircut! Princeton."

"Thanks." And back to road racing the boy went, then he paused with a new thought. "Dad, did you make this car? You know, the real one."

"Did I do work on the GTO?"

"Yeah."

"No, not me. But our shop did all the mock-ups for it."

Curtis smiled as he raced away, dreaming of working on cars just like his dad.

Marty descended the ladder below deck and Cam came up from below deck immediately after.

"Why aren't you going swimming, Curtis?"

"I don't wanna."

"You scared?"

"Nope."

"Yes, you're a little chicken liver!"

"Shut up!"

"What do you have here?"

"That's my car, Cam!" Cameron grabbed the car away from his brother.

"You better be quiet Curtis or I'll hold you under the water like I did last time."

"Knock it off Cam," Caleb said as he stepped up on the deck in his bathing suit. "Quit picking on Curt."

"He's too chicken to go in the lake."

"So what, he's four?" Caleb stepped in close to his brother to intervene. At eleven he was a head taller than his nine-year old sibling.

"Let's go swimming, the raft is already in the water," Caleb insisted.

"Give me my car back, Cam!"

"I dropped it back in the bag, little dork," Cam pointed to the bag of matchbox cars beneath the co-pilot seat. But when Cam jumped from the boat to swim, he threw the little green car as far as he could out into the lake and smiled as he submerged beneath the bubbling waters.

"Cam!"

"Huh?" he said wiping at his face when he surfaced.

"I told you to wait until I got back on deck," Marty said.

"You did? Oh, yeah."

"Come out of the water."

"Dad!"

"You didn't listen, now come up out of the water and wait until I tell you to go in. You're your own worst enemy, son."

Cam obeyed and climbed out of the cool lake. He took a seat in the co-pilot seat while Marty swept the deck around little Curtis. Perfect Caleb, on the other hand, had listened to wait for permission to jump in and was now sprawled out in the yellow rubber raft, smiling and soaking up the late afternoon sun. As Marty turned his back, Cam held his dripping hand over Curtis' head. Curt wiped at the water, not knowing that it was his brother's doing.

"Cam, stop it. Go back in the lake, and listen to me the next time," Marty said.

"Okay, dad," his mischievous smile faded with the thought of the refreshing water.

"Kamikaze!" he yelled as he jumped in right next to Caleb, splashing his unsuspecting brother.

Twenty minutes later Mags called from the deck while setting a tray of food on the built-in fold-out table. "Dinner, boys." Then, glancing southwest into the sun she had to block her eyes. The distant Detroit skyline was clouded by thick black smoke. Normally you could see the downtown buildings jutting into the sky from many places on Lake St. Clair, but today a heavy darkness covered the view in that direction.

"Mom there is something weird about the water," Caleb said climbing up the ladder.

"Yeah, it looks red," Cam said.

"That's why we brought you boys over here," Mags turned toward her wet invaders, choosing not to point out the eerie sky.

"Huh?"

"The Sydenham River runs red during the beet harvest."

"What?" Cam said.

"That's so cool!" Caleb said and looked out over the waters.

"It flows into the lake just to the north of here," she lifted her chin in the direction of the river.

"Mom, have you seen my green car?" Curtis asked from the bottom of the ladder below deck.

"No honey and it's time to eat."

"But, mom, it's my favorite."

"We'll look after dinner."

Marty came out of the tiny bath room and picked Curtis up and placed him on the deck, which brought a smile to the boy's otherwise sad face.

"Come on kiddo, time to eat!"

"Thanks for the elevator lift, dad!"

"Are you hungry?"

"Starving!" Curt said with a monster-like smile, which revealed his blackened front tooth. Curt had crashed into the corner of the wall a few weeks earlier while playing with Cam and his baby tooth turned color by the next week.

"Are we really having hot dogs for dinner, Mom?" Cam asked when he noticed the food tray.

"You don't have to," Marty said.

"Cool. What can I have instead?"

"Nothing. Or you could have hot dogs."

Caleb laughed at the look on his brother's face.

"It's kinda limited out on the water, you know that Cam," Mag said.

"I wanted your spaghetti."

"Sorry, Charlie," mom said.

"He's not Charlie!" Curtis said and laughed toward the sky holding his non-existent belly.

"Did you bring your binoculars, Marty?" Mags asked. She made eyes toward the horizon over the boys' shoulders.

"Yeah." He had noticed the growing black columns of smoke rising above the distant city.

"You boys eat your dinner because I brought dessert."

"Yay!" Curtis said.

"What is it?"

"Cookies."

Even picky Cam ate all of his hot dog and potato salad as sea gulls cawed around the boat, looking for a handout.

"The cookies are down in the galley on the table. You can have three each, but I want you to eat them at the table while I get this mess cleaned up."

Mags said. She sent the boys below and Marty grabbed his field glasses to get a closer look at the skyline.

"What is it?"

"It looks like the whole city is on fire. Columns of smoke are rising from all over the place."

"What?"

"We need to turn the radio on," Marty said.

"I'll go keep the boys below deck, you find out what's happening."

Marty stood and turned the radio's power switch on and waited for the internal tubes to heat. Twisting the nob, he dialed to 760 AM. The noise of static grew as the unit powered up. Then the powerful Detroit station interrupted the static with a grim sounding man giving a public service announcement.

"We gotta go, Mags," Marty whispered into her ear five minutes later. There is a huge riot in Detroit and many buildings are being burnt down. We need to get home."

"Okay. I'll get things put away down here, then I'll send the boys on deck as soon as you are under way."

"Right."

As the family raced across the calm evening waters, Mags did everything she could to calm her sons. Holding Curtis on her lap while he held onto his last scrap of his old blanket, and she gently caressed the other two boy's heads. The Canadian shore was growing distant behind them as Marty opened the boat up to full throttle and kept watch on the shipping lanes for the lumbering lake freighters.

Out over the bow of the boat a line of large airplanes filled the sky in a wide arch. The planes were circling, waiting to land at Selfridge Air

National Guard base just north of where they kept the boat on the Clinton River.

"What's going on, mom?" Caleb asked.

"Some buildings in Detroit are on fire and your dad wants to go just to make sure everything's all right at home, that's all."

"We're not spending the night on the boat?" Cam asked.

"Not tonight, honey."

"I thought you said we were staying in Canada?"

"I did, but sometimes plans change," Mags said.

"What's with all the planes?" Caleb asked.

"I think they're bringing in soldiers to help."

"Looks like a lot of soldiers."

Mags kept most of the details from her kids that night as one of the worst race riots in American history raged just fifteen miles south. A few hours after arriving home, the boys watched out their front window as National Guard units rolled south in huge Army transport trucks, through the barricaded streets, toward the growing chaos. Detroit was once considered the Paris of North America but had become a smoldering, hollowed out shell of herself, filled with racial strife, looting, and murder. Forty-three people lost their lives during those four summer days in 1967, and five thousand were left homeless due to over fourteen hundred buildings being burnt to the ground. The physical and emotional scars of the once proud and populous city would continue for decades.

* Sneaky Kid *

"This can't be right, I'm too old."

"I ran it twice and they both said the same thing."

"Marty's going to be surprised."

"Well, congratulations, Mags, this explains a lot."

Mags left the office stunned and made her way to her red Volkswagen Beetle where she sat and silently cried for a few moments. Starting the car, she made her way back to the bank where she worked in the bookkeeping department. Mags spent the rest of the day unable to focus and watching the wall clock do its slow walk until 4:30 finally arrived— a week later. Not one for much chit-chat after hours, Mags had responsibilities. Marty was still on afternoon shift, so she had to hurry home to the boys who had been home from school for a couple hours. Caleb was almost twelve and she thought he did a good job of watching over Cam in their absence.

This new revelation from Dr. Lindy however, would change so many things about their life. It made her mind wander toward all of the things that would be disrupted as she drove home, almost forgetting to get Curtis from Kay's house. She had to back-track a couple of blocks to pick up her preschooler.

Bewilderment was coursing through her as she pulled into the long driveway and up to the closed gate near the back door, nausea rose. Cam was playing in the back yard with the dog, which surprised her after Bonnie had scratched Curtis' face the week before. The youngest boy had startled the dog while he bent down to show her his Halloween ghost costume. The dog lunged at the unfamiliar figure with her paws. Now, with the news from the Doc, Mags knew the beloved dog would have to go.

"Maybe my mom would take her," she thought.

"Hey mom."

"Hi, honey. What are you doing?"

"Just playin' with Bonnie."

"Did you finish your homework?"

"I didn't have any today."

"Watch out Cam, Bonnie has sharp nails," Curtis said while climbing out of the backseat of the car. He touched the inch long scab on his right cheek.

"I'm not dressed up like a scary ghost, doofus."

"Keep your fingers off that scab, Curtis," Mom said.

"What's for dinner?" Cam asked.

"Swedish meatballs," the thought instantly nauseated her.

"Really?" It was not one of Cam's favorites. Being the pickiest of eaters, not many things excited him about mealtime.

"Unless you want pizza from Sila's," Mags said.

"Yeah!" Both boys said in unison.

"But it's not Friday," Cam said.

"I know, but I think we can do that." Mags was relieved she wouldn't have to cook raw meat on a day like today.

The next week a large family gathering was going on in the basement of the bungalow, as family and friends gathered for Thanksgiving. Julius and Helen came to celebrate and Cam was ready to put on his magic show to prove he was in line to take over for Mr. Houdini.

"That was a nice show, Harry. I see you learned a few more tricks"

"Thanks Mr. Jake. I read the book you gave me three times."

"Remember that magic is making the impossible seem possible. While using sleight of hand to cause your audience to look at one thing when the reality is happening unnoticed."

"I'm still working on that one."

"You're doing a good job, Harry. Do you know the number one rule of all magicians?"

"No, I didn't read that in the book."

"Well, I can tell you but it has to remain a secret, Mr. Houdini told me personally." Jake bent low toward Cam's ear.

"Houdini told me, and this secret has to stay between you and me."

"Okay. What is it?"

"You only get to see what I want you to see." Julius whispered to Cameron this basic truth of all magician's.

"Huh?"

"The real trick is to get your audience to see what you, the magician, wants them to see."

"Ohhhh. I get it!" Cam smiled and thought about the ramifications.

"You only get to see what I want you to see," Cam said and waved his hands.

"Exactly!"

Young Cameron took Mr. Jake's advice to heart and adopted it that day as one of his underlying life principles.

"We have an announcement," Marty tapped a bottle with a butter knife. The loud chatter in the room trickled off into silence. "Since this is Thanksgiving and all, I thought we should tell you something we are grateful for. Believe it or not, Mags and I are expecting again."

The shrieks of joy and spontaneous applause rose up from family and friends who all looked at Mags. She appeared exhausted from the day of preparation and her condition.

"When are you due?" Marty's mom called out across the room.

"May."

The three sons whispered among themselves what the information meant, while their aunts and uncles resumed their loud discussions around the table, offering congratulations and warnings. Many offered the hope for a daughter and a raise in pay.

"Where are you going to put the little goober?"

"In the back bedroom and I'm going to build a bedroom down here for Caleb."

"Your world is going to change, boys," Uncle Matt said. They had no idea what that meant.

* Up North *

Traffic on the expressway was heavy. The lanes were filled with every vehicle imaginable loaded down with equipment and expectations for the upcoming Fourth of July holiday celebration. Thousands of people crammed into every kind truck, car, and camper imaginable and made out for the northern woods of Michigan. Ropes holding duffel bags, coolers, and boxes, decorated the roofs of many cars. Trailers overloaded with motorcycles, tents, refrigerators, and luggage. Countless vehicles had to stop and retie their belongings along the shoulder of the highway which caused everything to slow for gawkers. There was the occasional poor soul that had to backtrack on foot to pick up some of what had been attached to their sedan from the roadway. These were the situations that brought the over-taxed expressway to a standstill and increased the level of anxiety for everyone.

Workers in Michigan who had vacation time used it for one of two hol-idays. The first was taken around Independence Day, and the second was for deer hunting season in the middle of November. The auto plants even scheduled their change over times during the first two weeks of July, which meant thousands of employees were idled and added into the holiday rush to relax.

Marty had been hopeful that by waiting to leave until Saturday morning they would miss a large portion of the traffic headed north on I-75. He gambled that, with the Fourth on a Tuesday that most Michiganders would want to squeeze every ounce of away time out of the holiday causing them to brave the road on Friday after work let out. Unfortunately for his family, too many folks held the same view, choosing to wait until Saturday.

Caleb was driving as traffic buzzed past. Marty was in the copilot seat giving his eldest son advice on dealing with the rising tide of vehicles, while wanting to drive. Mags sat in the back seat with the boys, chewing on the inside of her mouth trying not to call out instructions to her son.

"You've got to drive defensively when traffic is like this. Just assume they can't see you and don't care about you."

"Okay, dad."

The family of six was headed north to their little oasis in the woods. North of the small hamlet of Onaway, and close to the eastern shore of Black Lake. Marty had purchased six acres a quarter mile down the gravel road from Mag's sister's vacation spot. Their 1970 Coachman camper awaited the arrival of the family, as it had occupied the same spot on the lot for the last two years. The white travel trailer sat on the highest point on the six acres, about a hundred feet off the road. The long and narrow parcel had the highest elevation, near the road, while the ground fell off in the field to the rear, all the way back to the southern wooded border. Trees also grew along half of the western edge, connected to the neighbor's large swath of woods to the west at the back of his property.

The owner of a farm field needed to raise some money. He decided to sell off two, three-acre parcels from his twenty-acre lot. His motivation revealed the fact that he could not hold down a steady job in an area of the state that had little industry and fewer employers. Marty bought the center three-acre piece and when another buyer backed out from the deal for the remaining three acres, he bought the final piece the following spring.

The previous summer Marty had built a two hundred and fifty-six square foot barn on the property with an upstairs loft— complete with three twin beds for the boys. Curtis, who was now nine and a half, was going to sleep out with his brothers for the first time during this trip. Having the boys sleep in the barn freed up a lot of room in the travel trailer and offered the couple some needed vacation privacy. The only fear for the boys was the occasional bat that wanted to nest high up in the rafters and swoop with annoyance at the human invaders. Bees could also be a nuisance if they got into the soffit to make a nest. The beds would have to be shaken down and clean linens applied by all, while Marty made sure the pests were kept at bay. The access to the loft was a rudimentary ladder constructed out of two by fours nailed to the vertical studs in the corner of the barn. Bags and luggage were hoisted up through the front set of loft doors that acted as a window while occupied, complete with a screen to keep the mosquitoes out.

Katie, the four-year-old, would be required to sleep with Marty and Mags inside the 26' travel trailer turned cabin. The determined girl always wanted to hang out with her older brothers and often sought out their undivided attention through her loud antics, singing, and dancing. As it turned out, Katie and Cameron shared many similarities, but neither liked to admit it. Both were not afraid to be loud and rambunctious to garner attention from any of the frequent guests that visited their small suburban home, or even those who ventured the 250 miles north to the cabin. Overall, Caleb and Curtis tended to be the ones to stay back in the shadows, content with playing by themselves away from the crowds. Of course, these things were generally true of the siblings, but any and all of them could take on the other roles.

As the miles droned on, the frequent and annoying question was always, "How long until we get there?" Marty tried to shut that question down before it got out of hand. This was especially true starting out on vacation, the return trip was often filled with sun-burnt and exhausted adults dreading the upcoming week of work and routines, while the kids grumbled that the fun had to end, wondering why life could not always be spent on vacation.

The trip consisted of a hundred and fifty miles of freeway, then one hundred miles on a two-lane road called M-33. This had been explained to the children every single time the trip was made.

"Don't even ask if we are there yet when we are still on the expressway!" Marty became frustrated when either the kids argued or asked that one dumb question.

"We'll get there when we get there," was often his response after exiting onto M-33.

It had become a tradition to stop at the Dairy Queen in Rose City for lunch and a bathroom break, so long as there was not too many other families with the same idea. The four children lobbied for ice cream, while Mom and Dad just wanted to be out of the car.

"How are you doing?" Mags asked Marty from the back seat while touching his shoulder.

"Good," Marty said and smiled while looking back.

"This car rides so nice."

"I know, it's like sitting on the couch," Marty said.

"Especially back here," she replied.

Mag's thought the new car was comfortable and spacious for her entire family. The soft dark blue velour interior invited you to rest as you traveled.

Caleb drove on the expressway leg of the journey, Katie sat in the front, playing with her baby doll. Cam was behind the driver, busy reading a book about brewing beer, which was so foreign to Mags, she could only shake her head at her eclectic second son. She was grateful he was not needling his younger siblings. Curtis was reading his own book about the stars of hockey, leaning his small frame against his mother.

"My-lanta, there is lots of traffic," Mags said.

"It's like everyone waited to leave today," Marty admitted.

"Good idea," she teased.

Tires squealed and smoke rose up from many of the vehicles in close proximity. The nose of the car dipped low as Caleb slammed on the breaks in reaction. Mags cried out, while Marty grabbed at the chest of his daughter to protect her in case they crashed. Both the boys in the back dropped their books and looked up to see what was happening. Loud slams and the groan of bending metal came from in front of them. Glass shattered as cars spun in circles trying to avoid impact. Vehicles on both sides of them flew down into the ditches, throwing grass and mud into the air. Horns blared out their warnings while one in particular changed its tune to a growl. Steam and smoked mixed through the air outside the car, along with a rising cloud of dust. Then everything fell into a silent pause, just for the briefest of moments, as the entire freeway held its breath.

"Everyone all right?" Marty asked and looked.

Stunned responses came from everyone in the car, most from a nod, except Katie who cried out for her mommy.

"God job Caleb on keeping us out of the accident," Mags said as she pulled her whimpering daughter into the back seat.

"Stay here!" Marty said and jumped out from his door. After walking past two vehicles in front of their blue Oldsmobile, a pile of three cars was mangled unnaturally together. A couple of doors opened and people were beginning to stumble out from inside the steaming wrecks. A bloody forehead, and a broken nose on one woman, as she was helped to the shoulder of the road. Another door was forced open and several beer bottles clanked to the concrete. The man had begun his celebration a little early.

An older man helped him steady himself. Marty tossed the bottles off to the side of the road and made his way back to his family.

"Caleb, you almost got us killed!" Cameron said.

"What are you talking about?"

"You almost wrecked the new car," Cam insisted.

"No, I didn't," Caleb said. Then everyone began talking at the same time.

"Stop it both of you! You're frightening the little ones," Mags said.

Marty yanked the passenger door open, surprising everybody.

"Is everyone alright?" Mags asked.

"Yes. No one is hurt."

"What did you throw into the grass?" Cameron asked.

"A couple of beer bottles."

"I think you'll be able to get around on the left shoulder," Marty said.

"Do you want to drive, dad? Some people think I almost got us killed," Caleb asked.

"No. You are doing a good job. You braked like a pro, K."

"Okay. Thanks." Caleb smiled with the compliment and shot a glare through the mirror to Cam.

"Put your signal on, they'll let you over."

Forty-five minutes later Caleb pulled into the expanded Dairy Queen parking lot and breathed a sigh of relief over his leg of the driving coming to an end. The family took a lunch break inside the air-conditioned store, forgoing the sandwiches that had been planned for the ride, to eat while driving, and opting for a pile of hamburgers followed up by ice cream cones.

While licking at the side of his cone, Cameron commented to his brother as they sat alone in the booth. "I'm gonna be a better driver than you, K."

"Oh yeah?"

"Yep. I'm gonna check out a few books at the library and read all about it before I even take drivers training."

"You can't learn to drive in a book."

"Yes, I can."

"No, you can learn the rules and laws but not how to drive until you actually get behind the wheel."

"Well, I'm gonna drive better than you do."

"You're dumb."

"You suck at driving."

"Shut up."

"I'll race you on the motorcycles and prove it."

"Okay, Evel Kinevel."

"I am better, you'll see."

"What does Aunt say about you all the time, Cam?"

"What?"

"That you could sell ice to Eskimo's."

"So, she thinks that I'd make a good salesman, like uncle Al!"

"She thinks that you're a good bull-shitter, like uncle Al."

"Salesman!"

"You believe that stuff about you being a better driver than me because you have to. You've always wanted to be better than me, it's why you read all them stupid books about magic and now you're reading about brewing beer when you can't even drink it after you are done. You're crazy."

"You're an idiot. I am a better driver than you. At least I didn't almost get us killed today!"

"Neither did I, Harry Houdini."

"Enough you two. We are all tired. Go get washed up and use the toilet. We're leaving in five minutes," Marty said.

Two hours later the tires cruised off the asphalt and onto the gravel of the final road and vacation officially began.

Five

Cameron Lost

— Section Five —

"Three Amigos"

"The future is as bright as the promises of God."
Adoniram Judson

* Jacob's Staircase *

The soil was sandy and flat as the trio trekked away from the shoreline into the shadowy white pine forest. The air that filled their lungs was warm and moist as the brothers focused on the task while annoying stable flies buzzed about heads and legs looking for blood. A year of planning, training, and organizing culminated in an epic vacation. They strutted into the darkness of the unknown forest, a surreal cloud enveloped them, the palpable uncertainty that the day had arrived. Their joy spilled over as soon as the car was out of sight. Laughter surged from their mouths joined by words filled with hope and expectation. To anyone watching, they might have seemed boisterous and obnoxious, but to them, it was as regular as a sunrise on a summer day. There was not an ounce of pretense among them walking into their realized dream. Laughter and ridicule were familiar, yet even that came from within the security of their brotherhood.

Fifteen minutes later, they were still eager and marching with purpose across sand flats, in reflective silence while the trail meandered through pines, maples, and ash. They stopped to tighten bootlaces and adjust socks. Pack straps dug into shoulders. Crumbled T-shirts needed flattening beneath the pressure of harnesses. Hip belts were cinched and loosened with the low buzz of nylon straps passing through plastic retainers. Each sought a constant search for the most comfortable position as the heat of the day, and the burden of heavy packs became more than just a dream vacation.

"Where are these supposed cliffs, Curtis?" Cam asked.

"Are you sure we're in the right place?" Caleb said and laughed.

"Were we supposed to turn left at the Mackinac Bridge and not right?" Cameron's signature laugh followed this. It was a combination of "he, he, he," with an "uh, uh, uh," and a "ha, ha, ha," in short, loud, rapid bursts, like a human hyena, but more audible. Everyone who knew him for a long time referred to it as the "Cam laugh." His vocal outbursts were accompanied by extreme facial expressions with wide eyes, an open mouth, and a pointing finger, which only made it all seem more ridiculous.

When the three of them were together and got on a roll, most people near-by could not help but laugh along, but no one was sure if the cause of the hilarity was the jokes themselves or just three hyena's hysteria. Each of the brothers had their version of the Cam laugh, with Curtis coming the closest to the unique cackle. Caleb's genuine laugh was the least like it but still carried Cam-like undertones.

Caleb understood that Cam had developed the laugh to garner attention, while Curtis grew up with it being normal and continued his brother's antics. Everyone could hear the echoes of the three laughing brothers walking through the woods for half a mile in any direction.

"I mean, you didn't look at any maps; maybe you led us the wrong way," Cam continued.

"Wait for it, Cam. Wait for it!" Curtis said.

Three minutes later, as the trail bent right, a massive rock wall appeared through the pines and blocked their way. As far as they could see, in either direction, the barrier stood, which had them wondering how they were supposed to get to the top. Then the answer slapped them in the face.

"Holy crap!" Caleb said.

"How many stairs are there?"

"I can't count that high," Curtis said.

"Take off your boots. Then maybe you could use your toes, too." Cam said, and Cam's laugh ensued. Sometimes Cameron tried to annoy the people around him with all of the antics surrounding his cackle, but the brothers had become immune. Somewhere in time, Cam had discovered that any attention, positive or negative, was still, in fact, attention. This realization went all the way back to when he was the toddler who shrieked at the top of his lungs when things did not go his way.

The brothers' skin had thickened to the point that his acting out had become endearing, after three uninterrupted decades. Their sister Katie was the one to fall into Cam's psychological trap, but she was four hundred miles south, stuck in an operating room, helping repair someone's broken heart. God made Katie and Cam from the same magnet, but their poles tended to repulse.

"Funny."

"I guess I thought we'd be going up switchbacks or something, not a colossal staircase to the top of the cliff," Curtis said.

"Let's look at the topo map," Cam suggested.

"Grab it out of my back pouch," Curtis spun around to give Cam access.

After unfolding and flipping the large waterproof green map, the three stood over it as Curtis followed the trail they had been walking for the last mile with his finger. The map was an official National Parks topographical version, showing height differentials in twenty-foot increments. At the place where the trail ran into the cliff, seven lines became one, which indicated at least a one-hundred-forty-foot vertical rise was towering over them.

There was no other way to access the clifftop from Sand Point.

"Well, there you go. Now we know why there's a need for a staircase in the middle of the woods," Caleb said.

"We could walk back to Sand Point, drive to the Visitor Center, and start from there. It would add about three and a half miles onto the trip and put us at the top of these stairs," Curtis said.

"No fricken way are we are doing that," Cam said.

"Right, but this kinda takes away from the backcountry ruggedness of the trail, don't 'ya think?" Caleb asked while pointing up at the wooden colossus.

"What were you expecting, a stack of tires up to a rusted-out hillbilly trailer?" Cam's laugh was fully engaged.

"Yeah. But I don't want to strap on climbing gear to get up there. So, I will humbly thank the men and material sacrificed here on our behalf," Curtis said and pulled his baseball cap over his heart to complete the joke.

"You're such a dork," Cam said and laughed along.

"Maybe, but this is the only logical way forward, or upward, I guess."

"Lead the way, young one. Who picked this place to go backpacking, anyway?" Caleb asked Cam.

"Who was that idiot?"

"Both you sissies can wait in the car. I've got an adventure stretching out in front of me. Besides, I'll get dropped off in a week or so."

"You'd get lost," Cam said.

"Don't think so. The map is locked in this safe," Curtis said and pointed to the side of his head.

"We're doomed!" Cam replied.

"Just pace yourselves, take your time, old geezers, I don't want you to have a heart attack, 'cause I'm not doing mouth to mouth on either of your ugly asses."

"That's not how you do CPR anyways, genius," Cam said.

"Gross. Why are you always the disgusting one?"

"I was just born that way," Cam said and increased the decibels of the chortle.

"I'll wait for you chumps at the top." And off the kid went.

Curtis was not much of a kid. With three young children of his own and a real job, he arrived at adulthood with the other two. Curtis was in the prime of his life. He led an active lifestyle with plenty of sports and activities throughout the year to keep him in decent shape, plus he had a physical job working in a steel factory. But the most significant difference was his body type, which was dissimilar from his older brothers. He was lean, and an inch taller. One disparaging attribute from the older brother's viewpoint, which Cam incessantly pointed out, was Curtis' ability to eat whatever he wanted, whenever he wanted, and never gain any weight. This reality pissed the older two off because their genes demanded a different fate for both of them. That genetic destiny commanded any weight control for them would always come the hard way. Starving themselves with fewer calories, plus a lot of forced activity was the only way to reduce girth and stay in shape.

"Round is a shape," Caleb would often say, but internally he struggled against the idea of eating for comfort as a preferred coping mechanism. He wanted to stay in shape, but his sedentary job designing cars meant he spent countless hours at a desk in front of his computer, strapped down by obligation like an airline pilot forced to fly fifty hours a week. The auto industry rewarded high performance. It was one of the aspects that Caleb loved, but it also contributed to his struggle with his weight.

Cameron, on the other hand, was his own worst enemy. He fulfilled the prophecy spoken over him by his parents for the last thirty-five years in myriad ways. Sugar was second greatest enemy. The empty calories of a gooey candy bar or some concoction of chocolate with coatings constantly called out to him, bringing a flood of feel-good endorphins along for the ride. His eating habits were not great either. Late-night taco runs or burgers dripping their greasy goodness were always dancing outside his brain, waiting to hustle their waist-spreading ideas. On too many nights, the temptations won. They found their way inside his belly before crashing on the couch in front of the TV. His detox solution was to juice five pounds of carrots combined with a green apple. He would cram down a fist full of vitamins for breakfast dessert and call it healthy eating.

All of this had changed for the three of them about a year before their grand trip. It happened during a Father's Day celebration. Curtis suggested that the three brothers, plus their brother-in-law Lars, get away on an epic adventure. They would strap fifty pounds of a house on each of their backs and see if they could hike through Picture Rocks National Lakeshore. Curtis thought it was about fifty miles from the beginning to end of a primitive journey along the shore of Lake Superior. They would have to navigate a path threaded along the rugged coast, through old-growth forest, walking inches from a two-hundred-foot drop into the Lake, and then survive the dreaded twelve-mile beach. Curtis had done a respectable job selling them on the adventure. The rest of the family rolled their eyes. Spouses wondered about the financial cost of such a trip and the length of the separation.

The Lakeshore Trail begins on the outskirts of Munising, Michigan, and runs to the northeast. It takes hikers through a varied landscape— tramping across beaches, traversing rivers, down through murky swamps, and along 200-foot cliffs. The two most striking features are the view of the gigantic Lake from atop the escarpment and the rocks themselves. The limestone cliffs ooze mineral-rich groundwater, streaking the imposing walls' faces with a multitude of colors. It appears God himself paints living, breathing pictures on the rocks.

The massive Lake has a life of its own as well. On sunny days she is crystal clear, allowing hikers to see into her depths. Her green and blue waters sparkle, inviting weary travelers into her cold life-giving wonderland. Superior is a fickle beast, smiling and winking in one moment, then wielding her ferocious might in the next, pounding against all who dare trespass.

Summer boat tours running eight times a day out of the Munising docks brought thousands of visitors to witness the remote area each year, as long as lady Superior granted her approval. People come to see the rock formations and dozens of caves pounded into the base of the cliffs over thousands of years by the relentless Lake. Pristine beaches and waterfalls offer stunning evening views of water and sky. The boat tour is a two-and-a-half-hour passive ride sitting in a comfortable seat, listening to a narrator telling scripted stories over the intercom about ancient geology and native peoples who held the area in high regard. At the same time, passengers drink expensive and highly caffeinated drinks.

Hiking the trail was a different animal that did not require the Lake's approval. It is a challenge that resonates with men for various reasons—the chance to spend time together as brothers is the most compelling.

One collective agreement was the need for each of them to get into better physical shape before the journey. They all began to exercise individually and collectively, for a year before the trip. Walking and lifting weights were the primary focus. Caleb and Cam shook off pounds by dieting along with the physical regime.

The competitive spirit grew as they pushed one another along. They were looking forward to the day they would walk away from their families and onto the primitive trail.

Halfway up the stairway to the heavens, all three were breathing heavily, grasping for more oxygen to fill their lungs while streams of sweat rolled off their faces. Curtis paused for his brothers to catch up and to drink from his army surplus canteen. Each man had opted for the cheap and practical device to hold their drinking water supply.

"Better slow down, there, cowboy; you're going to run out," Cam said to Curtis while they waited for Caleb to take the final flight of stairs.

"Yeah, there should be plenty available to filter along the way."

"Hope you're right."

"How's the view from the top?" Caleb asked his brothers, their elbows perched on the railing. Their packs leaning against a nearby tree.

"Looks like it did twenty minutes ago, just higher."

"A lot of trees."

"Except you should look down, K," Cam said.

Caleb turned to look over the edge of the staircase and had to grab hold of the rail as the heights caused a surge of fear to shoot up through his legs.

"Oh, yeah, I don't like that!"

The pair at the ledge busted out laughing, knowing his fear of heights all too well.

"Yeah, buddy, it's a long way down!" Caleb said, forcing himself to peer over the edge while white-knuckling the rail.

Just as Caleb set foot on the final step, Cameron nudged Curtis.

"All righty then, ready to go, Curt?"

"Yep." They both stepped toward their packs.

"You're real comedians," Caleb said and removed his pack while the other two laughed at him.

They all felt the effects of the seven-hour drive north since they had left home at midnight and driven through the night. Exhaustion was the reason behind the long pause at the top of Jacob's Staircase, as Cam called it. They broke out a snack for a boost before moving on. The trio had not been alone in the wilderness for quite some time. Usually, one or two others tagged along for the adventure, but everyone came up with plenty of excuses to miss out on walking fifty miles while carrying a house. Even Lars, Katie's husband, who usually was game for a challenge, found other things to be doing during the expedition week.

* Popsicle Failures *

Their initial excursion to shake out their equipment happened ten months earlier. Four of them, Lars included, hiked a twenty-four-mile loop in the Lower Peninsula closer to home. That trip nearly ended in disaster. Vandals had destroyed all of the directional signs in the recreational area. This destruction confused the group when crossing many unmarked intersections not identified on any map. After the third time ending up in the wrong place and then retracing their steps back to another unmarked intersection, their confidence in their navigation ability had evaporated. It was then that a cold front blew through, bringing wind and rain. The wetness, the disappointments, the confusion, the cold temperatures, and improper rain gear caused both Caleb's and Lars' body temperatures to drop close to hypothermia. The misery index increased when they realized they had missed the lone trail that would have taken them to the camping area.

"Hey, we gotta stop," Cam said to Curt, who was bringing up the rear of the group.

"Okay. What's up?"

"Look at those two," he pointed forward with his eyes ahead on the trail as Caleb and Lars were weaving from side to side, as they walked like mindless zombies.

"Yeah, that's not good at all," Curtis said.

"How far do you figure we've walked?" Cam asked.

"I'd guess about eighteen to twenty miles."

"I'm beat; how about you?"

"I could be done."

"Hey! We're stopping here!" Cam called out. There was no response.

"Go get those two popsicles. I'll start clearing a spot for the tent," Cam said.

Twenty feet off the edge of the trail, Cam and Curtis carved out a campsite beneath a towering Jack pine. The hastily made camping area was rugged even by backcountry standards. They cleared out a spot to shoehorn in their four-person tent while Lars and Caleb huddled beneath the big pine, watching, and shivering against the cold. Each man had a separate part of the shelter tied to their pack. Neither Lars nor K could untie the knots and retrieve their respective pieces. Their shrinking motor skills had evaporated.

"They are further along than I thought," Cam whispered to Curtis.

"Yeah, they got to get out of their wet clothes."

"Right."

"Ah, nothing like thirty-eight degrees and rain, my favorite," Curtis said and feigned a smile.

"And being soaked to the bone," Cam said. Cam and Curt had invested in over-sized rain ponchos just before the trip that fit over their packs. Lars and Caleb had not.

No one in the party had brought proper gloves, so rather than fighting against the swollen knots with frozen fingers, Cam busted out his hunting knife and sliced the ropes, dislodging the poles from K's pack, while Curtis got the body of the tent from his own. The shelter was too large and heavy for backpacking, but they were only hiking for a few days to test things out. The tent failed that test. Part of the failure was on the guys because they didn't know enough to bring a ground cover along to protect the bottom, plus they set it up in a slight depression rather than on a rise, which would have shed the water away from their sleeping bags inside their orange dome. After fighting through their ineptitude for thirty minutes, the tent finally stood, with the rain fly stretched over the top, anchored to several small trees. Lars and Caleb went inside to strip their wet clothes and get into dry sleeping bags.

Cam and Curtis worked feverishly on trying to start a fire with wet wood. Ten minutes later, they stopped the fire-starting project. Curtis had purchased a backpacking stove a few weeks before the trip but had only started it up once, which was another failure. Fuel from the bottle leaked when his pack had fallen over while clearing out the campsite. The stench of white gas soaked through the side of his backpack. Only half of the fuel remained in the bottle. Cursing-laced agitation reigned while Curtis tried to remember how the blasted stove worked, with half his brain power used to fight against the elements and fatigue. His hands began to shake.

"You guys need to drink some water and try to eat something," Cam said into the tent to the two shivering bodies.

"Got you, little bastard!" Curtis said in celebration as the stove burst forth with a bright blue flame against the steady mist. The aluminum pot clattered down onto the grate, and his canteen was emptied into the pan bringing an instant sizzle.

"Watch this, Cam."

Curtis pushed a small wire lever on the stove, and it began to churn like an old locomotive.

"Sounds like a train," Cam said and stepped back.

Curtis fanned out his hands over the top of the flames for warmth. The fire darted past the bottom of the pot.

"Grab the pan for a minute."

Curt unscrewed the plunger and gave seven quick pumps, which increased the intensity of the fire, then nodded for Cam to replace the pot. Cam was hesitant, so Curt took it from him and set it down. A rolling boil pushed around a dried soup mix five minutes later. Curtis stirred the life-giving concoction.

"What's up with you and the stove?"

"Huh?"

"It seems you are afraid of the stove like it's gonna blow up or something."

"No, I was just watching how it works," Cam lied.

"Oh."

"Drink this," Cam handed full mugs in through the tent opening. The hot soup steamed against the cold, damp air. Lars grabbed his cup, but Caleb was unresponsive. Curt sprang into action and reached in and slapped his older brother across the face, "Hey Caleb, sit up, man. You need to get some of this inside your gut." Curt lifted while Cam pulled their brother upright, and he woke into a groggy reality.

"Drink this," they said, and Caleb complied, sipping at the steamy mug.

The salty soup had done its job against the cold, reviving the tired young men. Within half an hour, the four sat inside the tent, laughing at the day's events. Anyone on the trail could hear the growing crescendo of laughter for hundreds of feet.

"That may have been the best-tasting soup I've ever had," Caleb said with his goofy smile.

"I think I have enough fuel for breakfast in the morning," Curtis said after inspecting the tank.

"That little stove kicks butt," Lars said, lifting his cup in appreciation.

"We couldn't justify killing off our sister's husband on the first trip," Cam said and followed with a howl and his notorious cackle.

"No, but I hear those trails in Pictured Rocks are right along the cliff—which someone could fall off of." Laughter ensued.

A few hours later, another mistake caught up with them as the bottom of the tent gave way to the hydraulic pressure from the pooling water beneath. They all woke up shivering inside wet sleeping bags at three in the morning.

"Did anyone bring a towel?" Caleb asked.

No one had. The men tried to dry off with an extra shirt from their packs. The small stove was brought inside and ignited for the heat near the opening. Within minutes that mistake nearly choked them out with the fumes. Caleb extinguished the camp stove.

The darkness returned, and Cam clicked on their only flashlight to avoid the hot stove as Curt put it outside the entryway. Then the flashlight faded to black. Failure number— they had lost count, no extra batteries.

"Anyone having fun yet?" Cam asked. No one laughed.

* Castle *

The six miles they needed to cover to get to their first Pictured Rocks campsite was never an issue in any of the three men's minds. Yet, tired legs from being awake for over thirty hours had made the first four miles feel like absolute drudgery. The trail was challenging, with repeated ups and downs over steep hills and long stretches through swampy regions. Backcountry bridges made from a single line of 2" x 12s" nailed into cut pieces of logs bisected murky waters. These paths forced hikers to concentrate on the trail immediately in front of them. Passing hikers coming in the opposite direction was impossible, which caused those wanting to enter a swamp bridge to wait for the clumping boots to clear off. Good thing traffic was never an issue on this trail.

The men had to push through overgrown areas in some sections, as the trail edges needed trimming. Spider webs were a constant nuisance. Webs strung across the lead hiker's face, always leaving the creepy question of whether there had been a rider on the web that just snapped across the ears. The mosquitoes buzzed incessantly, and their tormenting friend, the biting black stable fly, had introduced themselves when they had first exited the car. Tricky roots embedded into the sides of the steep inclines helped with climbing but could easily catch a heel and cause a stumble.

Thirst was becoming an issue as the group discovered they needed to bring more water bottles for the journey. The summer heat drew moisture from them in their sweat and every breath. As the trail dropped them into the Miner's Castle visitors center, they made for the drinking fountain at the back of the restroom. People milled past from the parking lot to the trail. Part of the cliff had eroded to look like a castle spire. It was one of the main tourist draws of the shoreline in terms of the sheer numbers. The stunning aspect of the natural attraction was the contrast between the deep blue water and the white rock castle, making it a must-see stop from the platform and the tour boat.

Dropping their packs next to the building, the brothers drank a full canteen each, then doused their heads with the cool water. Cam grabbed a picnic table, and they sat for a late lunch with more liquids. Laughter returned. The brothers used personal slights, general vulgarity, and shared history to drive the jokes home. While their personalities were distinct, Caleb and Curtis were the most alike in mannerisms and temperament, but when they were alone, they were three amigo's in the truest sense of the word. Cam's laughter announced their presence to the entire visitor center.

After lunch, Cam threw away the wrappers they had opened and returned with a two-liter pop bottle filled with water.

"Where did you find that?"

"In the trash, well, laying on top."

"Your gonna drink from it?" Caleb asked.

"After we boil it. It's not even two miles to our campground, and I don't want a headache to start off the day tomorrow."

"Yummy. Hopefully, the guy who threw that away didn't have too many mouth sores," Curtis said.

"We're gonna boil it!" Cam insisted.

"Yeah, yeah, yeah."

"And who said anything about it being a guy? It was a hot chick that threw it out. I saw her."

"Did you see her oozing canker sores too?" Caleb asked.

"You guys are idiots."

* Water From Rock *

According to chatter, the Potato Patch camping area was not an awe-inspiring site. Located just off the main trail and buried in thick undergrowth, five numbered poles indicating the place to set up tents were camouflaged and could have easily been missed if not for the sign. According to the park rules, you had to erect all shelters within fifteen feet of the numbered pole, and the backcountry permit affixed to the permit holder's pack had match the site and date.

Park Rangers would patrol the waterways and trails, enforcing compliance with the rules by checking the camping permits of hikers, keeping an eye out for any abuse, and sniffing for fires that were not allowed at many of the sites. The ticket and subsequent fine for illegal fires were steep, but an uncontrolled forest fire would devastate the long but relatively narrow National Lakeshore. The goal for the National Lakeshore was a more even distribution of human traffic in the park to not overload the popular areas with people, which could negatively impact the natural habitats.

There was no overcrowding problem at the Potato Patch, as the three men were the only occupants. The long undergrowth verified that the campsite was underused. The scenic overview described in the park brochure for backcountry hiking was a narrow, overgrown slot trail to the cliff's edge. Large trees hindered the scene and offered little space to stand and take in the view of the Lake. For the brothers, late-day clouds had cast a low gray pall over the entire area as exhaustion took over. Sleep was welcomed, even on the lumpy ground.

The first morning brought a return of sunny skies and twittering wildlife all around the orange dome. Mosquitoes had discovered the campers and lined up for their early morning feeding. Cam and Caleb crawled out of their bags while Curtis continued to sleep.

"That kid could sleep through a bombing," Cam said.

"A nuclear one, at that."

"Curtis, get up and fire up your stove," Cam called.

"We need coffee!"

"Let's dip his hand in water, maybe he'll pee the bed, like when he was a kid." Cam's laugh, the human cackling hyena, penetrated Curtis' dream world.

"Why are you so freaking loud, Cam?" The question came from inside the zippered dome.

"I was born that way."

"Go ahead, blame God for your stupid."

"Curtis, we need coffee," Cam moaned.

"You come now, sorcerer, make magic with fire-breathing rock," Caleb said in his best caveman impersonation.

"Rock?"

"Yeah, his brown stove looks like it could be a rock if you were living a couple of hundred years ago."

"And blue fire came from the rock to boil our water."

"Oh yeah, the bottle of canker sore-infected water," Curtis said as he opened the tent.

"Ewe, you need more beauty rest. Your ugly is strong. Go back to sleep!" Cam said and roared.

"No magic fire rock for you two. Me pee now."

"The bathroom is two miles back at the visitor's center."

"This world is my toilet," Curtis waved his arms like he was introducing a group of people to his family.

"Looks like more than pee," Cam said while looking at the orange gardening trowel in one of Curtis' hands and the roll of toilet paper stuffed in a zippered plastic bag in the other.

"Nature calls."

"Nature is going to carry your butt away with her buzzing friends," Cam said as he swatted a mosquito on his bare arm.

"Hurry up. We are dying here!" Caleb said.

When Curtis returned, the insults began in earnest for the three amigos as they laughed the morning away while making and eating breakfast.

"Don't we have a long way to hike today?"

"It's about eight miles, but over Grand Portal Point."

"We better get the lead out."

Ten minutes later, they had dressed for the day with all their belongings put into their packs. The new dome tent was easily distributed among them. The poles and stakes were in Caleb's pack, the fly and ground cover tarp rode with Cam, while Curtis shouldered the central dome tightly pressed into its stuff sack.

All three had selected hiking sticks the night before. Cam had a lightweight hand saw to cut the wood they had rummaged from their trip to the cliff. They removed the bark and personalizing each walking stick. The length and girth comparisons started in the morning.

At about noon, they crossed the Mosquito River taking a break north of the beach. The slow rhythm of the waves hypnotized them while they ate jerky in the shade at the top of the twenty-foot bluff. A slight breeze was pushing in off the water, helping to keep the stable flies at bay, which was a welcomed relief. The little buggers know how to bite to draw blood and can swarm by the hundreds while hiking. Cam had reattached the leg-bottom of his custom pants with the zipper to keep the flies off his ankles. Had they waited a few more weeks, the stable flies would have died off— leaving only the mosquito to pester the warm-blooded human invaders.

"Got you!" Curtis had used his baseball cap to kill one of the biters.

"Only forty billion more to get," Cam said.

"I don't know how you can hike in pants."

"By sweating me arse off. Not really. These hiking pants are lightweight. But it's better than getting carried away by those little punks."

They left lunch behind at the sign saying they had 4.4 miles to Chapel Beach. Knowing the most scenic portion of the trail lay between them and that day's destination encouraged them. The views did not disappoint as they walked along the literal edge of the cliffs. Crystal clear water on their left and dense forest on their right as the trail hugged the rugged coast. Every single stop brought out one or more cameras to attempt to capture the scene's beauty.

"This is awesome!"

"Wow!

"Would you look at that?" Similar words were shared at every lookout. The two-and-a-half miles up to Grand Portal Point took nearly three hours, and they arrived with a couple of swallows of water left in their canteens.

"I'm out of water," Curtis admitted.

"Me too," Caleb said. They sat at the table on top of the point, watching another tour boat pass 250 feet below. The table is a flat rock on top of the bluff. People were pointing up in their direction in apparent disbelief.

"I got a couple of swallows left if you want some," Cam said.

"All backwash," Caleb said.

"Jerky floaters swirling about."

"Yum. Second lunch!"

"Is that the herpes water?"

"Gross."

"You know, I think we have enough rope between us to drop a cooking pot over the edge and get some water," Curtis said.

"From up here?" Caleb asked.

"No. We'd have to get down there," Curtis said and pointed to a ledge about a hundred feet below them.

"What?"

"I think we can get down by going this way."

"Let's do it!" Cam said.

"Get your rope. Is it a hundred feet?"

"Yeah."

"So, we got two hundred feet?"

"I think it will make it."

"Whose pot are we using? We only have two."

"All I have is the frying pan," Cam said.

"We can use mine," Caleb offered.

"Okay, you tie the knot on the handle."

They clamored down the steep incline toward the cliff's face. The loose sand and rock on parts of the limestone made the going treacherous. Curtis had an easier time with it and arrived first, peering over the edge. Cam was a few minutes behind, and he looked over as well. Caleb wanted nothing to do with looking down at the blue-green water.

"I think we should put a rock in the pan to get it to lean to the side."

"Okay."

Caleb had several near him and tossed one over.

"You both hang onto the end of the rope while I guide it down," Curtis said.

With that, they lowered the pan to the surface of the Lake. It reached the calm water and filled.

"Grab my hand, Cam." Curtis leaned out to see the remote pan.

"You're nuts," Caleb said.

"Ah, it's fine. We can pull it up now."

Curtis got down on his hands and knees and began to pull the rope up.

"Dang. This is a lot heavier than I thought."

"You have a rock, the pan, water, and all of the rope weight," Cam said.

The rope became much lighter in Curt's hand about the fourth arm-over-arm movement.

"Crap! We just lost the pan."

"Who tied the knot, K?"

"Shit."

Curtis finished pulling the rope and confirmed the knot had been the culprit.

"Now what?"

"We need water."

"But we only have one more pan to boil water with."

"You've got that fry pan?" Caleb asked Cam.

"Yeah."

"So, we could boil in that if we lost Curtis' pan."

"Right."

Curtis left to retrieve his pan from the pack beside the rock table.

"The kid's a dang billy goat," Caleb said to Cam while watching their brother scamper up the loose incline. Five minutes later, Curtis produced the pan. "You have to tie a different knot," he said.

"I'll tie a square knot with a hitch," Cam said.

When the pan returned from its journey over the cliff's edge, it was three-quarters full of clear and cold Lake Superior water. The brothers congratulated each other and then pumped it through their half-micron filter. They raised their canteens in salute and savored each swallow.

"Who would believe we could get water from this high up on the rock!" Cam said.

* Going to the Chapel *

An hour after Grand Portal Point, the trail opened to a window-like view of an abandoned beach in its pristine glory. A beige sandy beach lined the bright teal waters.

"Look! There's Chapel rock!" Curtis pointed and smiled at the iconic landmark.

A lone pine tree stood sixty feet tall on top of a flat table rock several feet thick. Four massive pillars of limestone support the rock. Those stones have been hollowed out by nature, making it appear that the legendary giant Paul Bunyan had his dining room table set next to the Lake. The tabletop is elevated at least twenty-five feet above the ground by the stone legs, giving it the distinct look of an altar in a church. In this case, the church was standing in nature's chapel and testified to the beauty and complexity of its Creator.

The gigantic altar sits at the northeast end of the beach. The untouched sand stretches back nearly half a mile. Three massive roots from the tree reach across a twenty-foot gap in the rock to the nearby cliff. The ground had fallen, scrubbed away by a ferocious storm, leaving the tree clinging to the ridge across the gap as it tottered on its table. Rooted fingers reach for water and nutrients the soil on top of the table cannot provide. It reminded the men of intravenous feeding tubes stretching from mother earth to a lost child stranded on an island surrounded by air.

Chapel River streams its light brown water into the teal lake a couple of hundred feet from Chapel Rock, zigzagging against the surf and bisecting the beach. If the winds are calm for a few days, the river makes its way down the bank in a straight line. However, when the wind blows, water slams against the river, the current is bent back against itself, causing wild curves to be formed in the sand like God moved a water rope across a silicon floor.

Even mighty Superior, with all her churning and fickled rage, cannot stop the river for more than a few hours. After a storm slams the area, the river's exit can become blocked by a new mound of sand heaped up by the frothing waves, but time and hydraulic pressure are patient opportunists, waiting until enough energy is stored in the pooling waters above the blockage and a simple drip becomes a rivulet breaking through the barrier. A trickle converted to enough energy, knifing through the earthen dam, destroying the blockade sweeping the mound of sand back to the Lake that gave it up, returning life to the river.

Coming from Grand Portal Point, the trail exits the forest at the top of a pale yellow sand bluff, a hundred feet above the beach. The moment Cam left the thick undergrowth, waves were rolling up on the sand like the Lake was caressing its lover's lower back as she lay out in the sun.

"Oh, wow!"

"Would you look at that!" Caleb said.

"I'm going down to swim!" Curtis said and bounded down the steep bluff with melodramatic steps as a small sand avalanche pursued each stride. Cam and Caleb followed. On the beach, they stripped off their sweat-soaked clothes and ran buck-naked into the cold surf.

"Man! That will take your breath away," Caleb managed.

"Woo hoo!"

"Crap. All cooled off in about thirty seconds," Cam said, returning to his pack.

"Dude, you got a blister on your heel!" Curtis said and pointed.

"Yeah, the new boots are grinding on that foot."

"It looks like it has broken open," Caleb said while getting closer.

"We are gonna have to do something about it, Cam," Curtis said. As the first aid kit keeper, Curt felt obligated to watch out for the three.

"Let's set up camp, and then we'll deal with it," Cam said.

"Hey, boys!" said a female voice from the top of the bluff.

"Hey," Cam shot back. The men were caught out in the open wearing awkward smiles.

"Looks like the water is really cold!" Another female voice said, drawing full belly laughter from both women walking past a hundred feet above and the three howling brothers.

"Very funny!" Cam shot back.

"She must be looking at you, K." Curtis said and dodged a feigned swing from Caleb.

"I thought we were alone!" Caleb yelled up the embankment.

"You can come down and join us, ladies," Curtis called up the hill.

"Maybe later. You wait right there," said one.

"Don't burn your biscuits," said the other while they laughed again, walking away.

With their bare butts to the water, a tourist boat filled with paying customers came quietly around the cliff in full view of Chapel Beach. This revelation brought even more laughter from the pair of female hikers on the bluff.

"You're busted!" One of them called down as the men tried to scurry for cover behind their backpacks. Meanwhile, people on the boat pointed and snapped pictures of the three neon white guys glowing naked on the beach.

The brothers looked at each other, threw their hands up, and mooned the boat.

"Put that in your photo album!" Cam yelled while smacking his butt cheeks, bringing audible laughter from the ship's passengers and the hikers on the dune.

Come to find out, Chapel Rock is the final stop on the boat tour, and the guide announced over the loudspeaker that they have "caught many people over the years skinny dipping on this hidden beach," well within earshot of the now waving brothers.

An hour later, the three Amigos' campsite area overflowed with their tent and their unloaded packs. Each of them ate from re-hydrated pouches of food with metal sporks.

"Man, when you're hungry, this stuff tastes awesome," Curtis said.

"Are you eating a second meal?" Caleb asked.

"Well, I brought a couple of extra just in case."

"His pack weighs a hundred pounds just from his food," Cam said.

"Very funny. We gotta take care of that blister." Curtis pointed with his utensil as he spoke.

The guys wore shorts and clean T-shirts after the bath in the Lake, and none had any boots on while they sat around camp.

"We should have brought some flip-flops," Caleb said.

"Really? Flip flops? That's what my wife wears." Laughter ensued.

"Think about it," he pleads his case. "They are lightweight and would let your feet air out after hiking was over for the day. Not to mention letting your boots dry."

"Hmm. Maybe. Plus, there isn't anyone to see your gay fashion statement up here in the deep dark woods," Cam howled and hummed the theme song from the Deliverance movie.

"Those two girls are camped just a few spots from us, and they would see you," Curtis said.

"And they would say what a sexy idea it is!" Caleb said.

"I'm going to light a fire in the fire ring after dinner," Curtis said.

* Growing Fires *

The fire ring was in a communal area of the backcountry camping site. It was on the edge of the bluff, overlooking the bay. Limestone cliffs on the left and Chapel rock on the right. The sun was hanging low on the horizon, growing in size and color. The brothers dragged a few downed and dead logs over to the ring along with an armful of twigs.

"Got some sap," Cam said with a large glob of pine sap on the end of a broken stick. Caleb arranged the twigs on top of a piece of birch bark, and Cam laid the sap stick inside the small pile.

"Got a match?" Curtis asked.

"Your breath and a buffalo fart," Cam said, repeating the old joke. "Yeah, I got my lighter," Caleb offered.

Within ten minutes, Caleb and Curtis stared into the dancing flames while Cam looked out over the calm waters. The pair of female hikers came over to take pictures of the setting sun with the sky arranged with an incredible array of colors.

"You want to join us?" Cam asked.

"Well, I guess we can hang out since you all got your clothes on." Everyone laughed.

"Why are you barefoot," the brunette asked Cam as she sat a day pack down next to the log seat. Three large logs surrounded the ring. Cam sat as far away from the fire as he could.

"Got a blister on my heel. I'm airing out." He spun his foot around so they could see the silver dollar-sized raw spot on the back of his right foot.

"Oh, dang!" she responded.

"Yeah, I got sand in my boots, and it ground out a hot spot."

"Should have stopped sooner to take care of that," the blonde said. Both women appeared like they were in their early twenties.

"So, what brings you ladies, out to the deep dark woods?" Caleb asked.

"I bet the same thing as you boys, summer adventure. We planned it when we were in college last semester and wanted to get away.

"My dad took me all of the time growing up," Blondie offered.

The talk went on towards types of gear, and trails explored, along with run-ins with bears and skunks, as the fire danced shadows across their faces and extrapolated out onto the leafy canopy surrounding them while darkness quietly enveloped their backsides.

"Our poor sister has to put up with the three of us," Curtis said in response to something Blondie had said.

"We're making her tough," Cam offered.

"Or causing her to hate you forever," Brunette said. It turns out the brunette had a name, Emily, and her roommate Kelly, was the blonde.

"Well, I am closer to her than these two buffoons," Curtis plead his case.

"How old are you?"

"I'll share if you do!"

"I'm twenty-two," Kelly offered.

"Twenty-one for another week," Emily said.

"Well then, we can share our flask!" Cam said and revealed a silver pint bottle and passed it around.

"Please do. We only brought this," Emily pulled out a full fifth of rum from the day pack.

"Right on!" Cam said.

Everyone laughed and sipped and passed both of bottles around the circle.

"Now that we have shared some spit, you gotta spill some stories," Emily said.

The brothers looked at each other and laughed.

"What?"

"We were just talking about hanging our sister," Cam said.

"You hung your sister?"

"Not in the traditional sense," Caleb offered.

"What other, non-traditional sense is there?" Emily asked.

"Well, if you must know, when she was about ten or twelve, we took her by the ankles."

"These two took her by the ankles," Curtis said while pointing with his thumb.

"And what did you do?"

"I was the catcher," Curtis said.

"Catcher?"

"Yeah."

"We held her by the ankles over the upstairs rail of our parent's quad-level," Cam said.

"And I was two levels down in case she fell. I was going to catch her."

"More like break her fall."

"She must have been horrified!"

"Not too bad."

"She only needed a few years of psychotherapy," Cam said, and everyone laughed.

"You guys are awful!" Kelly said.

"That's what I've been saying all along," Curtis said. He took a swig and sipped, then passed the bottle to Kelly on his right.

"We didn't drop her!" Cam said.

"Yeah, you guys probably talked her into thinking it would be fun."

"Yeah, that was him," Caleb said as he and Curtis pointed to Cam.

"Making her tough!" Cam said and flexed his arm.

"Does she even talk to you now?"

"Of course!"

"She only has a little stutter," Caleb said.

"You guys are terroists," everyone laughed loud and long.

Cam was looking at his blister and probing the area with his finger.

"You're gonna get an infection putting your nasty finger on that," Caleb said.

"I'm just looking at it."

"I'm going to get the first aid kit so we can take care of it." Curtis commented.

"All right."

"Can I come and check out your campsite?" Kelly asked Curtis.

"Come on, Blondie."

Kelly drew close to Curtis as they let their eyes adjust to the growing darkness. The pair left the light of the fire ring and stepped into the abyss.

"Crap, it got dark quick!"

"You can say that again," Kelly tried to speak clearly, but the booze was beginning to have its way. If she weighed a hundred pounds, it was only barely.

"I've got a flashlight in my pack," Curtis said, feeling her nearness behind him. He stopped walking, and Kelly ran into him, trying to suppress a laugh.

"Sorry I thought I saw something move," he whispered over his shoulder as she kept her body beside his. The moment he said those words, she grabbed him around the waist and pulled him in close, laying her head on his back.

"You smell so good," she whispered into his shirt.

Curtis spun around to face her blue eyes. He was five or six inches taller.

"You know I'm married, right?"

"Life on the trail is like visiting Vegas," she whispered and touched his neck with both hands, pressing herself into him as they breathed the same air.

"You mean what happens in Vegas, stays in Vegas?"

She pulled his lips into hers.

"What the heck took you guys?"

"You've been gone for fifteen minutes!" Emily said through bloodshot eyes.

"It wasn't fifteen minutes, maybe in booze time," Curtis said. "In case you hadn't noticed, its dark out there, you can't see squat, and we had to get the food bags down so I could get the first aid kit. Then hoist them back up."

"You put the kit up with your food?" Caleb asked with a snarky smile.

"Yeah, by mistake."

As the two travelers retook their seats, Emily touched her roommate's shoulder, then pulled a leaf out of her messy hair. She leaned in, showing her the leaf, and whispered, "Food bag, huh?"

Kelly smiled, took the bottle from her, and had another sip.

"What? We had to get it down," Kelly whispered into her ear and covered her friend's mouth with her finger as they shared a muffled laugh over an inside joke from college.

"All right, Cam, you gotta lay on your belly with your feet by the fire so I can see."

Cam slid off his log and onto the ground with a low grunt, ensuring he wasn't too close to the hot steel ring.

"I wish I could say this wasn't gonna hurt, but I can't." Curtis was enjoying the moment.

"What are you using?" Cam asked, looking back over his shoulder.

"Never you mind. K, sit on his legs," Curtis said.

Caleb got off his log and leaned over his brother's calves.

"Watch out for these two. They may want to take advantage while I'm down," Cam was talking to the girls, and they were giggling and enjoying the show.

"You ready?"

"Wait!" Cam tipped his flask and took a long draw. "It's gone!"

"You want some of this? Kelly asked, holding up the remains of her rum.

"I'm good."

"You ready yet, you big sissy?" Curtis removed the top of the small vial and carefully poured the iodine onto his brother's raw patch on his heel.

"Aw, man! What was that?"

"Just a little iodine."

"That burns like fire!" Cam was not happy, but everyone else was laughing out loud.

"Sorry, dude. Not really," Curtis said.

"You suck!"

* Backpacker Blend *

The sun came up behind the camping area through the thick woods, reducing the grandeur of the arrival of the new day. Chipmunks and squirrels were busy carrying on outside the tent when Caleb emerged to relieve himself. He noticed the stillness of the morning, slowly zipping up the screen entryway. In the distance, a gentle wave reached its destination spilling onto the beach. Cam was still asleep, stretched out on his belly with his injured and unbandaged foot outside his sleeping bag. His heel was stained bright red from the iodine. Caleb slipped into his boots and tip-toed fifteen feet behind the tent among the three-foot-tall ferns to relieve himself when the thought struck him that he had not noticed Curtis inside the tent. After he finished, he loosely tied his boots and walked toward the fire ring. Flames were dancing from three new logs when he noticed Emily making her way toward the ring with an armful of dead wood.

"Morning," he said.

"Morning, Caleb. Want some coffee?" she responded with her bright smile.

"I'd love some," Caleb said.

"It's instant."

"Backpacker blend. Coffee grounds and dirt," he said.

"That's about right," she said while dropping her armload of wood on top of a small pile a few feet from the ring.

"I gotta grab my mug." Three minutes later, Emily poured some black liquid into his lightweight blue steel cup.

"Thanks," he said over the rising steam.

"What a beautiful morning," Emily said.

"Have you seen Curtis?"

"Yeah. Kelly and him are down on the beach."

"Oh." Caleb wanted to walk over and have a look for himself but did not.

"They must have gotten up early."

"She was already missing when I got up to pee," Emily said.

"I smell coffee," Cam said while limping up barefoot.

"I got some to share."

"Does it have rum in it?"

"I wish. Well, not so much this morning. I kinda got a headache."

"Cause you're a lush!" Cam said to Emily with his signature he, he, he.

"What? You helped drink all that rum too!"

"Sad day. No rum for my coffee."

"You're a dork. My brother is a dork," Caleb said to her.

"He is, but he's a wounded dork." They all laughed, but no one could out-laugh Cam, even the pair on the beach below heard the cackle spill over from the bluff and bounce off the cliff walls.

The five gathered around the fire ring an hour later, sharing stories after breakfast. Backpacks, dishes, boots, and clothes were strewn about the area. They were commenting on the volume of stuff that exploded from each pack. Then a tiny skiff rounded the cliffs and made its way toward the beach.

"I hear a boat," Caleb said.

"More tourists to moon!" Cam said, and the girls laughed.

"Come on, girls you can join our mooning party!"

"No, I don't want my bare butt in someone's photo album," Emily said.

"It's a park ranger," Curtis had jumped up and looked over the bluff's edge.

"I wonder what they want?" Kelly asked.

"Probably checking permits."

Caleb and Curtis began organizing their things around their packs.

"Curt, you got the permit?" Cam asked.

"Yeah, right here." It was a white waterproof paper-like material written over with a black marker and wire tied through its eyelet onto the frame of his backpack.

"You got ours, Kel?" Emily asked.

"Yeah, but it's in the side pocket."

"Arrest her, officer!" Cam said and pointed at Kelly.

"Morning, folks." He was in his early forties, sporting the forest green Park Ranger coat zipped halfway up. His forest green baseball hat held the iconic National Parks logo embroidered with gold and black thread. The coat hung down to his belt, which allowed easy access to his sidearm in its holster.

"We're just out doing random checks this morning. Making sure fires are in the rings and the people are camping in the places they need to be."

"It's a nice morning to be out on the water," Caleb said, flashing back to the Three Sons.

"It is a beautiful morning," replied Ranger Rick, as his name badge indicated. Caleb had to suppress a laugh at the man's unfortunate name.

"So, you knew we had a fire going?" Curtis asked.

"Yes, I could smell it a half mile away."

"Impressive," Kelly said as she handed him her permit.

"Hey, Mr. Ranger, man," Curtis was doing his best Yogi the Bear impersonation.

"Never heard that one before, Boo Boo," Ranger Rick shot back, and everyone laughed.

"Ranger Rick got jokes!" Cam said much too loud for the situation.

"Our permit is on my pack," Curtis pointed.

"You guys are all set."

"We've got a question," Cam said, turning his heel so the ranger could see.

"Oh. That's a nasty blister."

"Yeah, my dumb ass brother put iodine on it last night."

"Good job, brother."

"So, we think we aren't going to make it to Trappers Creek today and wanted to rest for a day here."

"Do you have moleskin?"

"Yes, but it needs to air out."

"You know how to cut a doughnut with it?"

"Yes, sir."

"If you don't think you can make it, we can evacuate you by boat up to Hurricane River, where you can catch the bus. Where are you parked?"

"Sand Point."

"Yeah, the bus will take you there."

"I want to try to continue, but if we can stay here an extra night, that would be a big help."

"Let me radio back to check what tomorrow looks like for campers here. We can't kick out other backpackers to give you a zero-day."

"I get it," Cam said.

"Four-Two to base," the ranger said into his handheld radio and walked away to listen more closely.

"Well, I don't want to quit, Cam," Curtis said.

"I don't want to either."

"Even if they don't have a spot, we could hike half a mile down and pick a place to hunker down in the woods," Caleb said just above a whisper.

"True," Curtis said.

"You can have two tents on a site, right? I'm sure someone would share their site with you guys," Emily whispered back.

"You could come with us to Mosquito River and share our site," Kelly said.

"Sure," Emily agreed.

"Well, that's going backward and hanging out with girls!" Caleb said, emphasizing the girl's part, and then chuckled.

"Cam likes backward, but not girls," Curtis said, and everyone howled enough to cause Ranger Rick to look over his shoulder.

"I oughta' kick your butt right here in front of everyone," Cam said.

"You'd have to catch me first. Your Black Belt won't help you if you can't keep up."

"Black belt?" Kelly asked.

"Yeah, these two doofuses have a Black Belt in Korean Karate." He put his hands together, fingertips up, and bowed slightly in jest.

"You've gotta sleep at some point, Curtis," Cam said and boomed out a sadistic laugh.

"Is that the only way you can take me, Cam? Sneaking up on me at night," Curtis smiled.

"Okay, there is one site available here tonight, and you guys can stay to rest. But tomorrow night, you must be at Hurricane River or off the trail. The question is, can you make the twelve miles of walking through sand?"

"Yep, I'll make it," Cam said.

"Okay. Now you two are off to Mosquito River tonight?" Ranger Rick asked the women.

"Yes," Emily said.

"Alright, I hope your foot heals up enough for you. You folks have a good day."

"Thanks, Ranger," Cam said.

Ranger Rick walked off down the bluff and toward his waiting boat.

"I've got some flip-flops you can have," Emily offered.

"You need those," Cam replied.

"We are almost done with our little adventure. Mosquito River tonight and hike out tomorrow."

"You have tiny feet!" Caleb chimed in.

"Yeah, I don't think they'd fit him, Em," Kelly said.

"Well, you could try them, at least."

"There's no way his fat feet will fit," Curtis said.

"You're right, but maybe you could use them for something."

"I appreciate it. You've already shared your rum with us," Cam said.

"I wasn't sharing. I just was sick of carrying it!" Emily said.

"Got anything else good to offload?" Cam asked.

"You guys should hang out here for the night. You could move your tent to our site, and no one would be the wiser," Curtis said.

"Then we'd have to hike all the way out tomorrow," Emily said.

"I'm game," Kelly said and glanced Curtis' way.

"You two need to get a room," Cam said and followed with his goofy laugh.

"What are you talking about?"

"It took you forever to get the first aid kit. You were both down walking on the beach, probably spent the whole night there."

"We were just looking at the stars," Curtis said.

"Whatever."

"What? You need to stay up to see the sky tonight instead of passing out drunk," Curtis said.

"Yeah, it was so beautiful," Kelly said.

"We don't have any rum left anyway," Emily said.

"But I have a flask full of moonshine."

"I thought you ran out?"

"I did, but I reloaded," Cam said with his goofy smile.

"With what?"

"I had a bottle in my pack."

"That will work!" Emily said.

"You have not tasted his moonshine," Caleb said. "It will make you blind."

"What?"

"I know what's making you go blind, Curtis," Cam said, and Curtis faked a laugh in response.

"His stuff tastes like battery acid," Curtis said.

"Come on!" Cam said.

"What was in your flask last night?" Kelly asked.

"Whiskey."

"We should get our stuff moved over, Em." And with that, the girls were off. Three pairs of eyes watch the coeds bound away.

"What are you doing, Curtis?" Cam asked, his voice lowered.

"What are you talking about?"

"With the blonde, you know what I mean."

"Hey, what happens on the trail stays on the trail. Isn't that the rule?"

"It's only a joke."

Caleb was keeping out of the conversation by poking around in the fire

"You also have a wife and kids."

"Not out here," he tried to smile and joke reality away. "Besides, weren't you the one who pointed out that I should make friends with the hot neighbors?"

"You're living a fantasy, and this one will bite you in the butt."

"Nothing's happened, Cam."

"She's far too pretty and perky for it to stay that way, brother. Believe me."

"Curtis! Could you give us a hand with the tent," came the call from the girl's campsite, and off he went without a second thought.

"I hid from Him and under running laughter. Up vistaed hopes I sped." Cam recited a line from the ancient poem to himself, worried for his younger brother.

"That girl ain't in it for the long haul," Caleb said.

"You might be right, but what he's running toward right now will only hurt his family."

"We'll just have to keep an eye out for him and stop him from diving over that cliff if you know what I mean."

"I'm afraid the course has been set in his heart, and the pull of the fantasy is strong."

"This fantasy gives sweet kisses just before the venom."

"Plus, she's young, willing, and has curves in all the right places."

* Heel *

Curtis and the young ladies walked past the fire ring toward the guy's campsite. He was carrying the girl's tent upside down. The tent was still assembled in all its teal glory. They had their packs slung over their shoulders and hands full of bedding.

"Hey, we are going to teach these college girls how to play Mumbly Peg," Curtis said. Caleb was sitting on the log and staring into the fire while Cam stood near the bluff.

"They're girls. I don't think they can!" Cam quipped and laughed.

"Bring it!" Kelly said.

"You have no idea what you are in for!"

"I hope you don't use your broken foot as an excuse when you lose."

Cam's eyes widened with excitement as he started looking for a suitable peg. A two-inch long twig less than a quarter inch in diameter was the official correct peg size for the game. Mumbly Peg is a game played with a sharp pocketknife. The object is to stick the knife into a circle drawn on the ground from various positions on the body. The first obstacle is to lay the knife on your open palm blade parallel to your fingers and flip the knife upward with a flick of the wrist, so it flips over and sticks in the ground inside the circle. After completing this challenge with both hands, the next move is to lay the knife across the fingers, blade toward the thumb. Participants turn each hand over in one motion with a throwing action, like shaking salt out of a saltshaker to plunge the knife into the ground. This game portion must be successful from both the right and left hands. Then stand the knife up on one's wrist, blade down, while using your fingers from your free hand to flip the knife off your wrist and, with one spin, stick the blade into the dirt. The action is attempted from each wrist, elbow, and shoulder. The next phase includes once from the chest, chin, mouth, nose, and each eye, during which the knife blade is held between two fingers in front of the various body parts and flipped into the ground.

The final three positions are tricky. Each person has to go over the shoulder after setting the knife on the open palm and flinging the knife over her back to stick it. Then the final move is to jump the fence. This begins with the knife stuck in the soil. The left hand is placed horizontally in front of the blade, acting as the fence. Then, using the right hand to strike the handle of the knife with enough force to flip it over the hand acting as the fence and stick it into the ground.

The unwritten rules state that each person takes one try, and then they have the opportunity to "chance" it by taking a do-or-die turn, which, if they don't stick the knife, they have to start over at the beginning position, the palm. A proper sticking of the blade requires two fingers to fit beneath the end of the handle for it to count.

Now, the peg in Mumbly Peg is the loser's punishment. At the beginning of the game, one of the newest members of the competition picks a random number from one to five. So, if they choose three, each person gets three whacks at the peg. A small wooden dowel is carved from a dead branch and used as the game peg. It is placed upright on the ground and driven into the dirt with the knife handle. It sounds easy, except you must carefully hold the blade with the thumb and index finger as a hammer. Most beginners struggle to hit the small peg, which is why they go first. The more experienced players can get a couple of good hits on the peg, driving it below the surface of the dirt, which is crucial for the game's hilarity. The loser of the knife-sticking portion has to dig the peg out of the ground using only their teeth, as the rest of the participants laugh and enjoy the loser's misfortune.

Each of the girls took turns losing and came up from the ground spitting out a mouth full of dirt, as the brothers laughed mercilessly.

Early the following day, they were all again gathered at the fire ring, this time with their packs filled. Curtis was working on Cam's heel to get the Moleskin cut properly. The moleskin has a sticky side that adheres to the skin. The intent being the material rubs against the inside of the boot instead of the skin.

"This stuff isn't holding very well," Curtis said.

"Hey, what if we cut the back of the boot off?" Caleb said. "You know, just the heel."

"Might work. Then if we put the moleskin on the sides of his heel to protect against the edges."

"These are new boots!" Cam said.

"No kidding. You should have broken them in before hitting the trail, genius," Curtis said.

"You have to make the call," Caleb said.

"Well, I'm not making it to Hurricane River with this foot in this boot."

"Afraid not."

"Cut it," Cam ordered.

"Alright, guys, we've got to hit it," Emily said and stood, grabbing her pack. "we've got a lot of miles to cover."

"It was a highlight of our trip getting to know you," Kelly said to everyone while looking at Curtis.

"I almost forgot, there is a place called the Oasis a few miles east of the gate in Grand Marais. If you have time, you should check it out. He would know where you could get some boots."

"I'm pretty sure the guy on the bus could drop you close," Kelly said.

They exchanged hugs, and like a morning fog, the coeds disappeared into the lush green vegetation.

Watching them leave, Cam whispered, "I swung the earth a trinket at my wrist."

Six

Cameron Lost

— Section Six —

"At The Table of Saunterers"

"I know not the way God leads me,
but well do I know my Guide."
Martin Luther

* The Nova Galaxy *

"Jumper!"

"Another one? That makes three this week!"

"I'm not gonna let 'em get away with this."

"Monkey, what are you doing? Get back here!"

The young man bolted out of the station, watching the purple Charger speed south on Woodward Avenue as he ran toward the silver Nova he had driven to work that day. Fumbling for the keys, he was determined to stop the criminal or get his license plate number to tell the cops. He feared the station could close and he'd lose his job. The number of people pumping gas and driving off without paying was skyrocketing. It was already hard enough to make a profit.

The Nova roared to life, and Monkey pressed the manual transmission into reverse, bolting out of the parking space. He threw it into first and checked the traffic. With a quick rev of the motor and dumping of the clutch, both rear tires broke free from the concrete. The light turned green for the southbound traffic to his immediate left. Punching the accelerator, the car lurched forward like a bull charging out of the starting gate at a rodeo. Smoke billowed from the rear wheel wells as the muscle car shot onto the road— just as the four lanes of traffic were released from the light. Monkey quickly hit second gear, and the tires kept spinning. The Posi traction rear end was causing both wheels to spin violently, leaving two long black marks on the pavement behind him. The stealthy car was already doing eighty, and out of the corner of his eye, the purple Charger shot past him going north. Woodward, or M-1, is a ten-lane boulevard with five lanes of traffic in each direction with a broad and lush grassy section in the middle. Monkey had to break hard, downshift, and turn left through a Michigan left turnaround in the middle of the boulevard. The Super Sport version of the Nova was up to the task, and he blew the stop sign at the turnabout, fishtailing out onto the northbound side of the road to a couple of horn honks from angry drivers. He banged hard back into third and smoked his brother's new tires as the hood lurched upward in response to the torque from the souped-up small block Chevy motor beneath the hood.

Monkey and his brother had spent many hours working on the hot rod, which from the silver paint job, looked like any other 1970 Nova SS.

But the power plant beneath the hood was anything but ordinary. The black interior was immaculate, and the bucket seat fit the kid's body. The eight-track player banged out some hard rock band's guitar groove through the double six-by-nine speakers mounted near the rear window, which echoed the music from the angled back glass.

Ahead, the light he jumped in front of wanted to change to yellow for the north and southbound Woodward lanes, so the east-west traffic on Fourteen Mile Road could be freed. Monkey was determined not to stop. He changed lanes to avoid the pickup truck that was being too careful. He banged into fourth gear and raced through the rose-colored light with a roar. The purple Charger was about twelve cars ahead of him.

Catching up on the pump jumper the growing traffic was beginning to swallow him and slow his progress. He downshifted and slid right then left as a car ahead put its signal on. Flashing past the old lady in the Pinto, he went two lanes over to his left and stomped on the accelerator. The purple Charger was only two cars ahead of him in the far-left lane, as he strained his neck forward to see the guy's plate, and that is when the line of cars in front of him hit their brakes. Grease Monkey slammed the brakes, which locked up the front tires on the hot asphalt. The screech and the bang were almost simultaneous as the pristine Nova slammed into the rear bumper of a rusted brown Galaxy. The bumper, grille, hood, and fenders did what they were designed to do in a crash and crumpled like an accordion, absorbing much of the kinetic energy to protect the young passenger.

The first cogent thought Monkey had as steam spewed from beneath the crinkled hood was that he had destroyed his brother's trophy car— only a couple weeks after they had finished working on it. His head slumped to the steering wheel, where he began to cry tears filled with fear, anger, and regret.

* Humpty Dumpty *

Finding parts for a 1970 Nova SS was easy in Michigan. Finding rust-free parts not from a chop shop was a bit more complicated. Monkey must have made fifty phone calls to junk yards around the state searching. Finally, a week later, he located a front clip at a place out near Lansing. By that time, the Nova was already sitting disassembled in the garage back at home. Getting the parts from a Lansing junkyard all the way home was a problem.

"You think Weed would drive his brother's pick up out with me to get the parts?" Monkey asked his brother, who was unwrapping the paper off a sucker from the bowl on the counter in the gas station.

"Maybe if you buy him some beer."

"How am I going to do that?"

"Don't you have that fake ID?"

"Yeah, and it looks fake, too," Monkey admitted.

"Just give him the money for beer, he's over eighteen, you idiot." He put the lemon-flavored sucker in his mouth.

"You think?"

"You'll have to buy his gas, too and probably some food."

"Right."

Monkey's brother went back to reading the comics from the newspaper— feet up on the dingy station counter, enjoying his candy.

"Do you want to go with us?"

"Yeah, I'm going. I want to see the parts before you spend good money on them, doofus."

"I didn't think three hundred bucks was too bad."

"It's not if the parts are pristine."

"Okay. You know I'm sorry about all of this, right?"

"You're an idiot."

"Yeah, I know."

The service bell rang twice as a car pulled up to the gas pumps.

"Ohh, look at that!" Monkey said, admiring the red sports car full of gorgeous women.

"Mine!" his brother called out and exited through the open door, which was propped open with a used wheel that had a vertical post welded in the middle and was holding up an inverted hub cap that was used as an ashtray— classic gas station art.

"How can I help you ladies?" he asked while approaching the car, sucker in his right hand.

"Can I get five dollars of premium?" the hot driver asked. She had bent forward to talk through the passenger door window, blonde hair cascading over her bare shoulders. She revealed the tops of her breasts as her thin white tube top stretched against the weight, much to his delight. The other young woman sat with her head leaning back into her headrest and chuckled at her friend's antics while twirling a finger through her own long brown hair.

"Ye-ye, you bet."

Monkey watched from the doorway, unwilling to remove his eyes from the pair while his brother moved around the driver's side of the car to start pumping the premium fuel. A broad smile lit up his thick black beard over the car's roof toward Monkey mouthing a "wow!" while stealing looks at the woman's long, smooth legs through her open window.

After he was done with his pump jockey work, she thanked him with a wink and a smile, along with an extra dollar tip.

According to both brothers, this was the best time of year to work at a gas station. Searching for tube tops and bikini's ruled their summer workdays. Plus, both being car guys, there was not a better place to see all the hot rods on the iconic Woodward Avenue. Burning rubber from one car or another was a constant scene, along with zero to forty-five drag races off the light, especially at night. Cops had a field day handing out tickets, but there was not enough to stem the tide of people cruising in their rides or the countless wannabes out watching for their favorite cars, doing risky things with their own vehicles.

The body parts turned out to be in great shape, with no rust on the fenders or hood. The grille had one broken light, the left turn signal, but those were easy to find. The only downside of the clip was that it was painted a medium brown. The driver's side door that Monkey had gotten from a guy up in Pontiac was midnight blue. At first, the original door was not damaged, but the hinges had been partially ripped away in the crash and wouldn't line up. With nowhere to weld, the door had to be replaced— to the tune of a hundred bucks.

"Man Monkey, you're gonna go broke fixin' this screw-up," Weed said on the ride home from Pontiac with his cigarette hanging from his lips.

"Yeah. I was gonna buy a new ride but that will have to wait another year."

"Getting rid of Little Red?"

"I want to. If I can work some more hours I might be able to get a car before winter. Maybe I'll look for another job," he said out loud for the first time.

"Cool." Weed drew in long and hard on his half-spent cigarette while looking tilt headed at the teenager. His long black hair threatened to block his view, but his thick horn-rimmed glasses held it at bay.

"So what kinda car do you want?"

"I dunno. A Nova maybe."

"Following after big brother. I tell you what, I think your brother has the fastest car in the city."

"Really?"

"Yeah, I mean street legal, daily driver types."

"Huh." That news made Monkey feel even more guilty.

Three days later, after working a Saturday morning shift, Monkey came home to a group of his brother's friends helping put the car back together. On the one hand, he was happy to have the help lifting the heavy body panels in place while the bolts were being installed, but he knew the avalanche of relentless teasing was rolling his way, and nothing was going to stop it.

"Look who's home!"

"Did you finally wake up, Crash?" With that revelation, the entire garage roared with laughter.

"No, no, he's the cop from that movie with the '68 Shelby," said another.

"You sell whatever you want, but don't sell it here tonight," said the kid from down the block that everyone called "E." He was quoting the movie that had played as the second half of a double feature a few weeks before at the drive-in.

"Don't you mean that you can crash whatever you want— just don't crash mine tonight!" The uproarious laughter echoed off the garage walls, along with the rock song pushing out from the speaker of the old radio on the bench. Monkey laughed along with the older guys from high school. He had seen all of them walking the halls, a few had the same class. His brother's friends came in a few times a night for gas or to talk about the top three subjects on all of their minds— cars, beer, and girls, in that order.

The teasing began to let up when Monkey's brother put him in a head-lock, ruffled his hair, and handed him a beer.

"Come on, let's get these panels hung."

The following Friday night, the Nova roared back to life, although it looked like something like a Frankenstein car. Monkey had found an old scoop air cleaner, which, when mounted to the brand-new carburetor and high-rise intake manifold, made the car appear like it had a supercharger.

"Let's go crusin' without the hood," Monkey said to his brother.

"Yeah, okay. But I'm driving," his brother said and flashed a mischievous smile.

And the brothers and the now ever-present Weed did a few laps around their circuit on Woodward. South from Twelve Mile to Nine Mile and then back north just before Fifteen Mile Road. The Nova was running well and sounding mean. The new headers and full dual exhaust dumped out just before the rear axle. Several times over a couple hours, another car would come up alongside the tri-colored car— thinking it was a kid driving an old pile of crap, but then when they caught sight of what they thought was a blower sticking out of the engine compartment, they backed right off.

An hour into their cruise, at the northbound light at Eleven Mile, a purple Charger pulled up next to them and gave a quick rev of their motor. Monkey recognized his pump jumper right away.

"That's the guy I was chasing," he said to his brother— as a surge of anger shot through his eyes.

"You wanna go?" Said the passenger from the Charger to Monkey's brother.

"I just rebuilt the motor, I'm takin' it easy on her."

"Come on, that old hunk of crap couldn't get out of the way of it's own shadow."

"What are you running?"

"440 six pack."

"Oh, the boat motor?"

"More like an anchor," Monkey said from the back seat.

The light turned yellow for Eleven Mile Road traffic, and both drivers increased their RPM. Boom, the light turned green for Woodward, and both of the cars raced off the line with spinning tires, but the Nova with its small block revved up quicker and beat the Charger to the first block by two car lengths, which everyone who cruised the Avenue knew, was almost exactly a quarter mile.

As they backed off, the Charger pulled up next to the brothers.

"Hey I was only going half throttle to take it easy on you. Let's go again from a roll," the driver of the Charger was leaning forward to talk through the open passenger window.

"No. I made my point. Come back when you get a real car. Hey, next time, you should pay for your gas. Everyone out here knows you're the pump jumping douche-bag."

With those words, the Charger braked hard and steered left into a turn-around.

* Bye Bye Beetle *

Three months later, Monkey found his next car. He was driving his customized '67 Volkswagen Beetle that he and his brother had built over the previous year. The wide tires, flared fenders, custom red metallic paint with flames on the front fenders and hood, plus a built powerplant turned some heads, but it still was a four-cylinder running in an eight-cylinder world, and the only thing Monkey could think about was getting his own hot rod. He was headed home when he passed a lime green Nova for sale in front of a house on Coolidge south of Eleven Mile. At the first opportunity, he swung his car around. He went back to look at the Chevy, shifting and accelerating, then braking hard into the concrete driveway ahead of oncoming traffic.

He bought that car from an old lady whose husband had recently passed away and did not need a second car. The Nova was ugly— lime green plaid cloth bench seats inside and a metallic lime green paint outside, but it had the motor he wanted, the 350 cubic inch small block as his brother's car. He bought the Nova and sold the Beetle a couple weeks later for almost the same price. Over the next six months, every spare hour and dollar went into building himself a cruiser. Cam, intake, carb, headers with full dual exhaust, better tires, traction bars. He only had two regrets about buying the car— it wasn't the Super Sport model and had an automatic transmission. So Monkey dumped a bunch of money, the last of his savings account, into a stall converter and a new trans.

By the Spring of the following year, he was cruising Woodward whenever he could and winning as many races as he lost. After one particular win by half a fender, the other car guy said he had a fast "Key Lime Nova." That thought led to a new nickname for his car, and everybody started to call it Pie— the name stuck, and Monkey wore it as a badge of honor. He cut out two pictures of a piece of key lime pie from his mom's cooking magazine, mounted them to card stock, and stuck them in each rear seat window, just behind the doors.

Monkey soon discovered that even ugly cars attracted cute girls, so long as they were fast. About every few weeks after that, he had a different large-breasted co-pilot riding his route with him. It was also when he discovered he no longer had any extra money or time to invest in his car. It was all going to his new dating habit.

* Stripper Cult Hangovers *

Within a few years, Monkey graduated high school and got a job as a grinder hand in a local metal shop. His pay rate doubled compared to the gas station, as did the parade of women throughout his life. He was determined to move out of his parent's house and began saving for a down payment. He was out on his own within the year, renting a place in Ferndale. Girlfriends came and went, and so did the jobs. He took a job at a stamping plant for a year, and then he went to one of the Big Three auto companies, working on the assembly line during the midnight shift, where he fell into all kinds of destructive habits with his crew. Strip clubs and drunken mornings became the norm, and even though he was making good money, he never saved any cash.

On one sweltering night inside the loud manufacturing plant, the temperature was hovering right around the one hundred and twenty-degree mark. The contract between the company and the union clearly says they cannot work when it's so hot inside the plant. The men were edgy and falling like flies to dehydration, so much they had to slow the assembly line down. The thermometer outside the foreman's office never seemed to move past one hundred and five degrees. The union steward knew the old equipment was not allowed to go above that number, so the plant would not have to close. To combat this, he brought in his own thermometer, which was reading over a hundred and twenty. When he showed the supervisor, the man exploded in anger, and the steward called for an immediate walk out based on breach of contract. The third shift walked away from their workstations and flooded into the cool nighttime air.

The foreman tried to frame the strike as a wildcat, meaning an illegitimate walk-off, which would be an excuse to fire the entire workforce. The men were hooting and yelling as they paced back and forth across the entryway into the facility. Within ten minutes, printed union strike signs appeared, while phone calls were placed to the local media outlets.

Monkey skipped the protest and went with a group of guys to the local club to catch some nighttime action. This was a bit different from the early morning scene when they usually visited the seedy bar.

"I shouldn't be here," thoughts ran through Monkey's head as naked women did everything they could to pry his money out of his wallet. He knew it went against everything he had been taught growing up, and even his brother would be disappointed in him if he found out what he had been up to, but his brother was away at college now.

It was into this twisted life that they showed up. The persistent knocking on the front door had stirred Monkey from his bed. The pretty young woman asked him questions before he opened the screen door. After five minutes of listening and trying to wake up, the woman asked him if he wanted to know that he could go to heaven one day. The other smiling guy with her looked like a high school kid, and he was holding out a pamphlet with an unsteady hand. Monkey took it and noticed the cover art was trying to depict heaven or some heavenly-like place.

"I already know I'm going," he said and then instantly questioned his own words. The nagging question was planted in the back of his brain. Scenes from the seedy bars flashed in his mind, along with the unscrupulous things he had been doing with women. The attractive lady in front of him was relentless, and he was trying to break free from her unending inquiry.

"I, I really gotta get going," he said.

"Well, okay, thanks for talking with us!" she said in an overly cheery voice.

"Anytime," was the word that fell out of his mouth, but "Never again," is what he thought.

"We'll be back in two weeks," she said.

"Oh. Okay," is all Monkey could say while checking out her body again, trying to imagine her without clothes.

When he shut the door, he realized he didn't have a shirt on— only his thin cotton shorts, which wasn't a lot to hide behind. A wave of guilt and shame overcame him as he plopped down on his loveseat. He knew he had spent the past year feeding an insatiable beast. Every woman he was around he judged by their body appearance rather than who they were as a person— like they were a piece of meat occupying a place in the world for his pleasure and use. "Why had the visit from the door-knocking cult brought him to this place?" he thought as a wave of emotion brought unexpected tears from his deadened heart. Then, in an instant, he knew what he needed to do.

The day after his midnight shift, he did not hang out with the drunks or the strip club. Monkey drove to his parent's house. His boyhood home brought familiar emotions when he pulled into the drive. He did not bother knocking on the back door.

"Mom?" he said through the screen as he walked in.

"Would you look at that!" his dad said from the dining room table, holding his heart in a mocking gesture, but his smile gave away his pleasure at seeing his second son.

"We wondered if you had died!" his mother said while meeting him in the kitchen for a hug. Monkey never was much of an affectionate person, even as a kid. He always had to be encouraged to hug or show signs of emotional connection, but not this morning. He was genuinely glad to see his parents and embrace both of them.

"I'm sorry," he said, then explained the strike, working long hours, and the crappy shift he was on all had kept him away.

"Life is hard, honey," his mom said.

"I haven't been sleeping well either."

"You look haggard and worn out."

"I guess I feel like I look."

"You know you can pick up the phone and let us know that you're alright every once in a while?"

"You're right, mom," he said, eyes dropping, agreeing with her.

As they shared breakfast, small talk and laughter echoed through the house. Monkey noticed both of them had been reading from new leather-bound Bibles.

"So what's with these?" he asked while pointing his fork at the open books on the dining room table, then taking another bite of scrambled eggs.

"The pastor from church challenged us to start reading it through in a year."

"You've been going to church again?"

"Yes," she said.

"We've been going almost every week for a year now," his dad said.

"Oh?"

"Do you want more toast? You should come with us," she smiled and grabbed his hand. Tears welled up in the corners of Monkeys eyes. He struggled and fought against revealing too much of what was going on in his broken life.

"There was this girl who knocked on my door yesterday," he began, setting his fork on his plate and telling the detailed story in a rush of words.

* Changing Destinations *

Four years later, almost to the day, Monkey was seated in the front row of the wide pews. The guy in the robes doing the reading was his friend and mentor, Bob. He had met him during his first class called Doctrine. With that class, he also took the Old Testament with the retired Pastor Tony from Alpena. Monkey had enjoyed both courses, but the Old Testament class had so much homework he almost quit the program twice.

His dad was the one who had encouraged him to push through, and his mom offered to type out his chapter-by-chapter review of the entire Old Testament. His parents also went through the Bible college training course, but primarily for their own benefit and only one class at a time.

On the other hand, Monkey took the theological instruction because he had a new passion in his life. The beginning of his newfound drive was the bi-weekly visits he had gotten from the sexy cult girl. Somehow, God had used those meetings to open a part of his life. He had turned away from God so many years before. He knew she was wrong about her interpretation of the Bible but couldn't make a sensible argument about where she was in error.

She was attractive, articulate, had engaging eyes, was filled with laughter, and knew her Bible— at least, he thought she did at that point in his life. Whenever she showed up on those Saturday mornings, she smiled, smelled like springtime flowers, and brought a new trainee. Monkey was convinced she had to be one of the most effective recruiters for the area's cult, and new people were being trained by her in their twisted type of evangelism.

He started getting up earlier to take showers and clean up his living room. He vacuumed the dingy carpet and sprayed the couch with a scented fragrance to help cover up his greasy man-scent embedded into the fibers. He put on coffee for his early morning guests and skipped going to the strip club to afford to buy a new Bible like his parents. Kelly, the sexy cult girl— which was Monkey's secret name for her, was surprised after she arrived to find his new Bible opened on the coffee table with a green highlighter next to it. She commented on the verses he had marked but tried to move the conversation away from what he was reading toward what she wanted to point out. Her nagging questions ate at him throughout the week as he began looking forward to her visits. "A classic cult move," the Monkey, now sitting in the church pew, thought, thinking back on the girl who pushed him to go to Bible college.

All the guys he used to hang out with at the different seedy clubs knew he had experienced a conversion. They did not care. "Whatever works for you, Monkey," they would often say to him after work just before heading to one club or another.

"I think we're gonna stop calling you Monkey," one told him.

"Oh yeah?" Monkey replied.

"Yeah."

"Okay."

"Maybe we will shorten it to Monk," he said, thinking out loud.

"Does it look like I have joined a Monastery?" Monkey asked, pointing at his full head of thick brown hair.

"Not yet," as he said this, another guy joined the conversation. His name was Paul, but everyone in the group called him Rocky after he knocked out a guy hitting on his favorite pole girl. One quick uppercut put the guy on his butt and gave Paul a new name.

"What da ya think, Rock?"

"Not Monk, how 'bout Holy Roller?"

"Too long. I mean, we even shorten up Rocky 'cause we're too lazy to say two syllables, Rock," he said.

"Yeah, I s'pose you're right. How 'bout Preach?"

"YES!" I like it, Rock! No, I frickin' love it!"

On the day Monkey officially became Preach, he decided to never return to the seedy clubs again. That day, he decided he would try to share his faith in Jesus with his strip club buddies. His heart had been changed when thinking about those guys and their eternal destinations. Still, he knew he was not strong enough to go into a place filled with naked and available women and not fall back into his old habits of looking for a quick dopamine fix to counter life's ever-present pain. He hoped he was strong enough to stay away. He began asking God to give him opportunities during work or after to tell them about the love of God. He also began to see the desperate women who sell their bodies for money in a different light. Pastor Bob had helped him understand those truths a couple years before his graduation from Bible college.

One of the people sitting in the audience behind him, dressed in shorts and a tank top, was Rocky. Preach had been reassigned a couple of months after his renaming and began working side by side with Rock. They were a team that headed up a problem-solving unit that looked into quality issues on the assembly line. Things like scratches on fenders came from a guy working as a hood installer who was wearing a jean jacket to work that had metal buttons. Every once in a while, a scratch would appear on the front driver's side fender of a new car, and it would have to be sent to the repair house before it could get delivered to the dealer. It cost the company a lot of money to fix these silly mistakes, so they put two guys on a special task force to track down issues like this and make recommendations to solve the problems— Preach and Rock. They worked together for a couple of years, and Preach recognized the opportunity God had given him and began praying for a way to share his faith. Not three months into their new assignment, Rock told him that his wife was cheating on him, Preacher had many opportunities to share his faith with his friend.

Rock was not blind. He had been watching Preacher like a hawk. He knew the changes he had talked about were genuine because he had seen them happen in real time in his coworker's life. When the floodgates broke open, he told Preach what was happening and expected the kid to explain his faith in detail. Rock was on his knees within the month, asking Jesus to be his savior.

His wife still left him, and Rock still failed too often with seedy women, but he was trying to follow Jesus with a bit of help from his friend.

* Factory Zero *

A month after graduating, Preach took a job at a church just off the University of Michigan campus in Ann Arbor. He was brought on board to head up the outreach to college students. It took him a year to get acclimated to shadowing college life before he made a dent in the vast student population. His ministry grew steadily for five years, then he caught the bug to start a church. During the launch phase of his new outreach, Rocky came back into the picture, joining the new project, and the friendship started back up like they had not missed a beat. Six years later, the fledgling congregation moved out of the elementary school and into their building just off Main Street, and many new faces began to turn up for Sunday morning services.

Rock and Preach were talking with a group of guys after church and hit on a new adventure for the men's group. Eight months later, in early August, five guys stumbled across Tripwire Alley and were enticed to visit Butter's Oasis. They had passed five posters along the trail, all the while hearing stories from many travelers telling them they needed to check it out.

"You won't be sorry you walked the extra couple of miles," was repeated by every backpacker they encountered. Then Rock took a hard spill in the Tripwire, nearly busting his ankle. The guys had to split up his gear while the other two put their shoulders under Rock's armpits to help him make the final mile. When they began to smell the food cooking it drew them in like bugs to a zapper.

Upon arrival at the Oasis, the group dropped Preach and Rock off at the pavilion while they went to find a site and put up their three tents.

"You guys get us set up?" Rock asked one guy from the returning set-up crew.

"Yep, all set. How's the ankle?"

"You know, it'll be alright," Rock said.

His foot was elevated with a bag of ice resting on his sock. He was sitting in an Adirondack chair that had been pulled over from the fire pit area so he could sit in it and put his foot up on the seat of a picnic table.

"Yeah when you went down I didn't know if you were gonna get back up."

"Other than a twisted ankle and a bruised ego, I'll be fine," Rock said.

"Hey, I'm gonna go get the other guys so we can sit in a chair out of the sand and off the hard ground while we eat lunch."

"I hear ya," Preach said from the other side of the picnic table while elevating his arm and giving a thumbs up. He was lying on the bench seat, his boots off, knees up, and enjoying the rest. His backpack leaned against the table, and his socks were laid over his hiking boots to dry.

After eating a late lunch, the remaining guys dispersed to explore the Oasis while Rock and Preach hung out at the picnic table closest to the unused fireplace.

That's when an imposing black man entered the scene and walked right over to the two men while glaring at them.

"What's this? I hear you want to mark up my table?" he said, looking right at Rocky.

"I mean, if that's what you let happen around here," Rock said while sitting up straighter, clearly uncomfortable, and gesturing to the carved names scattered over the tables.

"What are you gonna carve into my property?"

"Umm, well, I thought…"

"You thought?"

"Yeah, by looking around your place, I heard people get to carve their trail names if they donate a buck to some trail organization. At least that's what I was told."

"Who would say such a crazy thing?"

"I don't know."

"You don't know who told you that you could carve into my perfectly good table?"

"I don't know, one of the guys we're hiking with," Rock was getting flustered and looked toward Preach for help, but he was still lying down and offering no support.

"So, you're telling me that you get to desecrate my table with your name for a single dollar? Has the pain from your messed up ankle gone directly to your head, son?"

"I thought so. No. That's just what I was told, man."

Butter let out a huge belly laugh. "I'm only messin' with you!" he said. Preach watched the show out of the corner of his eye while silently laughing at how uncomfortable Rocky had gotten.

"I'm Butter. Sorry man, I couldn't resist. Somebody put me up to it," he grabbed Rocky's shoulders from behind and gave him an apologetic squeeze.

"This here is my silent but best friend, Preach," Rock said, introducing his compatriot across the table.

"Preacher?"

"That's right, but most of us call him Preach," Rock said.

"Is that what they call you?" Butter was looking right at the man.

"Some do," Preach said.

"You're a preacher in a church somewhere?"

"Yeah, down state. Outside of Detroit, in Novi."

"Wow. How long you been doin' that?"

"We started the church about six years ago. I served at another church for five years before that."

"You don't say? Eleven years a preacher."

"Yep."

"We don't see many of your type out here in the middle of the wilderness," Butter said.

"John the Baptist and Jesus kinda liked the wilderness," Preach said while looking at the ceiling.

Butter smiled and nodded in agreement.

"Mom and dad must be real proud."

"They are. But I don't get to see them much, being so busy and all," Preach sat up.

"So you went to Bible college or something?"

"Yeah."

"That's good 'cause I got lots of questions for you, son."

Rocky watched as the pair embraced and got the vibe they might know each other.

"You know him?" Rocky asked Butter over his shoulder.

"Nope, never met Preach before," he said with a smirk.

"So can we carve our names now?" Rock had his knife out of its sheath.

"Not with that," Butter said and produced two carving knives from his back pocket. They had wooden handles, long steel stems, and razor-sharp blades curved in a half circle.

"This will do a much better job, just don't hit any nails with them, it will wreck the blade."

"Okay. So, where can we carve?"

"Rocky, you have to carve your name in the outhouse," Butter said and laughed again in the next breath, and Preach joined with a laugh of his own while he stretched.

"You're a funny guy, Butter."

"You can carve where ever you want, just don't screw up another carving."

"Got it. You want my dollar now?" Rock asked.

"Hahaha! Not after what I put you through, I got my dollars worth!"

"Is there a donation jar or something?" Rock asked.

"Somewhere 'round here, but don't you worry about it, Rocky Balboa."

"Thanks, man."

"No hard feelins'?"

"No way— I love what you're doing here."

"Me too."

"I bet."

"Alright— I got chickens calling out to me," Butter said while taking a deep breath, eyes closed, his hands extended palms up like he was listening for the calling chickens.

"What do you mean?"

"I make chicken dinners Rocky. You love what I'm doing here and you haven't had my world famous chicken yet?"

"Ah, yeah, and no, not yet, but we smelled something cooking a mile before we got here."

"Alright. Well you're in for a treat tonight, son."

"Cool!"

"Preach, you and me be talkin' later. You sticking around, right?" Butter asked the man who had laid back down.

"Yeah we'll be here resting up Rock's ankle for a day or two."

"Great, 'cause remember, I got lotsa' questions for ya." Butter smiled, pointed at the man, and walked off with a twinkle in his eyes and whistling a made-up chicken cooking song.

Rocky grunted his way off the Adirondack chair and onto the picnic table seat. He replaced the ice bag onto his ankle, perched up on the long bench seat. Then he smiled at his friend across the table and began looking for a place to carve his name in the soft wood. He decided his name would go under "Foxy '99'."

* Jaws *

His voice echoed loud off of the steel pavilion ceiling. It was louder than anyone else and non-stop. His laugh was like a cartoon character, and some would find the man's antics hilarious on a good night in the right mood.

But at the end of a cold, soggy day on the trail with high winds and surf battering the parts of the path that crept along the lake shore into a slippery mess, everyone eating beneath the pavilion was exhausted. Everyone except the guy they all called Jaws.

Jaws had spent the day catching up on rest, sleeping in his tent, which had energized his mouth for the dinner hour. Many of the hikers were far too courteous or exhausted to confront the man who was trying way too hard to get everyone's attention. Instead, they voted with their feet, taking their food and walking back to their campsite to enjoy their chicken in peace. As many tents packed themselves into the Oasis that night, half the expected crowd was absent from the scene Butter walked into.

To say Butter loved to work the dinner crowd would be a gross understatement. The man lived for the dinner crowd, and he would always make a grand entrance into the pavilion. On this evening, he went overboard—wearing a rubberized hat with horizontal spikes and a flashlight, mimicking the statue of Liberty.

"Give me your tired, your poor, your huddled masses yearning to breathe free. The wretched refuse of your teeming shore. Send these, the homeless, tempest-tossed, to me: I'll lift my lamp beside the golden door. And I'll feed them chicken!" Butter added his own ending to the famous Emma Lazarus quotation on the Statue of Liberty to the uproarious laughter of the crowd.

"Thank you! Thank you! Thank you, very much," he responded to the clapping and cheering hikers, then took a bow and began making his rounds checking in with every single person.

"What's going on around here tonight," he asked a table of four.

"Funny, Butter. Very funny," one man responded.

Butter was off to visit every table of campers in the pavilion. He loved spreading his festive spirit around the place, bringing laughter to everyone he saw. "Make them laugh," was one of his goals at the mealtime round-up. The other was to get to know a few by sitting at a table and chatting about anything. Butter knew his job at that point was to ask questions and listen to weary hikers spill their guts about everything from their tales of woe from their home life to tragedies and triumphs of the human spirit. Butter often went home feeling what he thought a priest or bartender would experience by listening to people bear their souls, and he found it very satisfying knowing he was helping them.

The growing buzz over Butter's presence in the room was stealing the show from Jaws, and he was not a fan of losing the attention of the dining room crowd. He was blind to the fact that no one knew him, so his antics fell on deaf and tired ears, chasing half of them off in the process.

When Butter made his way around to the table Jaws was occupying, only two other hikers sat with the wiry man. They were as far away as possible while occupying opposite sides of the table. They were talking to each other in low familiar tones like they were a married couple enjoying each other's company.

"Hey folks, thanks for coming out," Butter had approached the couple while Jaws tried to interject himself into the conversation that Butter had begun with them. They made no attempt to conceal the roll of their eyes when the man kept speaking over them, vying to get the famous owner's attention. Butter bent down low and whispered to them, "Some folk get lonely when they hike solo."

"But he's not hiking alone. I think his friends abandoned ship, if you know what I mean," said the woman to Butter.

"Oh! One of those!" Butter said and leaned back to laugh loudly. When he was done, he winked at the couple and sat down across from Jaws.

"Hey man, how are you doing, you having a good time?"

"I'm good. Really, really glad to be here Mr. Butter. I've gotta say your chicken is good but not as good as the chicken I used to get as a kid in Detroit. Back then there was this old woman at the end of my block who used to have my family over after church for Sunday dinners every once in a while and man could she cook the chicken! It was so good we tried to get her to give us some of the leftovers, my dad even offered to pay her. Yeah those were the good old days don't you think? I really enjoyed growing up in my neighborhood on the east side."

"Wow," Butter interjected the single word, hoping to get the guy to take a breath. "You can talk! What is your name, young man?"

"Well, I think the question you're really asking is what is my trail name, which I would like to point out it is not my favorite name in the world—that I've been given during my life, I mean. As a matter of fact I'd like to change my trail name. Are you the guy I'd talk to about making an official name change?"

"No. You can't change your trail name in the middle of a hike. Are you plum crazy?" Butter said with all the seriousness he could muster.

"No? But what if I just don't agree to the name and I think that I should be able to have some say in the process. It's almost like taxation without representation."

"Wait!" Butter had to cut him off again. "My head is spinning. What's this name you don't like?"

"Jaws," the man said.

Butter laughed so hard he nearly fell backward off the bench. The desperate man laughed along with Butter, but everyone around them knew he looked awkward while trying to mimic what the big black man was doing.

Then the man was off speaking so fast that Butter and the couple at the end of the table could hardly keep up. After a few nonstop minutes, Butter interrupted the man for the third time.

"Listen. Jaws," he said while holding up one hand like he was trying to stop someone from walking across a street. "I would like to get to know you a little bit, but that requires a conversation. A conversation between two people involves both people listening and both people talking. Right now you are the only one talking and everyone resents people who don't care enough about the other person enough to listen to them. You feel me, brother?"

Jaws sat and looked at Butter and did not know what to say. He could not remember how long it had been since someone other than his wife had talked to him in such a manner.

"What you're doing to me right now is kinda rude, dude. I don't know you, and if this is how you're going to treat me, I'm moving on. Like, apparently, many people already have," Butter said while holding the man's gaze. Heads from everyone within earshot were turned and watching the exchange between the two men.

"I'm sorry Butter. I am very excited to be here and I guess when I get away from my everyday life I don't think enough about others."

"I hear ya. It's good to get away, my friend. Many of the people who come off the trail solo then spend some time here have a lot to say because they have been quiet and have spent a lot of time mulling things over. That, I understand. Is that what you're talking about?"

"To begin to get to know me..." Jaws thought for a moment, wondering if he could trust the man with any of his information.

"Well, to be honest I am more than a little embarrassed to say, I lead a congregation in the L.P."

"L.P.?" Butter asked.

"Lower Peninsula," Jaws said.

"You know that's actually not a thing," Butter said.

"Really?"

"I can assure you as a man who was born a troll and lives up here, I have never heard it before."

"Well, you have just heard it because I made it up out on the trail. If the U.P. is a thing then the L.P. should be a thing too."

"No. It can't. People would start looking for a propane truck, like their pig was gonna get topped off."

"What?"

"You've seen the large tanks next to houses? Those are called pigs."

"Oh."

"You are a city boy."

"Yes I am!"

"So L.P. is not a thing and never will be a thing."

"We'll agree to disagree on that point, my friend. What's a troll?"

"Someone born under the Mackinaw Bridge."

"Under?"

"South of the bridge. Down staters."

"Oh. That's like ninety-five percent of the state."

Butter smiled at the man. "You said you led a congregation?"

"Yeah, but not in the traditional sense. My gifts are more in the administration, organization and training aspects of the faith."

"As opposed to preaching and teaching, or what not?"

"Yeah, I'm not particularly good at oration, or visitation either."

"But you found a place where God could use your gifts?"

"I did. It's a one in a million church," Jaws said.

"Kinda ironic though?"

"What is?"

"You aren't a good orator but your trail name is Jaws," Butter roared again.

Jaws hung his head. "I don't know what comes over me when I get out here. It's like the little boy in me overtakes everything," Jaws was talking in hushed tones and didn't realize the whole pavilion was trying to listen without being too obvious. But when he began to notice the attention being focused on the two of them his personality switched back to the lead pastor role for the first time in days.

"You get excited," Butter said.

"Yeah, I guess," Jaws sipped at his canteen to calm himself.

"How did you find this place?"

"I came here to see why my buddy loved this place so much."

"Oh?"

"Yeah. He spoke about this wilderness Oasis and the guy who ran it whenever we talked about backpacking."

"I knew him?"

"Yes, I'm pretty sure you did."

"You spoke of him in the past tense," Butter pointed out.

"Yeah. It's another reason I'm finally out here."

"What's that?"

"To overcome my fear."

"Fear of what?" Butter asked.

"My buddy got mauled while he was backpacking."

"Wait. What?"

"Yeah. It was Preach. My friend was the Preacher."

"Oh my God!"

* Rear View Mirror *

"Knew him? Yeah I knew him, he was like a brother. He was here just a couple of years back. He came through with another group of guys from his church for the fifth or sixth time," Butter explained.

"He was getting down near the end then," Jaws said.

"I remember he looked tired and we didn't get much of a chance to talk because we were busting at the seems," Butter was looking through the wood on the table, staring back in time.

"Yeah," Jaws said with downcast eyes. "I almost forgot why I was out here and got caught up in forgetting about my life for a while— just so excited to actually overcome something, plus when I get nervous, I like to talk. But I came here to say goodbye to him, finally."

"Where did he get killed?"

"It was just over the state line in Wisconsin. Down by Ironwood."

"I didn't know," Butter said.

"It's kinda strange because no one knew he was gone. He had this hiding thing he did every once in a while, and if he didn't want you to know something about his life you never were gonna see it. Like most of us guys we are good at compartmentalizing things, which helps with focus, but can lead to isolating parts of ourselves— usually the least ideal parts, and Preacher had his own dark corners."

"I thought he was always open and honest with me," Butter said.

"He was open about all the things he would let you see."

"What do you mean?"

"I knew him for years and began working with him in the same church five years ago. The Preacher version of himself he let other's see, was different than the man I came to know."

"Isn't that true of all of us?"

"Yeah, I suppose, but it felt like I could only get so close and then a wall went up. Like he was protecting something... something dark."

"You sure that wasn't just you? Not trying to put you down Jaws— but we connect with some folks and not with other's."

"Yeah, I've wondered about it. But we had many heart to heart talks, so I go back and forth on that one."

"I don't know how many talks I had with the man about significant things. Sitting right here spillin' my guts and getting my mind right— because of him. The guys that came with him over the years all raved about how he had touched their lives because he was real and raw."

"So true. All of it's true. You get no argument from me. He was an excellent outreach guy and people loved him, still love him."

"So what's the beef?" Butter asked.

"No beef. I wish I could have helped him. I'm not sure why he snuck off to get away, then he ended up getting himself killed in the process. I guess I feel guilty for not knowing him better on one hand and on the other, I'm mad at him for not letting me in closer, when it felt like he had."

"All of us struggle with letting people in," Butter admitted.

"And that's even more true of a pastor."

"I remember we had an ongoing argument, well more like a spirited disagreement for a few years," Butter said.

"Years?"

"Yeah it began the first year he brought a group from his church. He was having a discussion around his table after dinner when he and another guy got in an argument. So we start talking about it later in the night. We went back and forth on people being ready to hear the gospel. He was just pumping it out to everyone regardless of whether they were ready to hear it or not. I remember talking about preparing the soil for the seed he was scattering. I didn't think he was very loving at that point in his ministry, in terms of seeing the actual person on the other side of a gospel presentation. He saw it in terms of relating to them on their level, but not necessarily loving them wherever they were."

"Interesting."

"He told me that he struggled with his motivation for sharing the gospel. He had questioned himself a lot, like whether he was he just doing it for attention, or to prove he was right, and in so doing ultimately proving he was smart. I called him out on those things as well."

"I think we all need some truth tellers in our lives, he was that for me. He used to get on me about using the church to overcome my insecurities."

"Overcoming insecurities, what?" Butter said and was exaggerating his facial expression of surprise.

"Still working on it," Jaws admitted.

"Preacher finally came around to seeing things my way," Butter smiled.

"Yeah, I doubt that," Jaws said.

Butter looked at the man and smiled. "Here I was thinking I had to come over and calm down a crazy man," he laughed.

"You did," Jaws said, the embarrassment sneaking onto his cheeks again.

"So, how are you going to say goodbye to our friend?"

"Just by taking all of this in, I guess. I'm gonna head over to the Log Slide for a day hike tomorrow. Spend some quiet time at the lake. He liked that place."

"You, you like quiet time?" Butter teased.

"For a few minutes, then it begins to drive me crazy," Jaws said.

"You want some coffee?" Butter asked as he stood.

"Sure."

"How you like it?"

"Cream and lots of sugar."

"Alright. You know how I like mine?"

"No."

"Black," Butter deadpanned.

They both laughed.

"Preach used to tell about his friend who only liked his coffee black because it reminded him of his ex-wife's heart, dark and bitter."

"That sounds just like him."

* Hops *

"So what do you do when you're not walking through the woods or carving your name on tables?" She asked, pointing with her eyes to the

169

carving tool and the curled bits of wood scattered across the top of the picnic table and overflowing onto the concrete floor.

"I brew beer— at a micro brewery downstate," he replied.

"I've never met someone who did that before," she smiled to conceal her nervousness. Her dad left her sitting at the table with an old guy when he was taking care of an emergency in the kitchen.

"I brewed my first beer when I was thirteen," he said, and she knew she would hear the story no matter what. She considered wandering off to the bathroom but was not sure where they were. Instead, she began to listen to the disheveled man in front of her. He was a white man who looked like hadn't had a decent haircut in years. She was confident he was in a biker gang, although she didn't see any tattoos to confirm her developing theory.

"What? You couldn't even drink it. Why would you spend time on something you couldn't enjoy?"

"I dunno. I liked the challenge, I guess. Plus to see if I could actually make something just as good as anyone else."

"Did your parents know?"

"Yeah there was no hiding this hobby from them. In fact they bought me my first home brew kit. What was so funny was after I had brewed my first big batch of beer we left to go on vacation the next day. Then when we got back home a couple weeks later we were sitting having dinner in the dining room and then there was a pop, like a light bulb had blown up in another room. About every five minutes or so, another pop would interrupt our meal. I got curious and began looking for the source of the sound. It was my dad who happened to go down into the basement when a pop happened beneath his feet on the stairway. He called me down in the basement to show me that my exploded brown beer bottles had sprayed all over the closet beneath the stairs. The whole place reeked from rotten beer. It took me two hours to clean up the mess."

"Tonya, I'm almost done, honey," Butter said while sticking his head out from the kitchen door.

"Okay, daddy," she smiled and then wondered how long she'd have to endure hearing a lonely old guy's account of his life.

"He's not boring you with crummy stories filled with lies about me, is he?" Butter said and pointed his eyes at the man on the other side of her table who had stood to sweep off the table mess with his hand.

"No, dad,"

"Okay, 'cause I can put you at a table with people who actually lead exciting lives," Butter's big smile shone from the doorway as the man flipped him the bird in jest from behind Tonya's turned head.

"It's fine."

"You look tired," Butter said. She waved her hand and made him disappear back into the kitchen.

"That's impressive how you can dispatch the big man with a flick of the wrist," he said while sliding the large Plexiglas back on their table. He ran in the six screws with a driver, securing the top in its place while she watched.

"What does the name mean?" she pointed to what he had carved into the wood.

"Hops?"

"Sure."

"They are a flower that gives beer its bitter edge and depending on where they are grown, all kinds of other flavors too."

"Oh, I get it. The brewing guy takes that name as his trail name."

He sat back down straddling the bench on his side of the table, and just smiled his response at the pretty black woman in front of him. If he had to guess, he thought she looked like she was in her early thirties.

"Is this your first time out here?" Hops asked.

"Yes," she said while swatting at a mosquito flying around her head. "These bugs are about to drive me back home though."

"They aren't bad here cause your dad has the grounds sprayed."

"Oh yeah I bet he does. He don't like bugs either, don't let him fool ya."

"How long are you hanging around?"

"A week. We're supposed to go on a road trip to see the sights."

"Never been to the U.P.?"

"Never been north of Flint."

"Well, welcome to God's country," he said with a goofy smile plastered all over his face while he raised his water bottle.

"Thank you," she said. The phrase reminded her of what people in Virginia would say about their state when she attended college.

"You two know everything about each others lives now?" Butter asked as he set down a baking tray filled with steaming pretzels and wiped his hands on a white towel from his back pocket.

"No dad," she rolled her eyes toward Hops and shook her head.

"This old man try to impress you with his keg lifting stories?"

"What?"

Hops laughed at Butter's return and marveled how the man always entered the pavilion with his words preceding him and echoing off the walls and ceiling. Only two roll-up garage doors were open, so his voice thundered throughout the acoustically hot space.

"Tonight campers, we got some free pretzels," Butter was pointing to the tray, overflowing with fresh baked, golden brown pretzels encrusted with coarse salt. The room exploded with applause as thirty hikers made their way over to their table.

"Mustard is on the counter," Butter said as the ravenous wolves claimed their prizes.

"Your dad always has to have the attention of the masses when he speaks," Hops leaned forward and whispered toward Tonya, and she smiled a genuine full face smile in return.

With the tray nearly empty, Butter sat with the talking pair.

"Lucky your arm didn't get taken off in the rush," Hops said.

"It's all good," Butter said.

"I gotta tell you Butter, your ex-wife must have been Miss America," Hops said while he picked a pretzel out for himself.

"What 'choo mean?" Butter was trying not to smile as he pulled a steamy pretzel apart.

"I can see Tonya here is a beautiful woman, so your wife must have been the most beautiful woman in the world to counteract all your ugly genes upon procreation."

Butter's instant laughter sent sound waves bouncing off every hard surface in the place and drew looks from every table in return. Most folks were stuffing their faces with the homemade treat, smiling and laughing around their tables as Tonya finally grabbed her pretzel.

"You're killin' me Hops. She was a beautiful woman."

"Is, dad," Tonya said.

"Right. But I haven't seen her since she shacked up with the carpet-bagger, so how would I know?" Butter took a bite of the soft dough and approved.

"Come on, dad. You know you weren't right in the head after Grandma and Grand Pops died."

"You're right, honey. And I have forgiven her, it's just some days are harder than others."

"I get it. I had to work though my stuff when it came to my family melting down after I left. Man these are so good! Where did you learn how to bake?"

"Long winters up in here," Butter offered a toothy grin.

"Right," she said.

"I'm sorry about all of that stuff... I'm really glad you are here now, though!" Butter's eyes lit up, and his buttery hand reached out for his daughter.

"This place is really great, dad. I can't believe it has all come together like this for you. I mean I heard the stories but to actually see it. It's pretty impressive. And the food is top notch."

"Thanks. Never in a million years would I have imagined that I would have ended up here."

"It's a little different than the east side of Detroit," she smiled at the thought and looked for the mustard.

"Yeah, there is peace around every pine tree."

"And snow seven months a year," she said and hopped up to get some mustard packets.

"Hey, before you go, I want you to carve your name in this table," he said as she walked to the counter.

"He just screwed the lid back on. What's with all the carving anyway?" Tonya asked upon her return, dropping several yellow packets on the tray.

"It's leaving your mark— you know, that you were here. Everyone else puts the year at the end but your always my little girl, so you don't have to," Butter was beaming, and Tonya noticed how important the request was to him.

"Sure. Where do you want me to carve it?"

"At this table," he pointed to the table they were seated at."

"Um, it's covered with Plexiglas again, dad."

"Yeah, I'm gonna take it back off so you can sign it, then I'll put it back on."

"So, why is this the only table covered up?" she asked, looking around the room while munching.

"This table is special to me, only my closest friends get to carve in this one. It's kinda like the hall of fame for hikers. It's our Cooperstown."

"I'm not a hiker, dad and I certainly don't belong in some hikers hall of fame."

"No, you're not, but you are one of the most important people to ever visit this fine establishment," Butter said while tears of pride bulged in his eyes.

"Now, I saw two governor's pictures with you on the wall, over there behind the counter," she said and pointed in the general direction of the framed photo with her pinky finger while she pinched a bite of pretzel between her pointer finger and thumb.

"Yeah, you see their picture, but I wouldn't let them carve their names in the table unless they backpacked, which includes a night in a tent," he said and laughed. Everyone listening laughed as well.

"Besides you are more important to me than any dang governor of the great State of Michigan!"

"Go Blue!" shouted one enthusiastic hiker.

"What about Barak? Would you let him carve his name?" she asked.

"You know what? I was thrilled to finally see a black man get elected president, brought tears to my eyes, it did, but even he would have to hike before I'd let him carve into one of these hallowed tables or onto one of my precious walls."

"Wow. I guess I am special!" Tonya smiled, stood up, and embraced her big old daddy from behind, wrapping her arms around his neck while he was seated. Tears dropped onto his shirt as his hands patted her arms.

"I didn't think the forecast was for rain inside your pavilion tonight, Butter," Hops said, and everyone who had gathered around laughed. Several people, while laughing, were eyeing up the last four pretzels on the tray and had come over to see if they could stake a claim.

"So what's her trail name, Butter?"

Butter looked up at his daughter with a smile as his mind spun through different options.

"Since she's cryin' like a little girl, I think "Miss-T," Hops said, and everyone, including Butter, clapped their approval.

* A/R *

The rolling waves were slapping on the rocks far below the trio as they stood still with all their gear attached to their backs at the edge of a cliff watching the sun settle lower in the sky. The light was refracting through distant cloud formations in the western sky painting it with all the variations of orange and yellow, along with purple splashes. All those colors reflected off the surface of the vast freshwater sea in front of them.

"Never gets old," said the older man to his two sons-in-law. His backpack belt, the primary support for the whole unit, was unbuckled and hanging next to each leg as he leaned forward onto his walking stick.

"Thanks, man for bringing us out here," Duke said. Duke was a wiry man and married to A-R's eldest daughter. His physique and occupation led to his naming on the very first day of the hike. "Wire" became his trail name given to him by the other men. He would have ended up with something different if he had not worked in the cable TV industry running fiber optic to new homes.

Now Wire's brother-in-law may have had the oddest trail name on the planet for non-German-speaking people. He was as tall as Wire but twice his thickness because he relentlessly worked out, lifting at the local gym three days a week, plus cardio workouts the three other in-between days. He took Sundays off to attend church with his German-speaking family in the tiny hamlet of Frankentrost in Michigan's Thumb. He was accompanied to the German-only service every other week by his petite wife and their two little girls, so long as he went to her evangelical church service on Saturday evenings in Saginaw.

"Krankenschwester" was a long and clumsy trail name that stuck after he had made the grave mistake of speaking the term out of his mouth to the other men on the first day of their hike. The name means "nurse" in his native tongue, but his compatriots pronounced it like they were doing an old Hans and Frans skit on Saturday Night Live. Krankenschwester morphed into "Crank" whenever they were around other people, because they were sick of explaining all of the nuances behind the German term for a nurse.

The three men had stopped at the overlook three hours before watching the sky. That lookout on the island was near its northwest corner. The island is called Grand Island and lies a half-mile ferry ride north of Munising. The men went hiking its twenty-three-mile circumference as a summer getaway, spending four days on the island. The plan for the rest of the week was to spend over in Grand Marias at the Oasis with Butter, which they would cheat and drive over to camp.

This particular overlook had a unique feature which the two younger men had removed their packs to jump up on top of. It was a sizeable table-like stone about eight feet in diameter. The unique feature was that the boulder was like an inverted pyramid, and when they stood on top, the rock wiggled beneath their weight. Of course, that would not have been so startling except that it was on the edge of a two-hundred-and-seventy-five-foot cliff overlooking Lake Superior.

"That will give you the willies," Crank said after hopping down from the rock.

The men sat to eat a snack with their backs against the boulder while their feet dangled in the air.

"You know that old saying about a tree falling in the woods," Wire asked.

"Huh?" Crank answered.

"If a tree falls in the woods and no one is around does it really make a sound?"

"Of course it does," Crank said.

"How do you know?" Wire asked.

"It's still doing the same thing whether anyone is standing there or not."

"But if it falls with no ears to hear its sound it goes unnoticed, and therefore it can be questioned if it ever made a sound at all," the old man said.

"That's silly," Crank said. "No way."

"Is it?"

"Isn't it like a metaphor for life? Like if we isolate ourselves so much we never have any connections, then our life made no difference, no sound, if you will," Wire said.

"Oh, Wire has become the Island Philosopher." Crank said and took another bite from his trail bar.

"When George Berkely posed the question to his students, he was diving into the discussion of objectivism and subjectivism."

"Like does the falling tree in the forest even exist if I cannot perceive it?"

"Right. Tree or any object at all. The philosopher was asking if anything exists outside of our perception of them existing," the old man said.

"That's a stupid question," Crank said. "It's making man the center of the universe."

"Or is that just your perception?" Wire asked with a smile.

"So, this huge rock just appeared out of thin air right before we showed up to look out at the lake?" Crank asked.

"Now that you mention it when I was standing up there I did wonder how big of a splash it would make when it falls into the water."

"I wondered the same thing."

"Apparently, it will have no splash if we are not here to see it," A-R said, and they all laughed.

The idea struck each of them at the same instant, and they nodded in agreement without saying the words and began examining the rock together.

"I think if we can get those three pieces out from under the front edge we could push her over from the top using our legs," Wire was pointing at the rocks when he spoke.

"Lets do it!" Crank said.

Wire bounced up and retreated into the woods to find a lever.

* Bittersweet *

"It was colossal!" Crank whispered across the table but couldn't conceal his smile.

"You guys are nuts!" Butter said.

"It bounced and rolled so violently I thought we'd feel the vibrations on top of the cliff!" Wire said.

"The splash must of went out a hundred feet into the lake," Crank said.

"You're lucky you didn't get caught by a ranger."

"There was no one on the island."

"Except a bunch of bears," Wire said.

"Those bears are more like puppies," Butter said.

"I'm glad!" Crank said.

"Hey, Butter," the old man lifted his chin to call him up from his table. He was holding a black soft-sided zipper bag in his right hand and a green waterproof ammo can in his left.

"Let's go to your office," he whispered when the man drew close.

"Okay." Butter leads the way back through the pavilion's kitchen and then through the buildings to his log home. The new house was the replacement home he built after tearing the old hunting cabin down a couple years back. It was a small two-bedroom with modern plumbing and a propane furnace. Of course, Butter had a wood stove installed in case of electrical outages, but for the most part, he was done with chopping wood.

"Nice place, Butter."

"You've seen this place before, right?"

"They had just put the steel roof on but none of the interior was done yet."

"You haven't hiked in three years?"

"I stopped here two years ago, but I didn't come back to see the house."

"Oh. Sorry. I should've had you over."

"No biggie. You alright? You seem a little off."

"Yeah I'm okay. Got word earlier today that Charlotte passed away."

"I'm sorry to hear that Butter. I know you missed her."

"She was the love of my life until this place came along. I guess I had hoped for better," he paused and was lost in thought.

"We can do this some other time."

"No. I need a distraction," Butter said. "What did you bring me?"

"When we had last talked we were going back and forth between the Glock 17 and the Kimber 45."

"Which one was which again?"

"The Glock 17 we talked about was the nine millimeter, and the Kimber was the 1911 styled forty five caliber."

"Okay," Butter said and tried to recall the conversation.

"More weight but more stopping power with the Kimber against the lighter Glock with a smaller round, but its more agile."

"And which one did you bring me?"

"The Glock," he said as he pulled it out of the black holster.

"Nice!" Butter said as his eyes fixed on it.

"There's no mag in it right now," he turned it over and showed him the hollow handle. "The very first thing you always do is check to see if the gun is loaded. To do that with the Glock you pull the slide back to reveal the chamber. Never point the gun at anything you aren't willing to kill and that is true on safety checks as well, Butter. Failure to do these things is what kills most people in misfires."

"Gotcha."

"We're gonna practice this every time we go out. Every single time a gun touches your hand, you do a safety check even if the dude handing it to you is the chief of police."

"Safety check."

"And what does that mean?"

"I check to see if the gun is loaded."

"How?"

"The magazine goes in there," Butter pointed to the handle.

"If a magazine is in the handle, the release button is here," he pointed to the button on the left side of the handgun behind the trigger.

"Okay."

"Don't worry your gonna practice this a lot."

"Right."

"What do you check next?"

"The slide?"

"Yes. It slides back and reveals the chamber so you can see if there is a round. If you pull it all the way back it will eject any round that is inside. If the mag is in then another round will rack into the chamber. So remove the mag and then check the chamber."

"A-R, how did you learn all this?"

"Many years of practice and the last few getting my FFL."

"That's the government license?"

"Federal Firearms License. It allows me to sell firearms."

"You a bad mamma jamma now," Butter said, and they both laughed.

Over the next couple of hours, the pair practiced the safety protocols for the guns Butter purchased that day. He explained the unique trigger on the Glock, which always went to safety when you released your finger from the trigger. Learning the feel of the middle blade of the trigger mechanism was so crucial to A-R that he repeated that part of the lesson several times with no ammunition in the gun. As a matter of fact, he never brought any ammo out of the waterproof ammo can during the session. He explained that ammo was for shooting and it was too early to shoot anything.

"It's getting late, we can go over the Bushmaster in the morning."

"Sounds good, it'll have to be after breakfast though."

"It's all good," A-R said.

"You going back out on the trail at all?"

"Yeah, in a couple of days after training, I'm gonna hike out to the lighthouse and spend a night."

"Only one?" Butter asked while narrowing his eyes.

"I think so."

"Wait, training me to use the guns is going to take a couple of days?"

"At least, you big dummy, Lamont," he said and laughed at his joke.

"Oh, A-R got jokes! You pulled out the Sanford and Son!" They both laughed together.

"What are the boys going to do while you are training me?"

"I'm dropping them off down at the point, then they'll hike back here."

"What are they going to do without their daddy?"

"Who knows? Hopefully not fall off a cliff— I'd never hear the end of it."

"You know we had another one fall last month?"

"No way. Does that make three this year?"

"Only two. But they are talking about rerouting some of the trails away from the cliffs."

"That's stupid. It's the reason people come here, to live in the danger zone."

"Yeah we're supposed to have a meeting next month."

"You're in on the meeting?"

"I didn't tell you that I am officially on the civilian advisory board?" Butter said.

"Oh jeez, they don't know what they have done!" A-R smacked his own forehead with his hand.

"You're right!" Butter said, and the laughter returned between the men.

Crank and Wire spent their time without dear old dad-in-law searching around the facility. They read the articles posted on the walls of the Hiker's Store and the framed ones hanging all around the pavilion.

"I keep reading about the "table," what do you think they mean?" Wire asked.

"Is it the table rock up on Grand Portal Point?"

"I don't think so. They were talking about carvings in the table, and in another article they wanted to protect the old carvings."

"I have no clue," Crank said.

"It's like a sacred thing up here."

"We'll have to ask."

A female hiker was walking past with an empty water bottle headed for the filling station on the far wall when she heard Wire's question. "Hey guys, are you talking about Legends Table?"

"Not sure."

"It's over there by the fire place. You can't miss it, it's covered up by Plexiglas." She was pointing to the other side of the room.

"Thanks."

"No problem," she bounced away, black ponytail swinging behind her.

"She smelled so good," Crank whispered.

"And you smell like your funk got funkier," Wire said and laughed.

"We both smell, buddy."

"I saw a sign for the showers."

"I'll be taking mine alone."

"Gross."

They walked over to the empty table and stopped, then a wave of their own putrid smell wafted past and they both responded with sour looks and blowing air out of their mouths.

"I'm going to shower and then come back to have a look at this," Crank said.

"I'm with ya."

"No, no you're not!"

"There's gotta be more than one shower, right?"

"I sure hope so," Crank said.

"I think I heard it's a big room like high school, hang on to your soap big boy," Wire teased.

"What's wrong with you?" Crank said.

"I'm kidding."

Half an hour later, they returned to the pavilion and headed to the table. A couple of people looked at the names carved into the top, talking in hushed tones and pointing out different hikers.

"Hey there's Butter's carving," Wire said and touched the clear plastic covering above the carving.

"What's up with "Miles" and "The Hurricane" being so close?" Crank asked.

"Those were his first trail names on the A.T. and the N.C.T.," another woman said.

"Really?"

"Yeah he wasn't called Butter until after he started selling his chicken dinners."

"Oh. Good to know."

"Look," Wire was pointing now.

"A-R?"

"Holy crap!"

"You know him?" The woman asked the two guys, now standing with their mouths hanging open.

"It's our Father-in-law."

"No way! Did you know he's a hiking legend?"

"I had no clue," Crank said.

"I didn't know," Wire agreed.

"Have you heard the story of his hike with half a boot?" she asked.

They both looked at one another and then shook their heads in unison.

"It's legendary."

Seven

Cameron Lost

— Section Seven —

"Caveman"

"I fled Him, down the nights and down the days;
I fled Him, down the arches of the years."
Francis Thompson

* Intruders *

The stocky figure stood on a beach littered with millions of multi-colored rocks, facing the wind. He appeared to be staring off into the gray waters while his mind occupied another dimension. The onshore breeze was stiff, splitting his unruly beard at his pronounced chin. His thick brown hair hung past his shoulders and was streaked with gray throughout. The man was sporting the same woodland camouflage pattern on his hat, pants, and windbreaker. His thick black leather belt held his straight-bladed knife tucked in its cocoon at his side. The army-navy surplus store was the apparent benefactor for all of his wardrobe decisions in the recent past.

On the end of his bent left arm, his fingers clung to a lightweight mug of tea. A stream of steam flowed out horizontally, the breeze stealing both temperature and alcohol in the evaporation process, while the string and card from the tea bag flitted in the wind.

The fire ring twenty paces behind him crackled with life, using much more fuel in the breeze, even with the windbreak on the waterside. That curved wall was a simple stack of rocks about two feet high, built from materials from the beach. Natural gaps allowed the wind to serve as bellows, stoking the logs into a glowing red inferno. A half an hour earlier, he had forced himself to rekindle the smoldering fire after taking down his tent, cramming it back into its green stuff sack. He disassembled the two yellow fiberglass poles and gathered them up like toothpicks connected by an elastic rope, sliding them into their sheath. He forced the rain fly into its container and, along with the rest of the tent gear, rolled up in the ground cover and slid into its waterproof sack. The tent package was reattached to the bottom of his backpack by two black nylon straps.

His chest tightened as he moved the pack away from the fire ring by some thirty feet and leaned against a scraggly pine tree to protect it from flying embers— little pieces of dancing fire melt holes in lightweight materials, destroying their waterproof properties. Three gray duct tape patches on his pack reveal the hard lesson learned.

He also leaned against the tree to catch his breath as a dull ache inside his chest subsided, feeling the onslaught of the rash on his forearms trying not to scratch at them.

The thick low clouds produced a fine mist as they raced overhead. Pushed onward by the northwest wind, they squeezed out intermittent moisture in sputters and spurts. The gale forced the top of the lake onto the rocks in a thunderous display. The breakwater was not man-made; it was a natural stone formation out some fifty feet and clinging to the bottom of the shallows. Ferocious waves punished the rocks for some unseen sin they had committed against the freshwater ocean, forced to catch the wind-driven waves for eons and slow the liquid torrent before the rocky beach. The wind had pressurized the water for a hundred and fifty miles and released its fury upon the rocks. After they absorbed the initial violent crash, the waves were reduced to a minor ripple by the time it reached the shore.

The haggard figure stood lost in thought behind his sunglasses while sipping from his charred blue mug. Like a looming decision was banging inside his head, wanting to be solved and forgotten. He enjoyed pondering his thoughts, ordering them in a way he could disseminate. It had been his way since childhood. Making sense of his world was a bit easier out here in the wilderness, although looking at the man, most would not believe much orderly thought occupied his brain.

He appeared stereotypically disheveled. His go-to wife-beater T-shirt pushed the edges of his clasped jacket open, with the zipper connected for a couple of inches at the bottom. The various food and drink stains spotted the yellowed garment while it stretched across his bulging belly. A couple of rips in his now faded camouflaged pants near the knees, along with his weathered hiking boots, rounded out his current fashion ensemble, making him appear homeless and crazy.

He had spent the last few days camped half a mile west of a one-hundred-forty-year-old lighthouse. The white spire jutted almost ninety feet into the gray sky, peering into the lake eighteen miles with its piercing cyclops eye. Its sole job of warning ships continued to this day as the light from its beam swept across the waves, seeking to draw the attention of weary merchant sailors pushing through waters infested by dangerous shoals. This coast was littered with shipwrecks over the centuries, as the November gales were notoriously vicious. Wooden planks with remains of ancient rusted bolts and spikes testified to the horrors of sailing this sea. People still found pieces of wrecks up and down this section of beach, dredged up by the rough wind and waves. As if the initial sacrifice of merely sinking was not enough for the bloodthirsty sea, it continued to haunt and punish some of the dead sailors who had dared to trespass its icy waters.

"Excuse me."

"Sir?" A second voice said.

The beard turned away from his internal pondering and faced the two strange creatures making the inquiry and disturbing his alone time. He had to blink to bring them into focus.

"Yeah?"

"Um, I'm Kevin and this is Will."

"Okay."

"We were wondering if we could use your fire to cook some breakfast?" asked Will.

"And warm our hands," Kevin said.

"Have at it," he lifted his mug toward the fire in an apparent blessing.

"Thank you, sir," Kevin said while Will nodded in appreciation.

The crazy beard-man grunted and watched them walk across the unsteady beach rocks, heads down and arms out from their sides, like managing a balance beam. He was disturbed that he had not heard the dainty duo approach, and he chastised himself for letting his guard down with a shake of his head in disbelief. He knew he had been hypnotized by the water, deafened by the surf, and lost in thought. Wanting to shake himself free from its power, he followed the two overstuffed tan poncho's toward the dreaded fire, joining the pair as they removed their packs.

He threw a couple more pieces of driftwood on the burning pile and stepped back as his right eye spasm began in earnest behind his sunglasses. The two hikers sifted through their organized belongings and chatted with each other like no one else was around. The meticulous guys appeared to be in their early thirties, clean-shaven, with expertly styled haircuts and trimmed eyebrows.

"You, you guys haven't been out here very long?" he said to his mug as they overheard. He rubbed his eye with his index finger poking at it beneath the sunglasses.

"How do you know that?" Kevin asked.

"Just reading certain clues."

"Like what?" Will said.

"Your equipment is all brand new, for one. Boots, pack, food bag. Your pot isn't even charred yet."

"Yeah, we have been planning to come up here for over a year." Will said.

"And?" Kevin asked.

"And what?"

"Are there more clues?"

"You referred to each other by your given name, not your trail name."

"Trail name?" Will asked.

"You don't know about trail names?"

"What's to know?"

"It's kinda a right of passage among backpackers."

"What is it?"

"It's a name given to you by another hiker, usually older and more experienced, to quickly describe something you have done, or attributes you have, like "Chicken Legs, Hop-a-long, Stubby, Jaws, Trip. Things like that."

"Didn't know there was an actual trail culture."

"Those clues keep piling up," he said and raised his mug with a slight smile.

"I suppose you are right," Will said. "What's your name? Trail name, I mean."

The wild man considered the question for a moment, unsure he would reveal it to a couple of rookies. He thought that releasing his private information may somehow become polluted by their knowledge of it. Sipping at his tea, they gazed back at him in uncomfortable silence.

"Well, are you gonna tell us, or do we have to guess?"

"Caveman."

The rookies laughed out loud at the mangy-looking man standing before them. Their eyes flashed and connected like old friends do when they have insight into inside humor they share.

Caveman knocked the fire down with a long stick, so they could better use it for cooking, ignoring their laughter and evident scorn. His forearm rash began to bubble and blister beneath his coat.

"Sorry," they offered, trying to control their outburst, but they failed.

"Most trail names are evident to the people around you through observation, but you may not see what they are talking about, at first anyway."

"Well, I have to say they nailed yours," Will said, and Kevin nearly screamed with delight.

More laughter from them echoed through the forest, and more ignoring ignorance from him. His chest tightened beneath his shirt.

"Sorry we have a case of the giggles, a little slap-happy, from being out here so long."

"Three long days," Caveman said and laughed to himself.

"Who gave you your name?" Kevin asked after recovering, wiping at tears.

"An old friend of mine. He hadn't seen me in a while, since..." he trailed off in thought for a moment. He was peering into the past, just over their heads. There was no way he would let these two clowns inside that personal story, well, any more than what was necessary to remain polite.

"I had let my hair grow and he was surprised, you could say," Caveman offered.

"I bet he was!" Will exploded again.

"Was he hiking with you?" Kevin asked, fighting to get past his spasms.

"Na, we just bumped into each other along the way."

"How long have you been hiking?" Will managed.

"A long time," Caveman said.

"I meant this trip."

"You realize how long this trail is, right?"

"I read it isn't the length of the trail you hike, its what you get out of it." Will said.

"Huh? You read that in a book?"

"Yeah."

"So, John Muir, why are you asking, if it doesn't matter?" Caveman shot back.

They both missed the meaning of his slight.

"I imagine a lot of guys are out here trying to pound out miles, as some sort of machismo moment. You know, trying to prove something to their pathetic little world," Will said.

"There are those types out here, for sure," Caveman said.

"I want to..." Kevin cut off Will's voice.

"We want to."

"Right. We want to experience our time out here, not rush through it just to say we conquered something."

"Okay. I get that. You took time off from your everyday life to spend it out here in the wild. But the real question is why do you want to do this? Isn't your life hard enough?"

"That question can go both ways." Will said.

"Sure it can. But I have already walked down my why trail a long time ago," Caveman said.

"Oh really?"

"Yep."

"So, what is it? Please enlighten us. Your why, I mean?"

"You answer the question first."

"You're a rude creature." Will said.

"Sorry. Goes with the territory. Been isolated for awhile now. Not used to people wanting to hang around me."

"We didn't ask to hang out with you. You came over here. We just wanted to borrow the fire." Will said.

"Alright. It's all right in front of you," Caveman said.

Kevin shot Will a 'calm down' look as he returned to searching for his oatmeal.

"I'm looking for someone," Caveman offered the informational olive branch.

"Oh yeah? Tell it to someone who cares."

"Stop it Will. I thought we were all getting to know each other?" Kevin said.

"You don't even have trail names yet," Caveman barked at Will.

"So what?"

"How long have you two been out here?"

"Four days."

"Four days?"

"Yes."

"Well, I guess we all start somewhere," one corner of Caveman's mouth turned upward beneath his beard with the insult.

"I really don't like all the experienced guys we run into who always insist on lording it over us. It's like you guys are dying to project your superiority over us novices. We don't need anything from you. This isn't rocket science, Cave-man! We are all just walking in the woods down a trail."

"Okay," Caveman glanced at the fire to point out the obvious fact that they did need to use it.

"I mean, the arrogance of a guy, who in our world would be pushing a shopping cart up and down Woodward Avenue, and now, because he is surrounded by trees and camouflage, all of a sudden has something he can contribute to our life? Who died and left you the trail guru, Cave-man?" Will said.

"Say what you want." Caveman straightened up and peered at the two young offended guys in front of him.

"I will say whatever I want." Will said. "And no one like you will ever shut me up."

"You certainly don't need my help."

"No thanks, jungle man. Why don't you sneak back into the forest and eat a bear? Go figure out someone else' life."

"Will, come on, stop this."

"Alright then." Caveman reached down and grabbed his pot of water, the one he had boiled before the dynamic duo showed up. It was cooling on the lake side of the windbreak. He was waiting to fill his canteens before he struck out this morning, which was his everyday routine.

"Good riddance, freak."

With that final insult, Caveman dumped his pot of water on the fire, causing hiss and steam to rise from the embers and logs. Then he pushed with his foot and knocked the windbreak down. He scattered the burnt remains of the fire across the rocks with a swift kick and a grunt. The two guys yelled and covered their heads as hot wood and sparks flew everywhere.

"Have a nice day," he said and turned to march off to his backpack, grabbing at his tightening chest.

"You're a real asshole, Caveman."

"It's what I do best," he said as the bottoms of his arms turned bright red while blistering.

* Running Boots *

Propelled by his hatred of conflict, Caveman lumbered for a few hours. His trail took him up sandy hills and down to their swampy bottoms while his emotions played along. A few minutes of deep breathing exercises had released his tight chest muscles, and his eye had stopped the uncontrolled blinking after a continued massage, but his arms still burned with old memories. He struggled with the raw passions that surfaced under duress and the radiant heat. He sought to hide them from those who were close. Caveman was an expert at boxing up his failures in crates he designated for long-term storage. Yet, their covers sometimes bubble and spit out the fermented bitterness beneath their crusty lid. To combat these spurts and jitters, he used his emotional duct tape to close the gaps, hoping no one would ever experience the primal qualities of his darkness. There was no escaping the pressure of his internal containers needing to be bled off. The relief valve of his choosing was isolation. He convinced himself he had chosen the action to protect others from his brokenness, and for many years he had considered his decision heroic. His sneaking suspicion about his motivation now was the primal fear he had over the damage his fractured life would cause others. Either way, he knew he needed to be on this journey, whether for his or the sake of those he held in high regard. Isolation was the cure.

He struggled when he ran into other travelers with different mindsets, motives for the hike, or love for nature. Those folks want to milk him for something he can no longer give. The pulling, prodding, and tearing of the human heart was too much to bear. It was better to avoid it at all costs.

"How can anyone live back in that world," he wondered? People were the enemy. They were too willing to muck up his clear thinking and destroy the world he had worked so hard to create. People, in general, were to be avoided at this point, except for a select few, and those only occasionally. If he were, to be honest, it was the real reason he had grown the shaggy beard and kept sporting the knotted hair. It was why he wore his mirrored sunglasses even on cloudy days. He did not want others to look into his eyes and peer into his darkened soul. These things were his motivation for being out on the trail for all these years, his why. The wilderness was where he could best manage his world without interruption and distraction. It takes a lot of discipline, energy, and sugar, to live in a fantasy of your own making. Caveman smiled at the thought and stuffed a few more candy-covered peanuts in his mouth.

Deep down inside, he knew people were not the only adversaries to this lifestyle, and his smile faded. He knew that navel-gazing was feeding his doubts and fears. Like the box that needed duct tape to keep it from bursting, this line of thinking would take him to the place where the other was gaining control. Those situations were triggered after interactions like he had with the pair at the fire. It was not their fault they were being used, yet it angered him that he had let it happen.

"I am not giving that monster the power over my life!" he said through clenched teeth.

Needing a distraction, he thought about food again and stopped for lunch. His feet were already screaming at him anyway, so he slipped his pack off his back, leaning it against a thick trunk, and sat down next to the same tree, just off the trail. After taking a few moments to breathe and wipe at the sweat on his forehead, he removed his boots and socks. Freeing his feet was one of his favorite afternoon activities. It felt like he was relieving the built-up pressure from his overinflated ankles and legs. Wiping the sweat and trail grime between his toes was invigorating and exhausting. Reaching past his inflated belly had become a struggle. Getting that issue back under control would take time and discipline, the energy he did not currently possess.

The wind blew through the forest canopy, gently stirring the green soup where he lived. Caveman leaned back against the tree and took in all the sights and sounds around him. He paused to listen for the beat of unhurried feet and heard none. The pines waved and whispered their melodic songs, backed up by the not-too-distant rhythmic surf, while twittering birds sang soprano in nature's choir. The absence of the boots and the presence of the song rocked the old man into a deep sleep. Snoring and drool confirmed his complete departure from the afternoon. Within moments he was transported back in time.

"Would you like some tea?"

"Yes please, with lemon and two cubes of sugar."

"Sugar doesn't come in cubes!" said the indignant little voice.

"It does and I'd like two cubes please."

"I'll have' ta check on that. Right this way." They both walked into the room.

"Wow, it looks like you guys are packed!"

"Yes, it's been like this since Barbie has been our chef."

"Barbie, eh?" he said.

"Sir, you may have a seat next to Mr. Pickles," her brown eyes looked up at him from behind her plastic glasses without lenses.

"I'd like to sit at my own table, if that is possible, Miss."

"We are full today, but Mr. Pickles said he would share with a nice person. You are nice, aren't you?" she paused while clutching her menus.

"Mr. Pickles has nothing to worry about, does he?"

"He has nothing to worry about, Missy."

"Excuse me! My name is not Missy. Can you read my name tag?"

"It's upside down, sorry I can't read upside down gibberish very well."

"Penelope. It's Penelope."

"Miss Penelope it is!"

"Would you like some water?" she asked while he took his seat at the table in a most uncomfortable fashion.

"Yes and a menu please."

She handed the paper menu over; its surface was covered in different colors of crayon letters and numbers.

"Coming right up. Mr Pickles, how are your eggs?" She answered for the stuffed animal by nodding his head.

"He can't give you a thumbs up 'cause he's a cucumber and doesn't have opposable thumbs," the man laughs, but the young hostess is not happy with him and ignores his comment.

"Our specials for today are.."

He cut her off. "I forgot my glasses and cannot read what are your specials young lady."

"They aren't on the regular menu, so I will just tell you what they are." Her curly brown hair hung over her eyes. She brushed it back with her hand while holding the black crayon. She nearly knocked her glasses from her small but intense face. Without missing a beat, she continued like nothing had gone wrong.

"Green bean casserole for 5.99. Hummus and grilled chicken 7.99 . Be-sghetti and meatballs 9.99."

Excuse me, but it's early morning, and I'm here for breakfast."

"Yes, these are all our special ohm-lets."

"Ohm-let? What an ohm-let?"

"You know, it's made with scrambled up eggs and stuff."

"So your green bean casserole is an omelet?"

"Yes and I'm told it is very yummy."

"And you have a chicken and hummus omelet?"

"Yep. I mean, yes. Yes, we do. It's not my favorite, but some people love it, like mommy and Mr. Ken over there." She pointed Ken out, sitting at the corner table surrounded by beautiful, plastic-looking women.

"Oh I see and what was the other special?"

"Umm. Umm I forget."

"Oh because it sounded like it was going to be my favorite."

"Wait I be-member. It's Be-sghetti and meatballs— 10 bucks!"

"Ahh the prices keep going up."

"Yep, the longer you take to order the more you hav'ta pay, isn't that right Mr. Pickles? He just wouldn't tell me what he wanted, so he ended up with plain old cereal for ten bucks."

"He doesn't seem like the talkative type, Miss Penelope."

"He's sad cause Mrs. Pickles isn't feeling well."

"I am sorry to hear that."

"What would you like to eat, Mr?" When Cam looked up for the girl's brown eyes behind the dress-up glasses, she vanished into the fog. His heart snapped into tiny little pieces all over again.

* A Smoldering Fire *

Will and Kevin scrambled to save the fire after Caveman's outburst and exit. Managing to reignite the logs they had reassembled— then they fed the small pile with a steady dose of dry pine needles, leaves, broken twigs, and a gentle stream of warm air. All the materials were rescued from beneath a white pine tree except the air. It was borrowed from the wind, compressed by lungs, and directed through their nervous lips.

They celebrated their successful rebuilding of what was destroyed and talked about the experience with the crazy old Caveman. Will was still furious with how they were treated by the pompous hiker. He fixated on catching up to him at a campground and giving him another piece of his indignant mind. He couldn't remember being talked to in such a manner, at least for a long time.

Will was a respected business owner and ruled his company with a demand for knowing one's place in the hierarchy of his kingdom. Lessons needed to be taught to the arrogant, and apologies needed to be made, but not by him. His glaring error was based upon the false assumption that wisdom was always served alongside the knowledge. Because all of humanity's accumulated knowledge was available with a simple internet search, Will believed the old man was simply out of his league, even though Caveman continued to rent space inside his head by occupying his thoughts. He hated the idea that his way of life was challenged by someone unhinged, insane, and from a much lower rung on society's ladder.

Kevin was Will's best buddy since high school and was now the lawyer representing Will's business. It became apparent to Kevin that the wild man had triggered some deep insecurities inside his friend. This was undoubtedly something Kevin had not considered before asking Will to go on the trip. Over the last year, they had been diligent and detailed in planning for this adventure. Walking across half of the Upper Peninsula was going to be an epic adventure, plus Kevin had hoped it would restore their relationship. Getting the right equipment had been their initial goal before the trip. Now on the trail, they wanted to enjoy each other's company and time away from the pressures of life.

"This was going great until we ran into captain Caveman," Kevin said to Will over breakfast.

"I remember that cartoon! Captain Caveman and the Teen Angels. He was like a ball of fur, fighting crime, or something."

"That goes way back," Kevin said.

"So does the fire kicker."

"You gotta watch out for the crazies, Will. You kinda pushed him. Maybe too hard?"

"Yeah, maybe. But what a lunatic. He has a few screws loose. Maybe he's gotten too much of a good thing."

"Just a few french fries short of a happy meal?" Kevin asked.

"Apparently too much wilderness can mess with your head."

"I just hope he is hiking in the opposite direction."

"No kidding."

A couple hours later, they were back on the trail. It followed the shoreline, twisting in and out of the forest. The big lake was beating the rocks to their left as they headed east, soaking the parts of the trail that hugged the shore. The duo maintained a distance of about a hundred feet between them as they hiked, enveloped by their thoughts during the somber morning. This had become their hiking routine over the last couple of days, walking within eyesight of each other, and then reconnecting around their breaks.

Will, the usual leader, came out of a small wooded valley and almost stumbled over a snoring Caveman. He slammed to a stop to take in the scene. He turned to catch his partner's eye and placed a finger over his mouth while using his other hand to direct Kevin to slow down.

In this very instant, vengeance fully seized Will's heart, clinching it with both hands and encasing it in icy fingers. All morning long, he had been mulling over what he would do to the wild man if he ran into him again. Seeing the crazed old hiker completely vulnerable before him, he opened the door for anger to rush in unabated. The first thing he noticed was his pale bare feet, which triggered a knee-jerk reaction. Caveman's four socks were laid over his boots to dry next to the trail. His breathing remained deep and rhythmical.

Will reached down and plucked the dirt-encrusted boots up with one hand while holding both of his black walking poles together in the other.

Initially, he considered dropping the crazy bastard's boots about a mile down the trail and keep hiking to their next campground. But with every delicious step he tip-toed away from the snoring cannibal, his sardonic smile grew wider. Giddiness welled inside his gut, and he almost had to cover over his mouth to keep from yelping with glee.

"Revenge is a dish best served cold." Will remembered the Shakespeare quote and smiled at the thought of Caveman hiking on cold, bare feet.

On the other hand, Kevin was horrified by his best friend's theft, but he couldn't help but hold down a middle-school laugh at the outlandish prank. While Will was making his get-away, Kevin concentrated on taking intentional steps to get past Caveman without awakening the vengeful beast and giving away the scam. Each step Kevin took felt amplified, like he was shaking the ground he was trying to glide over while blaring every twig snap and leaf rustle over a loudspeaker. Twenty feet past the snoring body, he broke into a run to catch up, but Will was already sprinting away, far ahead of his partner.

Will had managed to take advantage of the sleeping man's slumber and pulled off one of his most incredible revenge moves. He was bound and determined not to get caught. Of course, imagining the barefoot and wild Caveman running after him, huge knife in hand, kept forcing him down the trail. Half a mile later, the realization struck him that he needed to conceal the extra boots and socks he held, just in case he crossed paths with another backpacker going in the opposite direction. They could inform the Caveman that someone in a beige poncho was carrying an extra pair of boots.

Will stopped, yanked off his poncho, and stuffed it under the lid of his pack, along with the two pairs of damp socks. He tied the boots on the back of his Osprey pack like his spare set was hanging out on the line to dry. He was finished with the deception before Kevin caught up to him and resumed his torrid pace away from the crime scene, laughing hysterically on the inside.

* Enter The Beast *

Gravity won and pulled the sleeping man away from the tree he was leaning against, tipping over on top of his pack. The movement jerked him awake just as he fell into a nightmare. Reaching and grasping for something to hang onto, Caveman returned to the conscious world with a frightened yelp. He pushed back the scary dream and pushed himself upright. Like a hand-cuffed prisoner, his sunglasses hung from their strap around his neck. He rubbed at his eyes with the heel of his palms. He stretched, yawned, farted, and groaned against the reality of his ever-sore body. His mouth was dry like it had been stuffed with cotton, so he grabbed his canteen in the side pouch of his pack, but it only held a single tepid swallow. Then he remembered he had poured out the contents of his water pot on the beach fire, which brought a shudder and a laugh.

"The look on those guys faces..." he approved of his message.

His feet had cooled and dried, which was why he stopped, along with his crying belly. After grabbing and munching through a dry fig bar, he smacked his lips, wanting liquid. Caveman rubbed at the dirt from his left foot and reached for his socks, confident he had stretched them across his boots to vent off the collected moisture, like always. His head twisted back and forth, searching. He pushed himself around onto all fours. Reaching out, he bent the ferns over in case he had kicked them during sleep. He swung his hands through the undergrowth, hoping to bump into what he had lost.

Fear seized his heart, and the dream returned with a vengeance. He stood upright while unbuttoning the containment strap over his knife. As his eyes rose above the foliage, he examined his surroundings without sudden movement. Sweeping the area back and forth with his eyes as his left hand grasped the leather handle of his razor-sharp weapon.

"Where are you?" he whispered while his upper lip pulsed with a slight quiver beneath his beard. Caveman rotated his head, listening, groaning after the sound of the familiar footfalls.

Glancing down to look for a place to put his feet without giving his position away through the snapping of a twig or the rustle of dry plants, he moved with intention, wanting to finish scanning his parameter before he took a breath. His vision had narrowed considerably with the surge of fear coursing through him, but his hearing power had increased.

"I know you are out here, you mangy beast," he said through unsteady lips while his right eye twitched.

Caveman's head was in constant motion now, probing back and forth. Up and down the trail, he peered. He searched through the trees above him to ensure the monster was not waiting to pounce. At last, a prolonged inhalation through the nose broke his internal tension, and he eased the grip on the knife.

"What did I do?" he asked himself, puzzled.

Then he returned his weapon to its sheath and looked for his boots. He combed over the immediate area a couple of times, then searched using concentric circles. He moved around the tree and expanded out by a couple of feet as each circuit was completed. Round and round, he went until he was fifty feet from his pack and still no sign of his boots.

"The beast took 'em. I got mad at those two guys on the beach, and the beast took my boots." He was angry with himself for his apparent transgression of one of the monster's unwritten and ever-changing laws.

"I should've known better," he said while he sat to rub his cold appendages.

"Damn it."

"Will this be the only cost?" he wondered.

"I can't imagine the price of kicking a fire would be any higher..." he answered his own question, talking to the wind above his head as it continued to sway the trees around him. Deep inside, he knew the answer, and the intensity of that fire grew.

"I'm sorry, alright!" he shouted deep into the woods and repeated the confession in the opposite direction, even louder. Only the wind answered him. Caveman sat and stared, lost in thought. The veins on his neck bulged, and his face reddened with the primal scream.

Unseen waves continued to crash on the rocks off in the distance. With bare feet planted on the ground, he felt an occasional rumbling and heard a distant thud. His heart jumped before his memory recalled similar sounds and vibrations from the recent past.

The noise revealed a nearby cave was receiving a pounding from the waves and water. After a deep breath, Caveman realized his heart felt like the rocks he had watched this morning. Battered and bruised but still standing, even though broken pieces littered the beach of his life. He wondered if the boot sacrifice would satisfy the presence who pursued him with an unrelenting vengeance, or did his transgressions require more to be given, like the sunken ships of old?

"Maybe one day, someone will find pieces of my life washed up on some distant shore, after I have given everything and all of my rough edges are ground off?" he said to the dirt. "Maybe."

* Push Through *

The sun was still hidden behind the conveyor belt of low gray clouds pouring out of the northwest as Will stopped for a rest. He was sweating profusely with a wet shirt and streaked face; he dug into his food bag twenty feet off the trail. Ten minutes after stopping for the rest, he heard Kevin approaching, boots thumping along the rutted ground. Will had picked the spot for the downed tree to sit on and its hidden quality.

"Hey, Kevin!" Will stood and called, raising his neon orange water bottle to grab his attention.

"Crap. I never thought that I was going to catch up to you!" Kevin said as he exited the trail. He grabbed for a small maple tree to steady him as he stopped.

"I got into a groove and didn't want to stop," Will said.

"Did your groove have a crazy guy chasing you with his huge hunting knife?" Kevin asked while panting after the air.

"What are you talking about?" Will flashed his conniving smile, the one he used whenever he won the best possible outcome over his competition.

"Don't you think he's gonna be a little pissed off?"

"Na, that old man is never gonna catch us," Will said.

"The same guy who kicked the fire in our face?"

"You mean the insane man who is so nuts that he's hiking on bare feet?"

"You know the dude with a foot long knife, who is gonna wake us up just as he slits our throat in our tent?"

They both laughed at what they had accomplished and the game they had played their entire life of one-upping each other verbally.

"We'll be fine. I wanted to get some distance between us and him. I'll drop his boots off somewhere he can find them. I'm just screwing with him the way he screwed with us. Besides I don't have to outrun him."

"Why not?" Kevin asked.

"I figure if I outrun you then you'd be the one he'd kill and I would escape Mr. Deliverance."

"Do you think he's the grown up version of the kid on the porch playing the banjo?"

"Definitely."

"Thanks for sacrificing me, by the way!"

"Survival of the fittest. I hear he is a cannibal," Will said and bit into an energy bar.

"I'm starving. Need meat."

They dove into their food bags, chewing silently as the wind stirred the trees around them.

"I thought we had done a pretty good job of preparing for this hike, but I never considered we'd run into crazy people." Kevin said.

"Yeah it took me by surprise too. I kinda assumed everyone would have the same motivation for being out here."

"I don't think we should stay at the next campground."

"What do you mean?"

"To diffuse the situation I feel that we should drop the boots off somewhere obvious and then continue on past where we were scheduled to camp," Kevin said.

"Sounds like we are running scared."

"Na, just avoiding more fire being kicked in our faces."

"Fleeing."

"I fled him, down the nights and down the days..." Kevin verbalized the childhood memory.

"Huh?" Will asked.

"It's from an old poem."

"Oh. Okay. Sounds like a good plan anyways."

"We'll find a place."

"It's gonna be a long day but it's probably worth it."

"You're right again, Will." Kevin smirked.

They hiked all day without taking breaks, and neither mentioned the Caveman again. Still determining where they would land for the night, they pressed on. Then, Will stopped in his tracks and turned his right ear further down the trail to listen.

"Do I hear a banjo?" Keven asked.

"No. I think it's a guitar."

"Whew. I was worried."

Nervous laughter filled their tired bodies.

They stepped into the private campground as the sky turned dark and nearly ran over another hiker.

"Oh sorry."

"You guys are late!" she said.

"Yes we are." Kevin replied.

"No, I mean you're late for the party," her perfect teeth gleamed in the purple twilight.

"Do you know if there are any spots left?

"There's always a spot at the Oasis. Come on, I'll show you."

* Happy Feet *

Traversing the next five miles consumed the remainder of the day. Caveman's internal map told him he fell four miles short of reaching the next town along the trail and seven short of his real destination. Walking in the leather moccasins meant only for use around the camp had cost him. Because he was striving to save his favorite footwear, he became very intentional about where he placed each step along the trail, which proved to be an exhausting way to hike. It did harken him back to some of his original motivation for being out here, which was determined in his anti-hiking days.

During that part of his life, he had been reading John Muir's biography when he stumbled across a quote he adopted for his own. "Hiking— I don't like the word or the thing. People ought to saunter in the mountains— not hike. Do you know the origin of the word 'saunter?' It's a beautiful word. Away back in the Middle Ages people used to go on pilgrimages to the Holy Land, and people in the villages through which they passed asked where they were going, they would reply, "A la Sainte Terre," "To the Holy Land." And so they became known as 'Sainte-Terre-ers' or saunterers. Now these mountains are our Holy Land, and we ought to saunter through them reverently, not hike through them." The memory brought a wide range of emotions for Caveman as he watched his charred metal pot roll with boiling lake water as he dared to warm his numb feet next to the fire.

He was still alert, wondering where and when the beast would show his ugly head again. The certainty was confirmed in his heart. The mangy hound would come, growling and howling as at the moon. He was sure the bruit had his scent burned into his nostrils and would forever pursue him, surprise him, dog him, challenge him, and chase him. The beast would extract whatever payment he demanded without question or remorse. This was the one thing that unnerved him about the wilderness. At least out here, you could hear his wretched approach as opposed to living in the city, where he had a million hiding places every square mile. It was for this reason alone Caveman spent most of his time out on the trail, hiding among the trees, communing with the clouds.

At the beginning of his wandering days, he could not comprehend the hideous monster had followed him off the trail to his home. He flashed back and shuttered at the memory. Caveman knew if he allowed those thoughts to linger, the beast could somehow pick up on the cosmic vibrations and use them to draw himself to his location. It was as if the monster had a type of radar that could lock in on all his enemies' thoughts directed toward him. Then, if your time for a visit was up, or your transgression was so insidious, he would hone in on you and pounce. Lives were wrecked and ruined by these visitations. The brute beast toyed and pawed with their lives as a cat played with a ball of yarn. People Caveman cared for were destroyed or twisted in unimaginable ways, like spiritual disembowelment, amputations, and even death.

When it came to his personal beast management, he had to fight off all attempts to ponder on the monster and his gruesome ways. He had to doggedly resist situations where his mind would gravitate toward him. He couldn't allow him to occupy any space inside his brain because the fear it stirred would call him and draw him. To combat his new reality, he had to do anything to busy his mind with other things, even though they were considerably less critical. His system worked to mitigate the damage the hellish beast could do to him and any sacrifice he might require. Some days it was a difficult task not to ponder his mysterious ways, but as soon as he caught wind of a footfall or whiff of his matted wet fur, fear surged and soared, which drove all of his desires for understanding away in a flash.

"I fled Him, down the nights and down the days; I fled Him, down the arches of the years," had become his mantra.

Caveman understood that this was his crutch, his coping mechanism, but he knew it worked and figured it wasn't harming a single soul on this

God-forsaken planet. Of course, using booze or drugs could accomplish the same goal, but they left you feeling like crap and wrecked your body in the process. Those drunken escapes happened on occasion and were why he kept his flask close and full. Yet, he knew he needed to control this as well. There had been too many unprovoked attacks while he spun on his bed without the mental acuity to defend himself because of the excess alcohol, where he would wake to find himself twisted with guilt. One fateful morning soaked in sweat, he decided he could not return to that place of helplessness, no matter the cost.

* Oasis Community *

"Holy crap!"

"That was the best meal I've ever had."

"The chicken was amazing!"

"Who knew?"

"Right."

Kevin and Will unzipped their tent and crawled inside with full bellies and nothing but sleep on their minds. They crashed for twelve hours, waking in a quiet camping area. The only noise they could hear was coming from the pavilion to the north, and the sun was higher in the sky than they had expected.

"I gotta pee," Will said and left the tent. Five minutes later, he returned to Kevin sitting up in his sleeping bag.

"Hey they got some awesome looking breakfast available at the pavilion."

"Really? I just want some real coffee."

"Let's do it."

The restaurant was a rustic cafe style. The food service lined the back side of the room with a long counter for hot food and several coolers filled with drink options, plus the coveted coffee station. Sliding the plastic trays along the counter of three stainless steel tubes, customers called out what they wanted on the plate and then paid the cashier at the end of the line. While the breakfast selection was subdued compared to dinner, there were still a few options, including eggs, pancakes, and steaming hash browns. Only two meals were offered daily, and Will and Kevin just made it in time to catch breakfast.

The seating was around rows of sturdy picnic tables beneath a large pavilion. Hidden up near the ceiling, between each thick wooden post, were rolled-up metal garage doors that could be lowered during lousy weather, enclosing the entire space. One end of the eating area held an impressive hand-cut stone fireplace, which looked like it was used primarily during the colder months.

The popular outdoor firepit was outside the pavilion to the south and surrounded by stained Adirondack chairs. Every single wooden surface, inside and out, was decorated with carvings. Some of the newer sculpted names had their grooves painted in different colors, which made them stand apart from the darkened, weathered carvings.

"Didn't notice all of the names carved in the place last night," Kevin said to Will, who was stuffing his face with buttermilk pancakes.

"They're everywhere."

"Even on the trusses and ceiling." Kevin pointed in amazement.

"How'd they get up there?"

"No idea."

"You see what they are, right?"

"Names?"

"Trail names, just like the Caveman said."

"Crap."

"What?" Will asked.

"You've still got those boots."

"I think we can off load them here."

"Like leave them somewhere?"

"Why not?" Will smiled at his plan.

After breakfast, the two separated and began looking at the unique sculptures. It was apparent that some people were talented artists while others were not. Standing back, the cacophony of names almost became a living thing, rich with texture and meaning. Kevin pulled his fingers along the tops of some of the carvings, like he was trying to get to know the person through a tactile connection. He was mesmerized, thinking about the hours people spent decorating and commemorating their visit to this remote outpost. This was more than graffiti by some random tourists. These carvings were a connection to a cause. More than that, they were like an adoption certificate into a diverse family spread over time and space.

"This place really is an oasis, Will. But it's more. It's like a monument to the struggle of life. Carving your name here says that you belong in the fraternity who has fought to get here."

"I was thinking it was more of a temple or shrine to the peace people find out here," his line of thinking was interrupted by a sudden discovery. "Look who was here!" Will was pointing at an inscription on the table closest to the fireplace. This table had a Plexiglas cover screwed down on top of the boards to prevent more carvings, even though there wasn't any room left.

"Holy crap!" Kevin said.

"Caveman '16, '17, '18."

"Do you think it's the same guy?"

"Yep. And I bet he's headed here," Will said.

* Throb *

The morning was calm and bright. Chipmunks and squirrels flitted about outside his tent as consciousness took hold. Caveman's feet throbbed from a day of hiking in moccasins, and his forehead followed suit from general dehydration. His water pot was outside and full of cooled liquid, and he knew he would have to drink all of it to solve the headache. Caveman wished there was some trail-side masseuse service he could hire for his aching paws. He would have to get to his destination riding the thinning moccasins unless, by some miracle, the grocery at the Eastern Gate may have his brand and size of a hiking boot. He decided not to hold his breath and struggled out of his sleeping bag.

A young couple hiked past just as Caveman put on his pack to head out.

"Morning," he offered. They smiled and responded in kind.

The hike to the gate was uneventful but painstakingly slow. Caveman's eyes scanned for his hijacked boots the entire way, hoping they would appear on a pole or in a tree. His ears strained hard to hear sounds that were not there, at least not yet. Caveman hoped the beast was preoccupied with another of its victims.

He searched through the store and found a boot he would be happy with, but they would cost him big money. He decided to look in one more place before buying those new boots. Caveman knew he'd need a week to break in the latest kicks. Seven days of slow walking, blisters, countless oil applications, sock changes, and a mile of sticky moleskin applied to his heels and toes. He was hoping and praying the beast would concede and return his comfortable boots. If it did not happen, he would grudgingly return and buy the new ones.

* Sweet Reunion *

The sign was new since his last visit. The original had probably rotted off its hooks. The painted oval mounted to a white oak tree was expanded to include more descriptions of the services offered and was no longer hand-hewn. The professionally engraved letters read; "Butter's Famous Oasis" across the top arch and "Restaurant, Store, Camping, & More" stretching along the bottom. A river flowed from a pine tree in the logo and cut the sign in half. Caveman had stopped to read and admire the shiny moniker in the twilight. He thought the sign hung in stark contrast to its wilderness surroundings and perhaps its original intent, but nonetheless, it invited him back in.

It was already quiet time in the camping area when he arrived, but the atmosphere was still filled with the collective sights and sounds of regular human activity. Conversational whispers were on both sides of him as he walked up Butter's legendary entry trail. As he sauntered along, he was greeted by a symphony of noise and activities emanating from the sites, tents, and even the pavilion. On the one hand, the sounds assaulted his weeks of solitude, feeling over-amplified, and at the same time, they invited him back into his community.

A hatchet's dull thump to split wood was breaking the rules. Nylon cords being pulled over branches to be used as a clothesline off to his left.

The clang of the door clasp on the metal bear-proof containers being shut after someone stored their food bag. Tent zippers and their long pulls, either open or closed, were common up and down the dirt walkway. Belt buckles tinged against themselves as pants were removed. Groans and sighs of tired bodies climbed into sleeping bags while others already snored away. The sounds of late arriving campers quietly eating with metal spoons against plates and pots while remembering their journey through gentle whispers. End-of-the-day kisses from one tent, while subtle words mixed with stifled giggles from a few others.

"Humans being human," he thought as he drew close to the fire ring.

"The Caveman returns!" Butter's voice boomed as he sprung to his feet to greet his compatriot, curfew be damned.

"You are a sight for sore eyes, old friend."

"Who are you callin' old, buzzard?"

Butter enveloped the man. They laughed like only people with a long history can. Backs were slapped, and eyes moistened with the reunion. People who had been talking with the legendary owner watched the reunion with jealous admiration and piqued curiosity.

"Man, it's good to see you! Where have you been hidin'?" Butter asked.

"Oh you know. Here and there."

"But you keep coming back home, don't ya? Ha ha ha ha!"

"It's the chicken, man. I've been smelling it for ten miles," Caveman smiled.

"Ran out. All gone. Don't make it no more!" Butter threw his head back and laughed more until tears broke free and streamed down his face.

He noticed Caveman's foot attire, and he pointed.

"Long story, but the bottom line is," he leaned in and just above a whisper said, "the beast took 'em."

A spark of knowing flashed in Butter's eyes, and he changed the subject.

"You look tired, son, and those dogs have got to be barking. Let me help you set up the house, so's you can tell us all about your heavy weight match with the monster, round the fire, like old times." Butter was feigning boxing moves.

"Sure, Butter. I'd like that, 'cept the fire part."

"Hey all, this here is the famous Caveman!"

"Caveman!" The chorus rose into the evening sky like the sparks on the fire.

"I'm gonna go help him get set up and then we will be back. You are not gonna want to miss this guy. Go tell your friends and neighbors, wake them up if they are sleeping, 'cause a legend has come home to visit."

On that night, all campers gathered around the two old hikers as they shared war stories from their decades out on the trail. They all got to hear Caveman's latest contact with the trail beast firsthand. After he warmed up to seeing people again, he enjoyed being on stage telling stories, being animated with his descriptions. Sitting on the edge of his seat, Caveman talked like a conductor, using his arms and hands to help his stories take on a physical meaning. His eyes twinkled and sparkled, reflecting light from the fire that Butter sat next to and a hidden light from inside him as his friend egged him on, just like in old times. Caveman paused, he looked to the sky. He sought divine intervention to supply the correct word picture, waiting long enough to gather more verbal ammunition.

To Butter, it seemed like his old friend walked alone, gathering enough words, energy, and ideas that needed to be off-loaded in grand displays like this night. He was happy to let his friend shine for a couple hours, even if some of his ideas had morphed into outlandish tales dredged up from a few years spent running away from everyone and everything. He knew his friend was lost to those around him, hiding in the wilderness gripped by fear, sin, and regret. He understood his peril, and his heart had been broken for the man a thousand times before, but this display may be the first step of a new journey in a different direction. Something here tonight could trigger him to return home to his first love. Butter had paved the way back for Caveman with thousands of desperate prayers, which he had feared had fallen on deaf ears for these many years. But he was not without hope. He was in this thing for the long haul, dedicated to seeing him return to sanity and rejoin the rest of society. Butter had walked Caveman's path and knew at just the right moment he was rescued, and now he was occupied with the faith to believe his friend's rebirth was just around the next corner, or perhaps the one after that. Butter knew change was coming while he continued to pray for the Damascus scales to fall from Caveman's dull eyes.

Butter and Caveman worked the audience like a couple of savvy comedians, playing off each other's compliments and self-deprecating humor. Butter was a good entertainer by himself, but his natural abilities were enhanced with Caveman at his side. After their performance at the firepit, Caveman's lifelong dance with the devil became the stuff of folktales. The growing crowd roared with life as the two danced their old dance, and most relished watching the spontaneous event unfold. It was a welcomed reprieve from monotonous trail life.

Kevin and Will slumped in their chairs as far away from the fire as possible while more and more campers joined the circle. The only thing the duo could think about was the pair of boots sitting inside their tent a few hundred feet down the path. They pulled their hats down as tight as possible and averted eye contact with either of the talent show stars in front of them. They were stuck until the party broke up, and even then, they would have to make their getaway as others left, hoping they'd be lost in the crowd. Each of them was reeling inside. They felt like a pair of condemned outlaw gangsters who happened to check into a hotel full of off-duty cops while trying to concoct a plan to get rid of the evidence of their theft.

* Shadow Names *

Before the sun rose, Will gently pulled the zipper on their tent. He and Kevin were wide awake. After stepping out into the predawn, he reached back, grabbed up the contraband boots, and tucked them under his arm. The four socks were stuffed inside. Kevin followed him out. The duo silently returned to the firepit, walking painstakingly slow. They whispered in each other's ears, discussing the best place to leave the boots. They agreed to set them down next to a chair and walk away.

"How about right there?" Kevin whispered with his lips nearly touching Will's ear.

"Perfect!" Will returned the whisper.

"Is that how you're gonna play it?" the voice asked.

"Excuse me?"

"I will bet you my paycheck those are Caveman's boots."

"What are you talking about?" Will said.

"We just found these on the trail, I, I, don't know whose they are," Kevin lied.

"I may be getting old, but I'm not dumb."

"I thought the monster took Caveman's boots?" Will asked.

"He did. The monster is one of you. I pieced together your story and Caveman's. I was hoping you'd two would fess up," Butter said from inside the darkness of the pavilion, his voice echoing off the walls.

There was a long silence as the two thought about what to say next.

"If you would have seen the way he went crazy," Will said, just above a whisper.

"Nearly burning us to death when he kicked a fire all over the beach, who does that?" Kevin said.

"The guy is insane. Speaking about some beast chasing him all over the woods for all these years."

"If you'd had listened, you would have heard a desperate man running from evil. But you two rushed to judge a guy, who is trying to figure out his own mess. You labeled him as crazy and treated him like what you thought he deserved."

"No, I disagree," Will insisted.

"I bet you do and I say you're blind to your own motives."

"I mean he does fit the description of someone who has mental issues," Kevin said.

"On the outside he does look nuts, I'll give you that. But if you'd had an ounce of compassion you would have taken the time to get to know the man beneath the beard, instead of condemning someone who doesn't look like you. Whatever happened to your generations diversity and inclusion bullshit you keep espousing?"

"That's not what this is."

"Really? What is it then?"

"He's intolerable and rude," Will insisted.

"And he doesn't think like you do." Butter was standing now and approached the men.

"That's not the reason we have a problem with the guy."

"I'm listening."

"You weren't there. You wouldn't understand."

"I wouldn't understand discrimination? I grew up a black kid in the heart of Detroit during the 60's. Try me."

"That's not what is going on here," Will said.

"Stealing a man's boots out on the trail is like carjacking a pregnant woman on the way to the hospital. Cold man, cold hearted."

"I don't know."

Butter cut him off. "Nothin'. You should say nothin'. I understand a good prank, I'll even help you pull it off, but this, and the way it worked out, was plain cold hearted cruel."

"We didn't mean it to be," Kevin said.

"It didn't start that way," Will said.

"But, it sure ended up that way."

"Yeah."

"In this community," Butter's hand pointed to the myriad of names watching from the shadows, "we don't treat each other like that."

"We are, sorry..." Kevin started to say.

"What's going on, Butt?" Caveman asked from the shadows.

Butter spun to look toward the voice. "Not too much, Capp-'em. Looks like these two may have found your boots."

"You don't say?"

"Yeah, I found them laying next to the trail, quite a way back," Will said.

"No kidding?"

"Just like someone had left them sitting around. So, I grabbed them and brought them here. I didn't know they were yours."

"He's lying," Kevin said.

"Kevin!"

"Stop it Will! You've been pissed off with him since before he put the fire out and I'm tired of your vindictive attitude. We took your boots, Caveman. I'm sorry. It started out as just a prank but the further we got away from you the less certain we became of our plan. It was mean and wrong of us to treat you like that."

"Oh." Caveman's head was spinning while his own narrative wavered with static.

"What about you, Will?" Butter asked.

"Yeah, it wasn't a cool thing to do."

"That is universally understood, young man," Butter said.

"Alright. Alright. The whole thing was my idea. Kevin had nothing to do with it. I was pissed off and wanted to get even," Will said.

"You don't say?" Butter said.

"I do say."

"What do you think Capp-'em?"

"Captain?" Kevin asked.

"My name for Caveman. It's from an old cartoon."

"Captain Caveman and the Teen Angels?" Kevin asked.

"That'd be the one in the same. But that's my name for him. The better question is what is Caveman's name for you two?"

"Huh?" Kevin asked.

"What are you guys talking about?" Will said.

"Caveman?" Butter asked.

"Well, I thought 'Cold' for Will, then it went to Rat, but now, Beam. His trail name shall be Beamer."

"Beamer is born," Butter said with a loud proclamation-type voice.

"What are you talking about?" Will asked while trying to fight back a growing sense of incredulity.

"When you walked across that beach filled with rocks after asking me to use the fire, it looked like you were navigating a balance beam, trying not to fall," Caveman explained.

"I like it," Butter announced.

"I do too," Kevin smiled.

"Okay." Will resigned to accept his adopted name.

"What about this one?" Butter asked while pointing at Kevin.

"Giggles. No doubt about it. Giggles."

"Giggles is trail born!"

"You know what you two have to do, right?

"Huh?" Will said.

"Carve our names!" Giggles '19 said.

Eight

Cameron Lost

— Section Eight —

"Cave Girls"

"I have never met the man I could despair of after discerning what lies in me apart from the grace of God."
Oswald Chambers

* Face-plant *

"Ready?" Butter's question went unnoticed.

Cam was staring out over the inland lake as the sunlight tried to push its way through the low clouds on the eastern horizon. The sky was painted with orange, purple, red, blue, and several shades of yellow— until shafts of light broke through and reflected off his sunglasses and the calm waters of Mirror Lake. His mind occupied a different time and dimension as the real world splashed over his face. Long buried memories flashed through his consciousness like an uninvited guest showing up at a holiday celebration.

The house lights snapped off and then back on. The cycle repeated itself two more times then a booming male voice came over the speaker.

"Ladies and gentlemen please find your seats, the show will begin in just a few moments."

The room was thick with a growing buzz as anticipation soared.

Darkness fell over the room while echos of applause bounced off the walls. The capacity crowd was engaged. As a single stage light popped on— revealing a sparkling red dress that glimmered beams of light in every conceivable direction. Somewhere in the darkness, music began playing, and the blonde haired girl pulled the microphone close to her lips. Her blue eyes and makeup shimmered. She seemed relaxed as if she was born for the moment.

"You can make it. You can make it.

Aww, this trial that you're going through

God's gonna show you what to do.

You can make it. You can make it.

I don't care what's going wrong

God won't let it last too long,

You're not in this thing alone!

You can make it. You can make it."

The crowd roared in approval, leaping to their feet and joining the chorus. It was a famous old tent revival song given new life on some TV preacher shows.

Cam stirred and clapped for the girl on stage.

"Sing another one!" he shouted as he sat back on his old couch.

"That's the only one I know, daddy. Daddy. Daddy..."

Cam snapped back into reality, the vision vanished, and a visible shudder surged through his body.

Butter was watching Cam along with the sky and felt uncertain about both. Cam appeared to have aged after the confession of the previous evening. He melted into the wooden decking on the cabin's front porch like candle wax spilling onto the floor. Cam's whole hidden world had poured out before Butter's eyes, or so he thought. Admitting to a crime like arson was a severe step in getting honest with who you are and who you had become through many years of avoiding consequences. Butter felt lost for his friend while watching water vapor rise off the warm lake. He was not sure what he should do next.

"We should get moving," Butter said. "Movement would be better than standing here," he thought.

"Yeah, okay."

After the zero-day, both men were physically refreshed, but the burning desire to be out on the trail was not as strong as it had been. The last two days of intense emotional revelations had left them both drained and uninspired. The eight miles standing in front of them was daunting, like scaling a ten thousand-foot peak from sea level, but their hike was descending to the Little Carp River Trail, which would take them out to their next campsite on the shores of Lake Superior. The trail between Mirror Lake and the Little Carp was what you would expect from the Porcupine Mountains. Lots of elevation changes, but the river portion was mainly downhill.

They stepped away from the lake into an old man trail shuffle, which had them walking twenty yards apart in the same direction. The first downhill grade was welcomed as the rising sun warmed their backpacks. The still-ness was only interrupted by the tinkling of their cook pots on the metal external pack frames and the twittering of birds in the canopy. They both knew they were walking through an active black bear portion of the park and wanted to give fair warning to the creatures they could be approaching. When they first checked into the ranger station, they had been notified that this particular trail section had seen the most bear activity in recent weeks. Both men were used to hiking through bear country and followed their typical hiking routine.

Cam was lost in thought again twenty steps away from the cabin.

* Tax Season *

"Excuse me sir, can I help you with something?"

"I've been sent to see you."

"Me? Why?"

"I hear you're the best."

"What do you mean?"

"You come highly recommended."

"I appreciate that, sir."

"And you're awfully cute."

"You're not s'pposed to say that to your tax prepare person!"

"I'm not?"

"No! You just sit down and give me your papers and tell me all your special numbers and I fill out the forms for the gov'ment."

"Is that what you do?"

"Yes, I fix your taxes!" She was very insistent. Her brown eyes said so. Her black horned-rimmed glasses without lenses made her appear very intelligent.

"Well, I certainly need someone to fix my taxes, because they are making me broke."

"You don't look broken."

"Well I am."

"Did you bring your W-23's and C-12's?" she asked.

"Yes. I have everything that you need to fix my taxes right here in this envelope."

"Let me have it, so I can get figuring. Please."

"Here you go."

"Thanks."

"Did you have to go to college to learn how to do taxes?"

"I'm not old enough to go to college, Mr."

"You're not?"

"No."

"Then how can you fix my taxes."

"Cause I just know how. Mom taught me."

"Oh? What if I get audited?"

"What does that mean?"

"If the IRS wants to make sure you didn't fix my taxes too good?"

"You just have them come to me and I'll tell them what I did. They'll listen to me."

"You are a very confident young lady."

"Yes I am."

Cam lay down on his side with his goofy smile plastered all over his face. The pink bed was made, its mermaid bedspread neatly arranged with several pillows leaning on the white headboard. Propped up next to the pillows were several customers patiently waiting for their turn to have their taxes fixed. A frog, a unicorn, and a mermaid all closed their eyes with him as the little girl scribbled with black crayon on a stack of papers, fixing his taxes.

* A Little Carp *

Several hours later, after not taking any breaks from their slow walk, hidden rolling waves welcomed them to their next home.

"Hey, you alright?" Butter asked.

"Yeah. Just lost in thought."

"I hear ya."

"You remember what site are we on?" Cam asked.

"Number three. According to the map we gotta go right, then over the river."

"Right on."

The Little Carp River Trail ends at the Lake Superior Trail, part of the North Country Trail system. A couple campsites were on each side of the Little Carp River, and all four were just off the beach, tucked into the woods. As their trail terminated, a footbridge came into view off to their right, connecting the campground's two halves. So the chances of encountering other hikers, even in the off-season, were higher camping here, which Butter usually loved and Cam wanted to avoid, now more than ever as the desire to itch his arms grew.

Their boots clunked out a hollow noise as they crossed the wooden bridge. They noticed that the whole area was covered in a sea of thick ferns, which were beginning to show signs of browning at their tips. Soon, they would all keel over to start the process of becoming another part of the rich soil. The first frost was getting closer even though the relatively warm lake water protected the shoreline areas longer; the cold was coming like a freight train, and there was no chance of stopping it. Old man Winter lived a long life in this part of the world.

As they set up their tents, it sounded like the lake was rolling out small but steady waves onto the shore in front of them while the river was gurgling through shallows off to their left. Both men smiled and caught the other man in the act.

"It's a beautiful spot, Cam."

"Sure is."

"Have you stayed here before?"

"Nope, I've never camped here."

Both men were done setting up their tents within ten minutes and sat down on a large log near the fire ring with their food bags in tow. The trees were tall and thick, but the undergrowth, except for the three-foot-tall ferns, was nearly nonexistent and gave them a partial view of the blue lake, which was a hundred yards west. One ancient tree, long dead, stood mingled among a forest of the living and looked down on the men's camp, waiting for its moment.

"We don't have to have a fire."

"Yeah, that would be good. I can get my stove out." Cam said and unconsciously touched his left forearm with his right hand.

"Naw. I'll just have a snack for now."

"Me too."

Butter noticed his friends sunglasses were off and he looked like he had hiked a hundred miles instead of eight. The dark circles only made his bloodshot eyes appear worse. To Butter, Cam's face had aged, and his beard appeared grayer than it had forty-eight hours ago. He was concerned.

"You look like you've been in a war and the outcome is still in doubt."

"Sounds about right, Butt."

"What can I do to help?"

"I don't know. Pray, I guess."

"I've been praying all morning. It's the only thing I got left to give you."

"You're giving me plenty— just, just by being here."

"So the stuff on your arms, when did it start?" Considering the topic, Butter tried to be as casual as he could. "How often does one get to talk to someone about their psychosomatic conditions that are triggered by a beast which has been chasing them through life after they've committed arson?" Butter thought while looking through his food bag.

"It's my curse. That's what I call it, anyway."

"Oh?"

"Yeah, and what is strange is I've had a sensitivity to fire all my life, but I still enjoyed them, until—" his voice dropped off, and he turned his head away. Tears bulged and broke free from the corners of his bloodshot eyes, and his upper lip quivered. The weight was pressing down on him again, crushing Cam's heart. His shoulders began to shake with the grief of the long-held secret. Another avalanche of emotion was about to break free from its mountain fortress and roar across his vulnerable heart.

Butter slid next to him and draped one arm over Cam's shoulders while his friend fought through the memories of failure.

* Hello Darkness *

"Hello, darkness, my old friend

I've come to talk with you again

Because a vision softly creeping

Left its seeds while I was sleeping

And the vision that was planted in my brain

Still remains within the sound of silence."

The old Simon and Garfunkel song had been playing on rewind for hours as Cam tried to sleep in his tent. Tears and sweat flowed from the man as he fought the horrific vision of his house engulfed in flames. It had been years since Cam allowed himself to feel the pain again, and it was ripping him to pieces. He knew this struggle would be calling out to the beast. It was only a matter of time.

Then another distant memory washed over him.

"... Oh say does that star spangled banner yet wave,

for the land of the free, and the home of the brave?"

The auditorium sprang to life, clapping and whistling echoing off the hot room. The blonde haired young woman placed the microphone back on its stand. She smiled; her blue eyes shined in the bright lights as she walked off the stage behind the three ROTC soldiers of the school's color guard holding crisp flags.

Singing the Star Spangled Banner was a tough job. Hitting the high notes and maintaining the nineteenth-century cadence required focus and skill. Doing it at your own graduation ceremony was a high honor reserved for only the best in the school's choir. The decision was made after senior tryouts, which took into account time spent with the choir and academic success during all four years of high school. It really hadn't been much of a competition. Blondie had the pipes, the grades, and the admiration of her choir director for all four years of her high school career. The tryout was nothing more than a formality; everyone knew she would be the one. She did not disappoint either, delivering a flawless rendition of the National Anthem for the packed house.

Up in the audience in a row near the top, seven bodies continued clapping long after the song was completed. Tears of pride flowed from all of her family, which included grandparents on both sides. They shared beaming smiles and looks of satisfaction before settling in for the two-hour ceremony.

"You were awesome!" Cam said and enveloped her in an embrace. Her white and red gown flowed while her graduation hat was dislodged from her head by his shoulder.

"Thanks, Dad."

Then she was gone into the night.

Hours later, with a head pounding at the insides of his temples, he drifted into the shadowy world of sleep while his right hand clung to his knife, waiting for the attack he knew was coming.

With a stillness in the trees, like before the coming of a storm, low moans could be heard emanating from the area surrounding his tent a little after three o'clock in the morning. Cam's calf muscle twisted from dehydration and sent the man grasping for his lower leg. He forgot that his hand was clutching the knife, and the sudden movement caused the blade to slice through the skin on the side of his knee, which sent another kind of searing pain, this time mixed with blood, shooting through his leg. A low growl was heard outside the tent.

"Urrggh," Cam yelled as a gust of wind came racing off the lake, which pillowed out his tent like large hands had grabbed it, along with another guttural growl.

"You're here!" Cam swung his knife and jabbed it upward through the nylon, which brought an earth-shaking snap from outside the fabric. Cam sliced more plunging his dagger into the beast. The tent ripped to shreds wrenched into the sudden fury of the wind. Blood from his knee streaked the torn material while tent poles sprung free from their eyelets. Cam's left hand felt for the cut and was covered in blood. His backpack, which had been resting next to him, was tossed through the air; its contents strewn about. Sweat pouring from his head and arms he stood on one leg ready to fight. Swinging his blade blindly through the thick darkness. Hacking, slicing, plunging the knife into the beast. He wiped the sweat from his face and unwittingly smeared a streak of bright blood from his knee across his brow.

"Get away you bastard!" Cam screamed and fell to the ground, desperately trying to suck more air into his lungs. The tree, which had snapped a few moments earlier, began to totter and then slammed into the ground, six inches from his head, shaking the earth. He became like a dead man.

* Christmas in July *

The crank was stiff on the side of the trailer, which usually meant it was out of level. The hidden cables that lifted the roof toward the sky were complaining. Cracking and squealing with each turn; sent the sounds echoing across the otherwise quiet campground.

"Is it supposed to sound like that?"

"No, the trailer must be going up crooked."

"Why?"

"The parking spot isn't very flat."

"Will it tip over?"

"No honey, it will be fine. Go play and let me get this set up."

"I'm going to the playground."

"Okay, find your sister and go."

Twenty minutes later, the trailer, which arrived three feet tall and twelve feet long, had expanded to over eight feet tall and twenty-two feet long. Each end was puffed out with blue canvas coverings over the slide-out beds, supported with two chrome bars, each slid into slots in the bumpers. The screen door folded down from its ceiling storage, and soft-sided panels were snapped and Velcro into place. The area, which had been collapsed into a single bed, was rearranged into a dining room table that seated four. The walls to the shower stall slid into place behind the dining booth, and the flexible hose with shower head was hung in its place.

The black electrical cord was uncoiled and plugged into the box on the wooden pole next to the trailer. That same pole had a potable water spigot connected to the trailer via a white hose. The valve of the propane gas tank on the tongue of the trailer was opened, and the hot water tank was lit. The stabilizers were lowered from each corner of the trailer and were used to compensate for the angled parking place. Cam knew when the trailer was perfectly level because the door could close without rubbing against any part of the frame.

Under the large maple tree, the tired old blue Safari van was disconnected and cooling after a long day of towing the trailer and hauling the family of four across the Upper Peninsula. The July swelter was well underway, pushing the thermometer above the ninety-degree mark, and everyone was exhausted before dinner was ready. The pesky biting stable flies were so annoying that the bug spray was placed on the outdoor picnic table to keep them at bay.

The two sisters came back from the playground with sweat on their foreheads.

"You two can get the tree and decorations out!"

"Cool!"

"You guys are crazy," Boo-boo said as she sprayed her legs and arms with the blue and white can of deep woods bug spray.

"Why?" Cam asked.

"It's so hot out and you are going to put up a Christmas tree!"

"No you are!" Cam said.

"But why?"

"Where are we?"

"At a campground."

"And where is the campground located?" He asked with his eyebrows elevated.

"Here."

"Where is here?"

"In the middle of nowhere!"

"Ha ha! No, it's Christmas!"

"No, its July!"

"Yes and we're in Christmas!"

"You can't be in Christmas," she said with her hands on her hips.

"Yes you can."

"How?"

"Cause the town we are camping in, is in the city of Christmas, Michigan."

"This doesn't seem like much of a city."

"A village then."

"So, why the decorations?"

"Because they have a big party on July 25th and call it "The July Christmas in Christmas Celebration.""

"Oh?"

"All the campers decorate, there is a Santa parade, candy canes, and elves. Even a sleigh ride!"

"Are there gifts?"

"Have you been naughty or nice?"

"Nice! Definitely nice," she said with a big smile.

* Yelling into the Pillow *

"Cam!" Butter yelled.

Butter was trying to unravel himself out of his lightweight sleeping bag in his pitch-black tent. The wind was blowing with fury through the trees, and he swore he heard Cam yelling and maybe a growl. He got himself on all fours, crawled to the zippered screen door, and released himself from his quarters. Cam's tent was only twenty feet away, but Butter could not see his hand in front of his face. The wind roared overhead, branches crashing out in the forest behind them. Leaves and sand washed across his face as he tried to block the onslaught with his hands.

"Cam!" It was like yelling into a large pillow.

"Was that a growl?" he thought and paused to listen between the chaos.

"Grab the flashlight," he thought and returned to the tent. He could not find the small LED unit in its usual place, so he grabbed the whole pack and drug it outside into the elements. Butter stepped a few feet toward the firepit or where he knew the pit was. He laid his backpack on the ground and began searching by feel for the metal tube. Zipping up each compartment after he searched through them. It was the fourth zipper he opened on the opposite side of the pack from where he usually stored the light where he found it. He clicked the button on the bottom, and light pierced the darkness with a solid narrow beam. As Butter turned toward Cam's tent, the dead tree just behind Cam snapped off and crashed to the ground, like it had been waiting its whole life to participate in their story. The tree carcass landed on top of Butter's tent, crushing it like a water balloon on a hot day, as a branch reached out and cracked Butter in the skull, sending his limp body into the dirt. The flashlight fell to the ground, illuminating the side of his bleeding head.

Cam stirred to life a few minutes after the tree nearly crushed his skull. The wind was fierce, blowing sand and debris all over his bloodstained face. Rolling over and sitting up, Cam noticed the tree that had nearly killed him was laying in the direction of Butter's tent. He struggled to his feet and looked around but could not see anything. He felt for the tree and followed it out into the night. The branches were thick and brittle, causing him to slide away from the trunk several times, limping around the limbs.

"Butter!" He called out to his friend several times and listened. Only the storm raged, with no response from his friend and no growl from the beast.

Then he thought he saw the light ahead on the ground. After several more minutes of pushing through debris, the light grew and revealed Butter's smashed tent. The poles were all bent and twisted, intermingled with the tree in unnatural ways. Cam imagined his friend's body was in the same condition as the poles, and he cried out in terror and raised his dirt and blood-covered knife to the sky in protest. Following the light back to its source, he saw his friend's lifeless, and bloodied head, and knew he was gone. Slumping to the ground was all Cam could do as rage boiled over. He plunged the knife into the ground with screams and fury. In his mind, he was stabbing the beast for taking his best friend.

"Why Butter, you unforgiving bastard?" Veins on his head and neck bulged as he sliced into the earth, screaming at the top of his lungs at the veiled monster.

"Not Butter! He was a good man. He was a good man."

Ahead of him and below the storm's rage, Cam heard the faint gurgle of the river and drug himself on his hands and knees through the ferns and dirt to the bank. He sloshed into the cold water, which smelled of fish and mud, rolling onto his back. The river's force pushed him sideways, but at that point, he did not care if he lived or died. The sky opened up and powered down icy darts onto his face and stomach. Flashes of lightning and booms of thunder rumbled against his chest. The roar of the rain drowns out all other sounds. Trees bent and were lashed by the ferocious storm, but Cam could only think about his dead friend and the vengeful beast who stole him away.

Then his rage resurfaced, and he plunged the knife upward into the throat of the storm, wishing it was the beast breathing and spitting in his face. He knew the monster had taken what he wanted as payment for his sins, leaving him to suffer the consequences. It was too much to bear. He didn't know how he would survive this. His arm slumped back into the water while the blade slipped from his cramped hand and was swallowed by the liquid darkness.

* Phoenix *

"Catch me!"

"Come on honey, jump in!"

"No you come over here, get off that floatie thing and catch me."

"I just got on and I'm relaxing."

"Not any more, I am here to go swimming."

The above-ground swimming pool was new to the family, as was the gray deck surrounding one-half of the 28' diameter circle.

"Yes you are," He was not even looking at the little girl standing on the wooden deck. Her curly brown hair was messy, but her feet were at the edge of the wood, just over the lip of the pool.

"Daddy, you didn't even notice my new swimsuit."

"Yes I saw your new suit, honey."

"But you never see'd it on me b'fore," she exclaimed.

"Oh yeah! It looks pretty, Boo-boo. I like the bright flowers," he said and then let his head fall backward on his new personal flotation hammock he had received from the girls as a Father's Day gift.

"And I got a new braid, too!"

"You did?"

"Yes I did. Are you gonna come over and catch me now?"

"Do you have your swim jacket on?"

"No, silly. That's why I wanted you to catch me."

"We talked about this before we got the pool. Until you learn how to swim you have to wear your jacket."

"I know, but I thought you could just hold me."

"Daddy's trying out his new gift right now. Get your jacket on."

"Okay." Her shoulders slumped, and she walked over to the round metal table and grabbed her jacket. She pushed her arms through the wet arm holes, struggling to make them move into the damp material. After a minute of grunting and groaning, she managed to zip up the front.

"All done! Now can you come and catch me?"

"AHHH!" The blonde haired girl attacked her unsuspecting little sister. Grabbing her and propelling them both into the cool water. Boo-boo came up, spitting out water and complaints as her sister laughed at her prank. The plunge had splashed dad off his water hammock, and he was swimming underwater like a shark toward the girls. He jumped up, grabbed both of them in each of his arms, and threw them over his shoulder as they screamed with glee.

* Beast *

Butter's head was throbbing with each beat of his heart. The light from the flashlight was not making him feel any better as the rays pierced his eyelid. As he felt around his head with his eyes closed, he found a large bump buried in the back of his curly black and gray hair.

"Ooof."

His body was covered in branches while he lay face down in the dirt. Butter struggled to get to his knees, snapping branches and grabbing the flashlight. The rain was pouring down cold, heavy droplets in sheets. With his left hand, he wiped off the water and grime from his face and then aimed the light beam at his busted tent.

"Man alive!" he said, realizing how close he was to getting pulverized. He had to push at more branches to stand up. He forced himself to turn toward Cam's tent and flashed the light around the area, but he couldn't see anything from that distance. He struggled against the stubborn tree, fighting for a path away from the carnage of his dome.

"Cam!" He called out, but the rain was so loud he knew it was in vain. Lightning flashed, and immediate thunder boomed as he struggled to regain footing. Blood mixed with rain and mud trickled down his arms from the scratches he received from the fallen tree.

"Cam, where are you?"

Butter broke free from the downed carnage and noticed the wind howling through the canopy above him. Fear flashed like lightning, and he wondered if another tree might be thrown down in his direction again.

Leaning against the wind, Butter found Cam's tent, or where it used to be. Light reflected off of a couple of titanium tent stakes that had been ripped from the ground, but nothing else remained.

"Oh my God!"

Butter turned his light away from the former tent site and began a frantic search. On the other side of the downed tree, he caught a glimpse of green fabric tangled in a branch. His vision was blurry, and he was feeling nauseous. It took an effort to get over the tree, through the storm and ferns, to the shredded remnants.

"Bet I got a concussion," he thought as he touched the knot again.

Grabbing at the cloth, he saw the dark red stain and knew it was blood. Fear shot clear through to his bones.

"Could the beast be real?" he whispered and looked around. He felt like he was at the bottom of a deep hole beginning to fill with raging water. More thunder boomed overhead. The rain was limiting the distance the light could penetrate into the night.

"CAM!"

The rain was washing the stain from the nylon, but he checked again to make sure it was real, and the wet red streak on his fingertips proved that it was blood, but the tent material looked like it was sliced clean. The edges of the tears were crisp, not like they had been torn from the outside, but like a knife had run through them from the inside.

"Was Cam fighting the beast and cut through his tent? That's crazy!" he whispered.

Shadows from his peripheral vision caught his eye as more lightning lit up the forest. Something white. He pointed the light and moved over toward the object. It was clothing from Cam's backpack. This led to a pair of gloves, a lighter, and a folded map. The pack was found at the end of the string of items, much like in the Hansel and Gretel story. Butter dropped everything else to examine the backpack.

There it was. Undeniable claw marks had ripped through the fabric.

"Ho-ly sh..." Thunder boomed. Butter was unable to process the information. The rain, the wind, the lump on the back of his head. The crazy story that he had listened to for years about a beast was real? He reviewed the evidence in his hand and began to search the area in concentric circles for a body.

Fifteen minutes later, he found himself next to the downed tree, except he was on the opposite side from where Cam's tent had been. Then he stepped on a massive pile of blood and guts which sent a shiver up Butter's spine and a guttural groan out of his mouth.

"No Cam. NO!" he screamed as he turned from the pile and wretched. After the second convulsion from his stomach squeezing out the remains of his dehydrated mac and cheese, tears fell from his eyes and joined the rain. Guilt piled up in his heart like ice in a springtime river.

"Why didn't I believe you, Cam? Why?"

The coughing and crying continued for several minutes when Butter took notice of something at his feet. He cleared away the tears, pointed his flashlight, and tried to focus his blurry vision.

"Was that fur?" he thought, reaching out to touch the matted black mess. The first thought that crossed his mind was that Cam had killed his beast. Maybe Cam had gotten the best of his monster right at the end of his life. That thought brought another wave of grief for his friend, which came like a hiccup, blowing snot and tears off his face. Butter wiped at the mess with his arm and noticed the rain and wind had slowed.

Looking at the dead mess at his feet, he bent to get a closer look, and that's when he saw the claws more clearly.

"Those are bear claws!" he said and smiled toward the sky. "Those are bear claws!" The smashed mess below the tree was a black bear which hopefully meant maybe Cam was lying unconscious somewhere close. Hope sprang to life inside Butter's heart, thinking Cam was injured but probably alive.

"Where would I go if I was injured?" he thought.

"The river," he said and swung his legs over the tree.

* Spigot *

"Miss Polly you need to get back in line right now!"

"Yes ma'am."

"There's no line jumping in college."

"No ma'am. I apologize. It's just that, I am wearing the wrong dress for college."

"Well then you need to go back to your room and change."

"But I don't want to miss my zoo-lol-gy class."

"Just inform the teacher 'bout your problem."

"Okay."

"What are you doing in here Boo?" The male voice asked with his head jutting into the room as he hung onto the door frame.

"Playin' with my girls.

"Your girls?"

"Yes my American Ladies dolls."

"Oh. What are you ladies up to?"

"We're going to college?"

"College?"

"Yep. The University of Michigan."

"Wow, I didn't know they let nine-year-olds into college."

"Maybe if your smart enough they do."

"Who is this one?" he asked while moving into the room. He was pointing to the third one standing in a long line.

"That's Miss Polly, she's my new doll from Gramma."

"She looks like you, Boo-Boo."

"I know she does."

"How many ladies do you have now?" he asked and sat beside her.

"Fourteen!"

"That's enough for a baseball team!"

"Ladies don't play baseball!"

"Why not?"

"I guess they could play, but they don't have any uniforms."

"You could take markers and put numbers on their backs and the black lines under their eyes like the big leagues do."

"I'm not drawing on their faces or their clothes, dad!"

"Come on it'll be fun."

"No. You guys tell me every time I get a new one that I have to take really good care of these because they're expensive. It's why you built me the special shelves."

"Well I'm sure you could give Miss Polly a bath and wash the marker off."

"You said no water on the dolls."

"You're right, I was just testing you."

"You are really frustrating sometimes, dad."

"I know. It helps me be a good dad to my serious daughter." He kissed her on top of her head, and she rolled her eyes as a slight smile worked its way across her face.

* Take Me To The River *

Butter thought the simplest way to access the river would be to go out to the trail and back to the footbridge to see if he could see anything. The rain was still coming down in sheets, but the lightning had moved east with the front. The trail was filled with water running toward the river and hiding all the sharp rocks that were finding their way through his socks.

"Calm down," he told himself right before he stubbed his toe on one of the three logs that served as the beams for the bridge. He reached out and found the handrail which kept him from crashing to the ground.

"Mmmm!" Butter knew he had just ripped his left big toe nail off his foot and bit down on his hand to keep from screaming out. His sock was holding the toenail up, and he had to dislodge it from the fabric and push it back down into place. He turned and sat down to accomplish the maneuver, not trusting his ability to stand on one foot with his sense of balance all screwed up from the tree strike. The toenail was ripped about halfway back, and he forced it back into position with a grunt.

"What a screwed-up night!" he said while gently touching the back of his head. Pulling himself up to his feet, he pointed the flashlight on the bridge so he could step up and not fall or bang his new throbbing wound.

When Butter reached the center of the span, he pointed his light down the river toward the lake and then tried to wipe the rain from his face to see through the downpour. The river was stirred by the sudden influx of water the storm was giving it, and the surface was pocked with the ever-changing impacts of the heavy droplets, but the only thing he could see was rocks, tree trunks, and ferns. The poor ferns were all bent over from the onslaught of water.

Butter swung his beam east, upstream. He worked the light back and forth in a systematic search pattern from shore to shore. The river was only twenty feet wide at this point, so he was able to make good progress. A couple of minutes later, he spotted a rock that was unnaturally lighter than anything else in the water. He needed to get off the bridge on the opposite side of his campsite, "or what was left of it," he thought, and he made his way upstream to the unusual rock.

Butter made his way off the bridge and stepped into the river, trying not to face a plant in the surging water. His flashlight was waterproof, and he moved slowly from rock to rock, reaching out to steady himself with his hands on the large boulders being careful with his injured foot. Walking in an unfamiliar place in the dark was always when you stubbed your hurting toe.

Five minutes in, he had cried out at least four times in pain from hitting his toe again. The last time he thought he may have finished ripping the nail clean off. He was getting closer to the anomaly and decided to stand up and try to see it.

"Cam!" Butter was convinced it was his friend's wife-beater t-shirt and began moving again.

"Hold on, Cam."

Butter couldn't see his friend's face, only his belly covered by the shirt. Ten feet from his friend, Butter crashed face-first into the water. His injured foot had found a hole in the river, and when he fell, he cracked his left hand on a rock forcing the flashlight free. The light went dark as it was washed away. Butter never thought twice about the light and crawled the last ten feet to his friend.

"Cam! Come on, brother, talk to me!" he said as he came alongside. He slid his right arm under the man's neck to elevate his head out of the cold water and felt for a pulse with his left.

"You stubborn old buzzard, you're alive!" Butter burst into tears while thanking God.

"Who you calling old?" Cam whispered through blue lips.

"You hurt?" Butter asked and tried to look at his friend.

"You dead?" Cam asked in return.

"Not yet."

"Are you sure cause I saw you trapped under that tree."

"How could you see anything?"

"Your flashlight was shining off your bloodied face, and I thought you were gone. I thought you were taken because my beast demanded an offering for my stupid stuff." Cam tried to sit up, but the cold water had seized his muscles.

"Let's get you out of this cold ass river."

"The beast got me too."

"What are you talking about?"

"My leg is cut."

"How bad is it?"

"Not too sure. I thought the cold water would be good for it. Plus I was hiding."

"Well the good news is your beast is dead."

"What are you talking about?" Cam pushed to sit up and grabbed for his friend's help.

"He's in a pile, smashed under the same tree that almost crushed me."

"You're kidding?"

"No. I'll take you to it just as soon as we get out of this river and have a look at that leg. Which one is hurt?" Butter was trying to see through the thick darkness.

"The right, by my knee." Butter forced his way up to his feet with a shiver. The rain was cold but felt much warmer than the river water. He got behind Cam and grabbed his armpits.

"Ready?"

"Yep."

"Three!"

The old pair would have looked like some slapstick comedy routine if not for the seriousness of the situation. The men's grunts and groans brought a new beam of light to their faces from the other side of the river.

"Hey! Are you guys alright?" Asked the male voice. The man didn't stop at the river's edge; he walked right in and over to Cam and Butter. He got his shoulder under Cam's left arm and began walking with them.

"Where are you headed?" he asked.

"Back to our camp, I think," Cam said.

"There's nothing left, Cam," Butter said.

"I gotta tarp we can get out of the rain," the guy said.

"Lead the way."

"I'm Roger."

"Thanks for the help, Roger," Butter said.

Cam's mind and body were numb, but it didn't stop the carousel of memories banging around in his head, even as they limped out of the Little Carp River.

* Creation *

"It was so good getting to know you guys."

"It was a lot of fun, we'll have to keep in touch," Don said.

"I got all your information already," she smiled.

"Good, good. We get up your way about once a year to see my aunt."

"That's what Gail said. Make sure you let us know and we'll get together."

They were both watching the parade of campers, trailers, and trucks, RV's trying to make their way off the festival grounds. When eighty thousand people decided to leave an area after being camped out for the better half of a week, everyone expected traffic issues and backups. The only honking to be done was with a goodbye in mind.

"That concert last night was amazing."

"Yeah, that band always does a great job."

"What was their name again?"

"Third Day."

"Right. I'm not sure why I have a hard time remembering that."

"Where's Cam?"

"He's supposed to be putting the trailer down, but here he comes."

"Hey Cam, you guys heading out soon?"

"Yeah. We've got an eight hour drive ahead of us."

"Well, we don't!" he laughed because they both knew he lived only an hour away from Hershey."

"Next year we will have to try to get sites next to each other again," she said.

"And we'll try to get them backed up to the river again, too," Cam said.

"Yeah it was good to be on these sites," Don agreed. "That water is cold. I couldn't believe you did those baptisms in the cold river," he said to Cam.

"He about froze."

"Naw, it wasn't too bad, after you got used to it."

* Freezer Burn *

"You must be about froze," Roger said to the both of them as they made their way out of the river.

"I just got in, I was looking for him."

"Not too bad."

"I had a fire, but I'm sure it's dead by now," Roger said.

"Let's get out of the weather," Butter said.

Fifty feet down a small side trail and Roger's campsite came into view between the raindrops. Roger's dome tent was fifteen feet behind the covered area. His ten-by-ten tarp was strung between four swaying trees, which caused the tarp to lift and fall depending on the direction each tree took in response to the wind. When it was drawn taut, the water jumped from the tarp with a splash. With the wind and rain beginning to let up, most of the water poured off the front side, which was lower than the remaining blue material. Beneath the tarp was a sitting log and a large rock that looked like it was used as a table, both glistening with moisture in Roger's light, but it was protected from most of the downpour.

"I got an emergency blanket, help him out of his wet clothes and I'll grab it."

"We just met."

"What?" Roger bent low toward Cam to hear him better.

"We just met and you're trying to get my clothes off?" Cam said.

"Don't worry about him, this is how he always acts," Butter explained and laughed.

"Good to know his sense of humor is intact," Roger gave a thumbs up as Cam began working on his soaked shirt.

Butter's pounding head forced him to sit down next to Cam.

"You alright?"

"Head's a poundin', think I got a concussion."

"Well considering I thought you were dead; I'd say you're doing better than I had feared."

"Yeah, I thought the same about you when your tent was gone and then I found your backpack ripped apart."

Cam peeled the shirt off his back, bumped his empty sheath, and remembered dropping his knife in the river.

Roger returned, unfolding the thin metallic emergency blanket, which reflected all the body heat back to the person under its shiny skin. He stretched it over Cam's back and head. The pair couldn't help but notice the examination gloves he was wearing right away.

"Keep your head covered, that's where most of your body heat escapes from."

"You a doctor?" Butter asked.

"Nurse."

"No kidding?"

"Yep. Emergency room RN for almost twenty years."

"You should have a look at his leg."

"And you should examine his head," Cam said, and they all laughed.

"I was figuring you both had some injuries. What's with the leg?"

"I got cut."

"Let me look," Roger pointed the light at Cam's bloody knee.

"Your skin has been ripped. Looks like you got gored to me."

"I was fighting the beast, but I thought I cut myself with my knife."

"You need several stitches."

"Can you do it?" Cam asked.

"Yes I have suture, but I don't have anything to numb it."

"I'm already numb, so now's a good time."

"Alright. I'm gonna have to clean the wound first."

"Yep." Cam's mind flashed back to his brother pouring iodine on his heel. Roger was a real pro, working fast while Butter held the light.

"You feeling this?" he asked Cam.

"Yes."

"Are you okay?"

"Keep going, I'm fine."

"You did good." Roger said and finished up with Cam, then had a look at Butter's head wound. He flashed his eyes with the light and confirmed he had a concussion.

"You're gonna want to stay awake tonight. I got some Motrin for both of you."

"You're a life saver, Roger!" Butter said.

"How'd you know we were out here?" Cam asked.

"The tree crashing woke me up. I came out of my tent awhile later, mostly to pee, and I thought I heard someone yelling across the river, but the wind was so loud."

"You came out in the monsoon to pee?" Butter asked.

"I really had to go, so I ran out beneath the tarp, but I wanted to check the ropes thinking I might have to take it down before it got destroyed. The storm was magnificent, really powerful. Then I heard you yelling in the river."

* Katie Storm *

"What are you doing, Cam?"

"What do you mean?"

The pair had walked away from the party and were standing in a long and narrow clover field by Curtis' vegetable garden. The Father's Day celebration had been tense from the beginning and was now to the point of boiling over. Katie drew close to her brother pushing her nose near to his chest while looking up into his eyes.

"All of this is such bull crap and you know it," she emphasized each word.

"I know."

"Well— do something about it."

"I can't."

"What does that mean? You're the only one who can do something about it."

"I know that I've been forgiven."

"Yeah Jesus does that, but he wants us to walk away from our sin and turn to him."

"We are all sinners."

"True."

"So, you can't ever say that you don't need the grace of God."

"Also true, but he calls us out of our sin, not into it."

"And I need his forgiveness every day," Cam said.

"What about the people around you? Plus all of the people you have led over the years?"

"Like who?"

"Your daughters, primarily."

"My girls love me," Cam insisted.

"Your girls may love you but they may never forgive you, Cam."

"I don't believe that."

"I think you're living in a fantasy world if you think you can hurt their mother in this way and then believe they will just jump in and come running back to forgive you."

"They will."

"Life doesn't work like that."

"But they know me, they know my heart," Cam said.

"They thought they knew you and you blew that image to smithereens. Besides, doesn't the Bible talk about the heart being deceitful above all things and desperately sick?"

"Like you've never have done anything wrong."

"I've never claimed that, and this isn't about me right now, quit trying to change the subject. I also know if this would have been me or one of our brothers, you would have held us to a higher standard than anyone else," she thrust her finger into his chest to make her point. "But because this is your sin you expect everyone to roll over and accept your lame-ass explanation that you're a sinner, like we didn't know that already. I can't believe how arrogant you've become, Cam."

"Arrogant? What are you talking about?"

"Yes. And selfish. What are you trying to do to our parents, for God's sake?"

"Huh?"

"Don't you think this is killing them? Watching their son blow his life to bits?"

"They know I'm not perfect."

"That was never in doubt, Cam. The whole Harry Houdini, 'only show them what you want them to see,' doesn't work as a life verse, brother. What they do know is you are bringing all of this hurt down on yourself and the rest of us as well."

"What are you talking about?"

"We all suffer when one of us does. Your brokenness is like an avalanche and it's running over everyone. It's like you have scales on your eyes and you can no longer see the world as God created it."

Cam had never seen Katie so animated. She was ten years his junior but was leading this conversation, driving her point home with blow after blow to his fragile ego.

"Why can't you see the damage you are doing to the people who love you? No, it's worse than just not being able to see it, it looks like you don't care about hurting anyone else, as long as Cam gets to feel better about Cam."

"This isn't about you guys, it's about me."

"And your wife, your kids, your parents, your siblings, your nieces and nephews, who have all looked up to you over the years."

"You're wrong, this is my sin, my shame."

"And this crap you're involved in is splashing all over the rest of us, too. Enough! You need to get on your face and do something about it."

The Katie storm ended as she turned away and walked back to the muted gathering on the patio by the pool. The rest of the family had been listening without making it too obvious they were. Cam stood still with his back to the small crowd, wiping tears away from his face, and struggling to accept what his sister had said.

* Right Time *

Roger was a godsend who had packed all his trail gear up the next morning and moved on. He left the guys his tarp, some over-the-counter pain medication, extra food rations, and his triple antibiotic ointment. He also promised to send help with the first Park Ranger he crossed.

"Unfortunately I still have thirty miles and only two days," he said.

"No reason to apologize, you have been more than kind," Butter said as he shook his hand. "If you're ever walking through PRNL you make sure you stop by the Oasis and say hello.

"Looking forward to it, Butter."

And with a final handshake their trail angel was off, headed toward Wisconsin.

"You cannot deny God had a hand in putting the right guy in the right place just when we needed him," Butter said to Cam as they watched the man fade into the forest. Cam was speechless and filled with gratitude while touching the gauze bandage wrapped around his knee.

The pair hobbled back to the log under the tarp to see what they could salvage from the pile of gear they had managed to recover earlier that morning. Cam still had not processed what went down during the storm. He believed it was the beast seeking revenge but could not deny the dead bear beneath the broken tree. He felt for his knife in his sheath. Roger had even found his prized tool in the river because the blade reflected enough early morning sunlight to be spotted on the bottom.

Both men still had their food rations, which was because they had stored them in the campgrounds bear proof bin. Cam's pack was ripped but it was limited to the rear outside pocket and the metal external frame was bent in, near the bottom.

Butter's tent was the final issue that they needed to resolve. Cam's tent was shredded, including the rain fly, both were destroyed by claw and knife. Cam rolled it up and stuffed it in the sack for a memento, although he was not sure how much of the previous twenty four hours he wanted to remember.

"Let's go see if we can get my tent out from under that tree."

"Okay," Cam said.

They headed back over the bridge to their former campsite. The felled tree had been standing dead for some time, so most of the branches were dried and crispy. When the two men pushed together they were able to snap them off and toss them aside. Forty five minutes later both of the men were covered in sweat but the tree over the top of the tent was whittled down to its trunk.

"Looks like your tent may be alright, except the mangled poles."

"If we work the material all over to this side of the tree maybe we can use that big branch as a lever to lift it just enough to get it out," Cam said and pointed.

Ten minutes later they were sitting back under the tarp at camp Roger, inspecting Butter's dome.

"Does your blade have a saw tooth edge on the top?" Butter asked.

"Yeah."

"Do you think we could cut your fiberglass tent poles to the right length to fit my tent?"

"Why not?"

"Yeah, why not. I figure we can put the one pole inside the tent since the sleeve is torn," Butter said.

"We can just secure the fly over the tent with cordage."

"Right."

"Your head must be alright, Butt, still coming up with good ideas."

"Even a blind squirrel gets a nut every once in a while."

An hour later and Butter's tent was standing upright again. Although this time it had four pieces of duct tape covering small puncture holes and one tear near the top.

"It should be fine, the holes are beneath the rain fly, plus we can set up under Roger's tarp."

"There's only one problem," Butter said barely able to control his smile.

"What's that?"

"I gotta sleep next to you! I have to insist that you leave your beast killer knife outside!" They both exploded into laughter which echoed all the way down to the waterfront.

* Tidal Wave *

The duo had decided to limp down to the beach to watch the evening sky. They were set up on Rogers's campsite, wondering if anyone else was supposed to camp the night there. After the previous night's experience, many would have thought they would have wanted to run away from the place, but they needed to feel better to run anywhere. So, they decided to stay put and try to heal up. It would cost them an extra day, but neither of them cared. No other hikers had walked past the site; apparently, Roger never saw a Park Ranger to send their way either. Both men would have accepted a boat ride out at this point. Exhausted and emotionally spent, they collapsed onto the sand using a significant piece of driftwood as a seat back.

"So, what you thinking about your beast now?" Butter asked as the sun dropped toward the clouds on the horizon out over the gigantic lake. Waves were pulsing up the sandy beach in a steady hypnotic rhythm.

"I don't know what to think. Everything that happened last night is still so vivid and raw." Cam sipped some green tea while watching the sky. The pain in his knee was significant as he tried to find the correct position for his wounded leg.

"Yeah." Butter's hand felt at the knot on the back of his head while keeping his eyes on the show in front of them.

Silence settled in between the old friends as they took in the scene. Dark water from the Little Carp surged into the blue lake, gurgling over their final rocks while the waves sought to stir the waters together. The current from the river bent to the will of the lake, and it looked like the river flowed through the lake along the shore out in front of them. The beige sand was littered with natural debris from the powerful storm. Sticks, branches, and leaves covered the area, reminding them of the previous night. The radiant sky pointed their hearts in a different direction. It was filled with brilliant and ever-changing colors as birds began singing their sweet lullabies to another day.

"Life really is a miracle in the middle of chaos," Butter said.

Tears streaked and stained Cam's face. He tucked his head down into his hands and moaned. Butter turned to his right toward the man and did not know what to make of what was happening. His first reaction to obvious pain was to try to encourage the one suffering. It was what his trail had taught him so many years ago.

"Come on, man, that old beast didn't get you. Found may be different than what you believe, but your life isn't over." Butter said and draped his arm over his shoulders. The move forced Cam's head lower. Then he began wailing and moaning like he was stuck in perpetual agony.

"Whats going on?"

Cam tried to get some control over his emotions but couldn't and just kept blubbering as Butter could do nothing but watch the man melt before his very eyes.

"I didn't know they'd be there, Butter. I just didn't know..."

Butter wanted to jump in with questions but bit his lip and waited for his compatriot to continue.

"I knew who I was going to hurt the most and I gotta tell you, at that point I didn't care anymore. My heart was calloused and dead toward her, but she didn't deserve it. She was an honorable person and I had gone too far."

"Who are you talking about?"

"I'll tell you but I want you to know that I'm not going to air her dirty laundry by ever talking bad about her. What happened between us will stay between us."

"Okay. Whatever you need to do."

Cam could not bring himself to look at his friend, so he raised his head and pointed his eyes to the water, but the only waves he could see were his dark memories.

Several minutes passed in silence while still more water drained from Cam's eyes, running like the river next to them, washing into the freshwater sea.

"You can't keep hiding from this pain, it will eat you up," Butter said just above a whisper.

"Yeah, I know."

"Just because you burned down your house doesn't mean that you are lost forever, beyond God's reach," Butter said.

"But I burned it down while all my family was inside. I waited for the lights to go out when that damnable poem went off inside my head— and I did what I wanted to do anyway."

Nine

Cameron Lost

— Section Nine —

"Ache"

"Being broken is the beginning of revival.

It is painful, it is humiliating,

but it is the only way."

Roy Hession

* Roping The Whirlwind *

The view from the balcony offered Cameron a nice view of the corn fields behind his apartment. Although he had to bend down to see the horizon, it was still closer to nature than he ever thought living just north of Flint would ever offer.

Six months passed since his final battle with the trail beast. He limped away from the conflict along with his best friend Butter when a couple of park rangers showed up at camp. The Rangers offered the men evacuation via a skiff to the park headquarters near Ontonagon in exchange for a debriefing on the storm, which had left a black bear dead and both men wounded.

By the end of the day, they were pulling up to the parking lot side of the Oasis in Butter's pickup truck, both men utterly spent.

"You're crashing in my guest room tonight, Cam."

"You sure?"

"Come on, man. You don't even have a tent!"

"Oh, yeah. Thanks."

"What a trip."

"You can say that again."

Before the sun could push away the darkness on their side of the globe, Cam was tiptoeing out Butter's front door, driven by a sudden need to run, even while his head continued spinning. His ripped backpack was still in the truck's bed, smelling like dirt, must, and sweat. When he threw it over his tired shoulders, he fell to the ground, landing on his back with the pack cushioning the fall. Even though his mind wanted to run, his body was telling him "no" with complete certainty.

He had no recollection of how he ended up in Butter's guest room upon waking the next day. At the time, he did not know how long he had been sleeping and felt like his exhaustion had not abated. Cam showered off his stench and tried to find some clothes that smelled not awful. He sat on a chair in the room for untold hours, staring out into the trees, his head still buzzing from the fatigue, when a knock came on the closed door.

"Yes?" Cam said but did not move.

"Butter sent me over with some food for you," the muffled female voice said.

"Just leave it by the door."

"Okay."

The setting of the fiberglass tray on the hardwood floor, the jingling of the metal eating utensils, then descending the stairs were all heard by Cam as he laid back down on the bed, but they were the last thing he remembered that day. The sun danced across the room as he slept, switching from one window to the next as it moved the shadows across his feet.

The next knock on the door was from Butter.

"Cam, are you alright?"

"Cam?"

"I'm coming in," Butter said, pushing through the entry.

"Hey, Butter," Cam managed to say, not moving from the pillow, not even opening his eyes.

"You gotta eat something, brother."

"She just brought me some food a few minutes ago."

"That was twelve hours ago. You've been sleeping for almost two days!"

"What?"

Butter reached for the lamp on the nightstand and clicked it on. The sun was hidden on the other side of the planet now as Cam looked up at the man through one partially open eye.

"So glad you took a shower, you were ripe, dude."

"Two days?"

"Yeah. I was starting to think I'd have to call someone and get you shoveled up out of my house."

"Huh?"

"Never mind. You needs to eat, and I got dinner downstairs waiting for you," Butter said. "If you don't show up in ten minutes I'm coming back to carry you down."

Fifteen minutes later, Cam appeared at the top of the stairs and paused for a few beats of his heart. He grabbed at the railing and leaned into it. He made his way down with his left foot stepping down first on every step like he was ninety years old. Butter watched the man descend and wondered what life had for him next. He knew what he would keep on doing, but he was confident that this would be Cam's final visit to the Oasis and that the trip out of the Porcupine Mountains, the one they had just survived, would be the last excursion for both of them.

Once Cam got situated, he looked at his friend, lifted his chin in appreciation, then looked back down at the carry-out container of food and devoured the crispy chicken, buttery dinner roll, and pile of corn. Then he slammed through the gooey brownie like a ravenous animal. Butter just watched the man while occupying the chair across from him.

"Thanks, man," Cam said. "The food was excellent, as usual."

"You're welcome. It's good to see you eat."

Silence reigned over the next few moments as Cam washed down dinner with an entire bottle of water in one long continuous gulp while Butter sat and watched his friend with curious eyes.

"I had the same strange dream over and over," Cam said, breaking the sound barrier.

"What's that?"

Cam raised his eyes to meet Butter's, then wiped at his mouth with the brown napkin that came with the take-out carton. He was pausing to reign in his wild emotions.

"Both my girls were banging on a strange window I didn't recognize. Their hands, arms, and faces were covered in soot as they slapped the glass with open hands," he paused to swallow down his dread. "Fire was rising behind them, crawling up the walls, licking the ceiling above them. Their hysterical voices were muffled by the thick glass— almost silent as they pounded. The strange part was they were both about the same age, like five years old, which makes no sense at all."

"Save us, Daddy, Save us!" Cam tried miming a little girl's voice and had to look away from Butter's peering brown eyes.

"I'm sorry," Butter said in hushed tones.

"I don't know if I can cry anymore tears."

"I think you have been catching up to the rest of us over the last few days, that's all."

"Yeah, maybe." Cam squeezed the life out of the napkin still in his right hand.

"Where do you go now, Cam?"

"I'm not sure, but I have to be done running."

"That old trail beast is dead, right?"

"Yeah. I think it's finally gone."

* Stoned *

"The rain fly!" Cameron was reaching up, trying to hold the tent from the inside. Wind and rain were battering the outside of the dome with a ferocity he had not experienced since his time in the Porcupine Mountains when the storm nearly killed Butter.

The condensation on the inside of the top of his new dome tent was being snapped off the ceiling by the outside fury. Beads of water were dripping like it was raining inside the structure too. That's when he heard a branch snap above him, and he tried to sit up in his bed with a scream—convinced he would be crushed in the next instant.

"NO!" he called out.

Then the pain punched him in the right side of his abdomen, like getting kicked by a horse, forcing him down, flat on his back. The storm turned off as the oak limb slammed through his roof and pinned him to the bed with a groan.

"Wait. What?" Cam said, looking around for what were only moments before so real.

Cam moaned, still on his bed outside of Flint, waking from a dream covered in a thick sweat. The pain under his rib cage was genuine, and the situation, just seconds ago, he was convinced an actual branch had pinned him down with a thud— but that was the dream world which was still hanging around like the steam in a bathroom after a long, hot shower is over.

The pain on his right side was familiar, and once his dream fog cleared from his head, he knew he had a gallbladder attack. Nausea began pushing at his gut and head. He knew what he needed to do.

Cam forced himself over and rolled out of bed, nearly falling down. The room was pitch black. For an instant, he was confused about the direction he was facing and grabbed for the side of the bed. He had to think about which side of the bed he had come out on and then reach out in front of him into the darkness. He could feel nothing, and then a flash of fear that he was still in a dream touched his mind, except for the pain in his side, which he knew was palpable. He forced his left foot forward and then his right like he was in a shuffle while his left hand probed the darkness, and his right countered the pain with light pressure, pushing up and under his ribs.

By the third shuffle, his hand clunked against his dresser, and as he felt along the front, he could orient himself. In two steps, he reached his hand inside his bathroom door and sent the darkness scurrying back into the shadows with a flick of a switch.

He pushed at the single round handle on the vanity and stuck his face under the stream of water falling from the tap. Cam knew he needed to burp to relieve some of the pressure inside his stomach, and then nausea would retreat into his memory. With a few gulps, he stood and let out an impressive belch that offered instant relief.

Another burp rumbled out, and a thought occurred to him— all of the unhealthy bar food he had been living on for the last couple of months had caught up to him. His mind went back and thought about what could have brought on another gallbladder attack. He knew it was the greasy tacos his bulging stomach had talked him into getting from the drive-through the previous evening.

He knew how to deal with the attacks. It would be a very long ten days of drinking only apple juice before he could push out enough gallstones to get the pain under control. Cam had discovered the method from a homeopathic doctor several years back as a non-surgical solution to the problem of gallstones. Of course, he also knew that if he changed his diet and lost a bunch of weight, he would not have to cleanse his body twice a year after another attack. The desire and motivation for the change were always at the apex during an episode, and as the days and weeks after a cleanse passed, those inclinations lessened.

"We forget," he thought.

"I always forget how fricken awful these are," he said while looking in the oblong vanity mirror above the sink, still grabbing at his side and shaking his head in disgust at himself.

He knew he would be running into town to buy their supply of apple juice and a couple bags of apples because that was all he would eat for the next ten days. He then remembered he would also need to stock up on toilet paper. Cam wondered why it was called fast when they went by so slowly.

"Do I still have the poo screen?" he wondered, knowing that after a couple days, he would have to have all his bowel movements pass through a filter. By that point in the process, his intestines would be cleared out of all solid debris, and the stones would begin to be released from the deactivated organ to pass through his gut and the colon. It was a weird game he played during these apple juice fasts, but it was proof the process, as odd as it was, actually worked. His record count was 146 gallstones, but he was not sure this attack was as bad as that one was. That epic attack happened five or six years back and had him bent over with the pain, laying in bed for days before a friend introduced the apple juice cleanse to him. He was skeptical since he had not done the research himself, but his pain overruled his skepticism, and with nothing to lose, he dove into the simplistic treatment.

Whereas most people would have gone to the doctor and had them figure out what was happening, not Cameron. In his mind, he was taking responsibility for his health, learning what he needed to know to treat himself.

Cam was amazed, at the screen full of little stones, which he pooped out over several days at the end of the fast. After the loosening process by the power of the naturally occurring malic acid inside the apple juice, the next step involved drinking extra virgin olive oil mixed with the juice of a lemon, which in theory, provided the gallbladder the needed lubrication and nutrients to expel the unwanted stones. Like some witch doctor's magic, his bile duct was clean from the foreign invaders.

* Alien Abduction *

While the early morning view from the deck is something Cam enjoys, he truly hates the late-night music pounding at the floor beneath his feet. It is why he spends most of his waking hours in one of three places. Cam was downstairs in the bar he lived above working a shift, eating the free food he gets as a perk for being an employee, or out riding his Harley exploring the back roads to clear his pounding head. For the last ten days, he had to endure the thumping floor as his body repelled the alien invaders from his gallbladder.

During his rest, he began noticing pain in his lower abdomen, down from his rebellious gallbladder. He thought he had a hernia from lifting up the beer kegs in the bar. Fully loaded with the frothy liquid, they weigh 168 pounds. He was changing out several a day, keeping the bar stocked with its best-selling commodity. He would have to find another way to get the job done without ripping his guts out.

The bartender lifestyle had caused him to gain twenty-five pounds since getting the new job and living quarters. His sleeping habits had been forced to transition. He was falling into bed around three in the morning and trying to sleep until ten or eleven.

While the gallstones passed, the pain in his lower abdomen increased. The pain became unbearable when he moved out of the crummy apartment and into a house ten miles west of his crappy job. That house backed up to a farmer's field filled with soybeans. Cam loved the place because it was stuck back into the woods and had an elevated deck wrapping the west and north sides of the house with the stained wood retreat.

His sleeping and eating habits soon returned to normal levels, and the weight dropped back when he started walking four or five miles in the morning. He was able to work a regular shift, noon until eight thirty, and let the new young guy work until closing with Mark, the owner. Life was looking up again for Cam, except for the growing stomach pain. Losing the weight had helped him reduce the sharpness of the injury to his core muscles, but he was confident he would have to go under the knife and get the hernia screened up, but Cam did not have any health insurance, so he kept putting it off. He had convinced Mark to get rid of the shelf the kegs had to be lifted up on, even tearing them out on his own time. Now they could roll the old barrel out and the new keg into place in the long refrigerator beneath the bar. He used a hand truck to move the loaded metal bottles around, which gave him hope that his wound would begin to heal.

Cam slept better at his new place— the nightmares were beginning to fade. One morning he was climbing up into his old suburban when an intense shooting pain that felt like his abdomen and right leg was on fire stopped him. He stood on the running board but fell back onto the ground, grabbing at his side.

One doctor visit led to another until he was driving up to the massive hospital complex in Ann Arbor, considered by many to be the best facility in the state for most illnesses. Some of the specialty centers were considered some of the finest in the world. Cam had been referred to a clinic on the third floor of the pristine facility. The concourse rose above him several stories as he struggled to figure out where he was going. The heavy traffic on US-23 had put Cam behind, causing him to run late for his appointment. He was relieved when he found the information center.

"I've got an appointment and I don't know where I am going," he said to the mature woman sitting behind the counter.

"Well let's have a look at your card, young man," she said with a twinkle in her eye and a broad smile on her face.

Four minutes later, he was in the waiting room filling out a stack of papers on a clipboard.

* The See World *

"I don't know, they drew some blood and I had a C.T. scan and then I was sent home," Cam said.

"Sounds like they shoulda told you more than that," Mark huffed.

"I go back next week."

"You're not missin' any more time are ya?"

"It's in the morning, I should be back before noon."

"Good, I just covered you for ten days," the red-faced man replied.

"It was only eight work days."

"Felt like a fricken month," Mark said while not looking at the man.

"I brought you something," Cam said and held out a small glass vile with a black metal lid screwed on.

"What's in there?"

"Look at it,"

Mark turned his attention to the vile, taking it from Cam. "Kinda looks like a retarded rice."

"Yeah, those are my gallstones," Cam said.

"You're a weird dude."

"Yeah, so what?"

"Don't you got some kegs to change?" Mark said and flipped the glass bottle back to the man with a goofy smile.

A week later, Cam was pulling out from the University hospital complex with a high-pitched ringing in his ears. The picture his eyes were sending his brain was blurred like someone had smeared grease on his life's camera lens. He could not think and pulled over several times, unsure where he was or where he was going. He stopped his vehicle in a park next to a river, not far from the hospital, put his head down on the steering wheel, and cried for a while. Then he went and sat on a bench, watching a pair of ducks out in front of his seat glide across the water, nipping at floating things. He pulled out his flip phone from his pocket, and after staring at it for a few moments, he dialed the only number he knew by heart.

"Hello," the female voice answered.

"Mom?" Cam asked.

"Cameron?"

"Yeah mom, it's me."

"Thank God. How are you?"

"Not so good."

"What do you mean?"

"Do you think you and dad could come over?"

"Yes. When?" Now Mags was worried.

"Today,"

"We'll leave now."

"Okay we should get there about the same time, then."

"Where are you?"

"Ann Arbor."

"What are you doing down there?"

"I was at the doctor," he said.

There was a pause. "How bad is it, Cameron?"

He didn't know how to answer her. "You're gonna need my new address."

"You moved?"

"Yeah."

Marty and Mags left their home ten minutes later, wondering what their second child had gotten himself involved with.

"I'm concerned, Marty," she said.

"Let's find out what we're dealing with before we go off worrying, Mags."

An hour later, the tires from their pickup truck crunched the limestone gravel on the road Cam had told them to turn on.

They prayed for him several times together while driving. It was a favorite coping mechanism over the last several years whenever thinking about their wayward son. Everything else was out of their control, so they laid their troubles in God's lap again as they pulled into their son's drive. As they approached the door, they were each holding two things, their collective breath, trying not to get out in front of God, and the two dinner dishes they were all going to eat together.

Four hours later, three more cars from various locations around the state joined the gathering. All of them had been called by Mags into an emergency family summit at Cam's new house.

"Holy crap, Cam, you've shaved your face and cut your hair!" Curtis said, poking fun at his older sibling.

The pair hugged, but Cam remained seated in his recliner. Caleb and Katie repeated the gesture with their brother when they arrived.

"I wanted to have you guys over because I need—" Cam began crying, and the siblings looked to their parents, who were seated on the couch and looking like a pall of gloom had settled over their life.

"I need to tell you something."

"What is it Cam, " Katie asked and went to his side.

After a few snorts and deep breaths, Cam regained his composure and then wiped his nose with a tissue.

"I have cancer," Cam said. He didn't like hearing the words come off his lips. It felt like admitting defeat.

"What kind?" Caleb asked.

Cam had to swallow a few more times before he could continue.

"Colon cancer."

"What stage?" Katie asked.

"Four. It's stage four. I wanted my family around me to pray. I know I haven't been in the greatest place these last few years, but I knew I could count on you to at least pray for me."

"Of course," was the response from everyone as the harsh reality sank into the dimly lit room. The six prayed for healing, a sense of peace throughout the process, and wisdom.

* Dirty Scoundrels *

"Listen, I need you here. You told me you'd be here and you didn't show up," Mark said, still ticked off at his best employee.

"I missed one day," Cam said.

"Where were you? I had to cover your shift— again, Cam."

"I'm sorry, I got some bad news. I should have called you."

"I tried reaching you for a few hours and you ghost me like that? It's getting old, dude."

"Like I said, I'm sorry."

"Don't ask me for any more time off, Cam. It ain't gonna happen."

"Well that may not be possible."

"What do you mean?"

"I'm gonna have a few more doctor appointments to get to."

"Down in Ann Arbor?"

"Yeah."

"Make sure you schedule them for the mornings. Why?"

"It's a medical condition, I'm dealing with."

"Well, what kind of medical condition?"

"You can't ask me that," Cam said.

"What are you talking about?"

"HIPPA laws."

"Nonsense," Mark said, backpeddling a bit.

"As an employee I don't have to reveal to you my medical condition."

"I thought we were friends, Cam?"

"So, you're asking me as a friend then?"

"Absolutely," Mark said and knew he was lying.

"I have cancer, Mark. Stage four colon cancer. I need to meet with my doctors to come up with a plan to fight it."

"Sorry, Cam."

"Really?"

"That's a horrible question to ask."

"I'm finding I don't have a lot of patience for silly things."

"Alright. Alright. Fair enough."

Five days later, Mark had called Cam into the back office before his shift. Cam had been training a new guy he was told was brought in to help while he got treatment.

"Hey, how are you doing?" Mark asked. "Sit down."

"Sit down? You've never told me to sit down before."

"Well, I don't want you standing up if you can take a load off."

"Okay," Cam said and sat his suspicious butt in the chair.

"Listen, I don't deal with this kind of stuff very well," Mark said.

"Cancer?"

"Well that too."

"Then what?"

"Cam, I gotta let you go," Mark said while looking at the floor.

"You're firing me?"

"We're going in a different direction, that's it."

"A different direction?"

"Yeah."

"I've been training a guy to do my job and now you're going in a different direction?"

"That's what I said."

"That's complete crap man. You're firing me because I have cancer."

"No I'm not. We're taking a different direction. That's all."

"You said you were my friend. I told you my diagnosis because you said you were my friend, and now you have used it against me?"

"No."

"You're a real piece of work." Cam left his office and slammed the door. As he walked through, he announced to the entire bar, "Mark just fired me because I have stage four colon cancer. Did you hear me? He fired me because I'm sick."

The patrons looked at Cam and then at each other. Everyone followed the unemployed man out the door, leaving their beverages and food at their tables. Some vowed to never return to their former favorite dive bar.

Mark didn't know it yet, but he had just committed economic suicide.

* Visitors *

Cam couldn't remember why he started admiring them, then the image of Mr. Jake from childhood washed through his mind.

"Oh yeah, he was a cigar smoker," Cam remembered.

Cam was sitting on his back deck enjoying the morning and his final Cuban cigar. He usually washed down a small shot of bourbon or whiskey with his indulgence, but he had walked away from that after the war with the beast was over. Cam did not care if he ever had another drink again, but he did care about leaving his occasional Cuban cigar habit behind. It was not so much the idea that he would choose to walk away. It was more the thought that when he decided to quit, it would then be off-limits. He didn't like to put too many things into the off-limits category. His mindset had changed. Spending a few years wrestling a demon and then turning around to face stage four cancer will change your perspective.

Cam was losing control over his life and was not a big fan. It turned out he had also recently discovered what most people around him knew—Cam liked being in control. It's why he ran away to the woods to hide for all of those years. Exhaustion caused Cam to resign to the idea that he was just along for the ride, like when his family had taken their countless trips up north. He was a passenger then and was able to enjoy the experience. All of the introspection after years of avoiding thinking deeply about anything because of an all-consuming irrational fear was wearing him down. He was wrestling with the old cliché of "letting go and letting God."

Cam hated being categorized as a cliché, "But if the saying was true," he thought, but he still did not like it.

"What's wrong with me?" he asked the breeze.

"You're weird," he thought was the answer in his head, but it had come from the large black man standing next to him.

"Butter?"

"Sorry for sneaking up on you, Cam, but I called out a few times."

"Sorry, I must have been somewhere else. It's good to see you. Why are you down here?"

"Caleb called me, man," he began tearing up, affecting his speaking ability. "I'm so sorry, Cam. I don't know what to say."

He embraced his friend and dropped more than a few tears on the back of his flowered shirt. Cam also cried, not knowing where the new tears were being produced.

After several moments in the embrace, they pulled apart, and Butter had a look at his friend.

"You look good, Cam, and I don't think I have ever said those words before. I didn't want you to get the wrong idea." Butter could not help but laugh, and Cam joined in with him. Then it was like the thing they did not want to talk much about faded into the background, and they were whisked back to the trail or to their favorite table under the pavilion, three hundred miles and another world away.

"I see you haven't given up the stink sticks."

"Last one I own, last one I'll smoke," Cam said. "Besides I'm not really worried about getting lung cancer, now."

Butter slapped his friend on the leg. "It was good to see him again even thought the conditions were less than ideal," Butter thought.

"It's more than just the cancer, Butter. I've been thinking it's more like a hacking and tearing process. We are called to die to ourselves, I've heard it hundreds of times, but I've never lived through the death of myself."

"You're not talking of physical death, right?" Butter asked.

"No. I'm talking about the idea that when we follow Jesus we are supposed to die to ourselves and our own motives. I have spent so many years trying to figure out how to have it both ways. How can I follow him and seek the pleasures of a hedonistic life? It was like I was living to avoid the pain of dying to myself. Like, pain avoidance was, or became, the most important thing."

"What's the part in that old poem you like?" Butter was trying to remember. "All which I took from thee I did but take, Not for thy harms. But just that thou might'st seek it in my arms."

Cam was silent for a few moments. He drew a long draw on the cigar and slowly blew the smoke up into the sky above him.

"Why have I never seen this before?" Cameron asks.

"Because you weren't ready."

"I guess so."

"The letting go, the tearing process, as you called it, is never fun. The deep seated lies and unbelief has grown it's roots way down into chambers of our hearts that we don't want to ever open up again. Let alone go excavating our old stuff. But that's what God does Cam, so we seek our satisfaction in him, instead of the walls we have built."

"Coming to the end of ourselves," Cam said to the blue sky.

"Yep."

"Do you think cancer is part of that?"

"I think everything is a part of it, Cam."

"How so?"

"The question we all face every day is— will I trust him? No matter what is in front of me, the question is still the same. Will we trust him?"

Cam just watched his friend's face as he talked to him. He was able to hear what he was saying.

"Why do you think I had to go through all the crap I went through, Butter?"

"O Lordy, Cam. How am I supposed to have your life figured out when I don't have my own figured out?"

"What are you talking about?"

"None of us have it figured out, that's why we walk by faith not by sight, my friend."

"I guess you're right," Cam said.

A car pushed into the driveway on the other side of the house, and both men listened as the motor shut down. The sound of two doors being closed bounced off the house and trees. Cam and Butter looked at each other, puzzled by the intrusion.

"Cam?"

"Where you at?" Another voice called out from the front porch.

"Back here," Cam barked.

Caleb and Curtis came searching around the corner, and the four men had themselves a loud reunion moment which only people who have spent significant time sweating together can have.

The men joked and laughed the afternoon away, sharing lunch and good memories.

"Cam do you remember what you did in the basement when we were kids?" Curtis asked.

"I did a lot of stupid things in the basement as a kid."

"He's trying to deflect," Caleb said.

"Speak it out, son," Butter said to Curt.

"I don't know how old I was at the time but Cam told me to come downstairs, he wanted to show me something."

The three other men were watching with their minds as they listened.

"Which was a bit weird. I think I was like six, maybe."

"Which would have put him right in the middle of his Harry days."

Curtis and Caleb laughed as Cam made a goofy face at his brothers.

"Harry? I feel left out," Butter said.

"For a while Cam was going to be the next Harry Houdini," Caleb said.

"You guys were just jealous of my magic skills," Cam said.

"Go on with the story, Curt."

"So when I get down the stairs and it's completely dark in the basement. I thought he was going to try to scare me again so I turned to go back up. He told me that I wasn't going to believe what he was going to do. Apparently he had been practicing the activity for some time. Caleb had a lighter in his basement room. He made candles for people— like for Christmas gifts and he was allowed to have a few in his own room. Well Cam knew this and because we had eaten beans the night before, he was more than just his usual gross."

"Huh?" Butter asked.

"Cam is a gassy guy even without beans."

"Okay. Yeah, I shared a tent with him."

"When I move into the hallway, he is standing in his underwear and alarm bells are going off all around me," Curtis said, and they all laughed again.

"He had been downstairs lighting his farts on fire in the dark and was so amazed by the blue flames shooting out of his rear end that he needed to show me. But this time he had removed his pants to get a bigger flame."

"It was all about the efficiency," Cam said.

"What he hadn't realized was how thin underwear really are. He laid down on the floor and lifted both his legs," Curtis continued.

"And he was watching with his face close to the action," Cam said.

"You guys were some screwed-up kids," Butter said as he looked at all three brothers.

"He flicks the lighter to get a flame and places it near his butt and blows a huge fart, almost like he could do it on command. The flame shot out six inches, but when it does he also screams in pain, grabbing his butt and rolling around yelling at the burn. He singed the hair off his rear end and was sore for days."

The men erupted with laughter and howled at Cam's expense.

"The jeans he had removed were the thermal protection," Curtis said.

Butter couldn't help himself, "I always questioned if Cam was a flamer, now I know, now I know!"

Cam was confident all his neighbors could hear the four brothers howling.

"I gotta pee," Caleb said and stood from his seat, took a few steps, and let go off the side of Cam's deck while no one else batted an eye at the sight of a grown man urinating from up on the deck out onto the lawn.

Cam leaned over and wretched out his lunch, which brought an immediate end to the hysterical nature of the visit.

* Stillness *

The months he spent enduring treatment were made more palpable by the offsetting hours he spent sitting and watching. Spending extended periods of lovely days out on his back porch continued for Cam. The birds and deer calmed him. The time also allowed him to think about his life. It was a different mindset from all of the running and hiding.

Cam understood with renewed clarity that God was honing and grinding off his ignoble will— while replacing it with his own, but it was a painful task for humans to endure. Learning how your satisfactions are ultimately crushed by the will of God, so you can possess something better, something eternal, drove him to his knees, even while sitting still. In the stillness, he contemplated the intensity of his self-worship over the years and the depth of the sea of his deceit.

"Father, I know I have been consumed by my own stuff. I still struggle with getting in the way of your work in my life. I am sorry for the things

I have made more important than you. I know I deserve nothing from you other than retribution for my actions. You would be just to demand payment for my mistakes. For the people I have hurt, abandoned, and destroyed. My girls, Father I traded for a fantasy. There is nothing good that lives in me aside from you Lord. Oh, Jesus help them to see you in all of this mess that I've made."

Tears flowed heavy and often on Cam's back deck, flowing from his broken body that was growing a brand new heart, as the maples swayed in the breeze, clapping their hands in worship to the Creator who was not done with his work of recreating hearts inside of human lives.

Ten

Cameron Lost

— Section Ten —

"Spun"

"Ah, fondest, blindest, weakest,

I am He Whom thou seekest!

Thou dravest love from thee, who dravest Me."

Francis Thompson

* The Oasis Visits *

"Cameron."

"Mr. Cameron." The soothing voice almost sounded like she was singing his name.

He felt her warm hand caress the side of his cheek and then feel his head for a fever with the back of her hand.

"Cam, you have a visitor."

"Who is it?" Cam asked and tried to force his eyes open, but they were not taking commands so early in the morning.

"This is Sheryl," she said while warming the metal end of her stethoscope in the palm of her hand.

"No, I know who you are, you're the annoying lady who wakes me up every morning poking and prodding around my broken body. Always wanting me to take deep breaths, roll over on this side then that, and stuffing food in my face," Cam said with a hidden smile.

"Oh the lady keeping your ungrateful self alive? That lady?"

"Well I never said I didn't appreciate you being a pain in my butt."

"You've got a heck of a way of showing how much you care."

"It's a gift," Cam said.

"Your visitor is trying to make his way inside and he is being escorted by a very pretty lady."

Cam's eyes opened.

"Oh I see how you are," Sheryl said with her broad smile.

"You've made me curious."

"Mmm hmm. You're just like all the rest of your kind."

"What are you talking about? My kind?" Cam asked.

"Take a deep breath for me," she said while placing the scope over his right side. Cam complied.

"Another."

"What are you talking about?"

"You gotta shush while I listen to your lungs. We can't have you getting pneumonia."

"Alright," he said and gave her four more deep breaths.

"You're just like all the other men I see, is all I'm saying."

"How's that? And when did you go two timing me behind my back?"

"The only thing I have to do to wake you up is mention that a pretty woman is around and all of you men start reaching for a hairbrush or tooth brush— 'cause you gotta impress the pretty ones. You're all the same." Sheryl reached in her bag for her blood pressure cuff.

"Well I'm not dead, yet. And you said very pretty."

"I have six patients to visit every week. Four men and you're all the same."

"And here I thought I was the special one."

"Oh, you're special all right. A special pain in my butt." She pumped up the cuff and listened to the heartbeat disappear under pressure. Then she released the pressure and watched the gauge to find his systolic number as his heartbeat returned to her ears.

Cam could hear the air being released from the pressure cuff on his arm. He could also hear a clank, shuffle, shuffle coming down the hall of his home, and he was straining to see around Sheryl's body to catch a glimpse.

"Clank shuffle, shuffle. Clank shuffle, shuffle."

"Mr. Cam? Are you decent?"

"No he's annoying and cantankerous," Sheryl said and laughed, having just removed the stethoscope from her ears.

"I know you're not lyin'. I just want to make sure we didn't run into anything glowing white and naked."

"Who is it?" Cam asked Sheryl while looking toward the spot where the hall dumped into the living room, which had been converted into Cam's personal nursing station.

"It's Tonya and I've brought a guest with me."

"Miss T?"

She came into the room smiling and as radiant as he had laid eyes on her the first time.

"Put my bed up please, Sheryl."

"Okay, cowboy. Hold on. Hold on." Sheryl grabbed for the controls and elevated the back of his bed.

"Thank you. Are you, are you, done?" Cam asked his nurse, swishing her away with his eyes.

"No, but I will go do some chart work while y'all visit."

"Hey Mr. Cam," Tonya drew close and met his eyes.

"Don't mind him being all star-struck by how lovely you are," Sheryl said to her as the clanking and the shuffling person came into view. The large black man had shrunk a little since the last time he had visited and was hunched over his walker.

"Butter?"

"Hey, Cam!" Butter said with a tired and raspy voice.

"Let me pull up a couple of seats," Sheryl reached for the wooden chairs that were pushed under the dining room table and brought them over to Cam's bedside.

"Thank you," Tonya said.

"Hey anytime we can get someone to come over to take the pressure off of me!" She was laughing at herself by the time she finished the sentence.

"Sit down over here," Cam said to his friend.

Butter walked to his bedside and grabbed Cam's hand, the one without the IV. Both men said nothing while looking into each other's tired eyes.

"I didn't know if I was gonna make it back downstate before you left me for good," Butter said.

"I'm glad you did, old friend. Very glad you came all this way."

Tonya circled to the other side of Cam's bed, leaned over, and kissed the man.

"Thank you for bringing him to see me." Cam grabbed at her hand, and she took his cool hand into her own. Tears bulged from every set of eyes in the room, but Sheryl was trying to hide hers behind her opened laptop.

"We've been trying for a few weeks to get here— dad hasn't been feeling well lately. Yesterday he told me that we were going on a road trip downstate," Tonya said.

"Well you've made my day, my week," Cam's smile was plastered all over his face.

"I needed to see you," Butter said.

"Are you sick?" Cam asked.

"My ticker's been actin' up. Doc's sayin' I eat too much fried chicken." Butter wanted to remain standing, but the pull of gravity won. As he sat in the seat, he was glad for the cushioning of the maroon pillow top— which was tied to the wooden dowels of the seat back.

"You're looking tired," Cam said, watching his friend sit.

"Have you glanced in a mirror lately?" Butter shot back.

"No I don't want Sheryl to have to clean up any more of my messes, all that broken glass."

"That's an entirely different attitude from the one I've been dealing with all week, Cam," Sheryl said from the dining room table— now turned into her workstation.

"Naw, she's all right. You just gotta get used to her mouthin' off." Cam said and tried to laugh, but a raspy cough came out.

Sheryl just smiled and kept on typing on her digital chart.

"You want some water?" Tonya asked Cam and held up the Styrofoam cup with a clear bendable straw.

Cam took a sip and thanked her with his raised eyebrows.

"You should ask her what she is doing for a living these days," Butter said to Cam while pointing at his daughter.

Cam looked toward her again, which he didn't mind at all.

"Well, for the last few months I have taken over as the CEO of Butter's Famous Oasis, L.L.C."

"Ha! Really?"

"Yes, Mr. Cam. I'm his boss now."

"I love it!"

"It has been hard on him the last year or so," she said.

"He told me he was sick in the letter he wrote. He's as old as dirt," Cam said and looked at Butter.

They all laughed.

"Yep, almost at the end of the trail on this side of life," Butter said.

"I know just what you mean," Cam said.

"There's a reason he wanted to come down to visit with you, but I have to go get it out of the truck."

"You do whatever you want to," Cam said and closed his happy but tired eyes.

* Mirage *

Cam's head was woozy, and something was pounding outside his head, but it felt like it was on his skull. He didn't have the energy to open his eyes to see what was happening. The medication Sheryl had slipped into his IV had made him groggy, pulling him further down into his pillow, away from his visitors.

"Butter!" he thought, forcing his eyes open to see the man's backside across the room tapping a nail with a picture hammer.

"What are you doing to my walls you crazy old coot?"

"Shut up and go back to sleep," Butter said.

"He is so proud of this," Tonya whispered to Cam as her vanilla perfume danced across his face with her words.

"You smell delightful!" Cam said.

"Mr. Cam, you say the nicest things."

"Watch that one," Sheryl said, "He'll charm the pants right off ya."

"Oh he's a charmer, all right," Tonya touched Cam's head and smiled.

"Not with you hounding me night and day, day and night!" Cam said over his shoulder.

"I think I need to up your dose of shut up medicine," Sheryl quipped and offered a half laugh.

Butter began his return trip toward his chair next to Cam's bed, aided by his shiny aluminum walker.

"What, you came all this way to stick a nail in my wall? Is this one of your life lessons, or something?"

"Ha ha! Better than running one through your head," Butter responded while he clanked his walker closer to the side of Cam's bed.

"I think you'd need a bigger hammer."

"You're right."

"So, what are you doing?" Cam asked.

"It's time you had this," Butter said and tried to hold up a board leaning against Cam's metal bed frame. Tonya came around and picked it up for him.

Cam instantly knew what it was and looked at his friend as tears welled in his eyes.

"I, I don't know what to say," Cam choked on his words.

"Thank you is the normal human response when someone gives you a gift, Cam," Butter's mouth turned up at the corners.

"But that wouldn't be enough."

"Oh come on. We both know it was yours just as much as it was mine," Butter said.

"You know how many hours we sat right here?" Cam was touching the notches in the wooden plank.

"Those were some of the best times of my life," Butter said.

"And now you're giving all the memories to me?" Cam asked while wiping at his wet face.

"Don't let him fool ya, he had two copies made. One's back on the table and the other hangs on his wall in the living room," Tonya said.

"But you're giving me the original?"

"Yeah, Cam. After all— you carved into it the most."

Cam's finger traced his own original carving, "Camshaft '94."

"Look at the blood stain from you carving that one," Butter pointed to a different trail name.

"Yeah, I sliced my finger pretty good that day."

"Got you some stitches, as I remember," Butter said.

"It was a long time ago, Butter."

"And it's like it was just yesterday, in so many ways... Speaking of stitches look who signed late last year. Over in the corner," Butter said and pointed.

"Doc Roger '20?"

"You remember Little Carp River in the Porky's?"

"How could I forget the end of the beast?"

"The guy who helped us out of the river?"

"He came up to visit you?"

"Yep, just like he said he would. Same guy. Was wondering how you were doing."

Tonya took the plank from their famous picnic table and hung it on Cam's wall while the two men watched. The memories leaked out of the wooden sign for each of them, like a cool morning fog rolling in off warm water.

The men cried silently for the final time— watching in their minds-eye as the distant scenes passed before them with a renewed energy.

"You remember what I told you about your trail beast?" Butter broke through the silence.

"You told me lots of things." Cam was lying back and resting his eyes after the emotional drain.

"What I wanted to remind you, before I go on and get up outta here, is that it wasn't the dumb old beast chasin' you all those years, Cam. It was Abba pursuing you with his love, and still is. Even why you are layin' here in this bed."

"Well, I have nowhere to run anymore."

"Sure you do."

"What? Haven't you seen me stuck in this bed?"

"You run to him, Cam. You run to him."

With those words, Cam opened his eyes and looked at his friend—Butter seemed like he was glowing with a light from a different world, beaming the rays right next to him.

"I see you Billy Cantrell and I can hear you, too," Cam said.

The amber light pouring in the window illuminated the hand-carved names on the board, turned wall hanging. "Camshaft '94" had "K – '94" and "Cutter '94" carved next to it, which was from Caleb and Curtis, after their original backpacking trip all those years ago. Then, there was "Hurricane '92," "Miles '93," and finally, "Butter," with no year indicated— all tooled from Butter's own hand.

"Preach '04," "Hops '12," and "Miss-T" were next to the upside-down "A/R '14." However, the largest and most elaborate carving on the entire board was the only one with four years next to it— "Caveman '16, '17, '18, '19."

Cam smiled as he closed his eyes again.

The swirl of sleep carried Cam away from his memories as his best friend in the world said goodbye, then clanked down the hallway and toward the front door. What Cam could not see was the stream of tears that were dropping from Butter's reddened eyes with each and every step.

"You take care, Mr. Cam. I'll never forget you." Tonya said, kissed his forehead, and left out after her dad.

* Undone *

A couple of weeks after Butter's visit, Cam's health had descended closer to his departure. He was experiencing fewer lucid moments, vertigo, and much more pain. Sheryl and others working on his behalf did try to get him outside a few times, rolling his bed out the double doors and onto the deck where he could see the sky and hear the birds singing their sweet songs. The main difficulty was the threshold on the door was too hard for one person to get his bed through. Sheryl had to wait for help to move the man to his preferred location outside his home.

Caleb came to visit and brought a couple of boards he had cut on an angle to act as a bridge over the doorway. Then one person could easily maneuver the bed in and out of the house. For Cam, those times on his porch breathed some life into his weary bones. He was constantly asking to go out. Sheryl complied, even moving the large umbrella from the picnic table and sliding between the rails on his bed and the frame to protect the man from the ultraviolet rays. Two times she had put him outside and gone to catch up on some computer work at her workspace when a sudden, rouge rain shower had pushed its way across the state. The second time it happened, Cam asked her to stay in the rain with him and put down the umbrella. They got soaked and were overcome by laughter when the sun returned a few minutes later, and Sheryl toweled him off, then changed his sheets and clothes.

This was the same day a small gray car pulled into the drive, and two women walked up to the front door of Cam's house. They hesitated before ringing the doorbell. Cam tried to hear as Sheryl answered the door, turning his head and pointing his ear toward the entryway conversation. Everything was still too muffled, and the sun had darkened his house's interior so that he couldn't make out anything inside.

"Who's there, Sheryl?"

He heard more muffled sounds coming from what he knew to be her voice but could not make out anything in particular.

The screen door slid open, and two women stepped through the shad-ows into the afternoon light.

"Hey, dad."

Cam groaned at the sight of his daughters and covered his face with his hands. His girls came to him, one on each side of his bed. He could not contain himself— crying with deep groans. Moaning through an internal flood as his emotional dam ruptured. Sheryl teared up as she delivered a box of tissues and then disappeared back into the house but still within listening distance. All three people on the deck grabbed at the top of the tissue box, pulling out several to wipe.

"I thought, I thought, I thought I had lost you," Cam said, wiping the crud from the corners of his mouth.

"You never lost us, dad," Jamie, the blonde, responded. "You ripped my heart out of my chest, but you didn't lose us."

"You lost me for a while," Jenna, the younger woman admitted. "I had to work through so much to bring me to this day, dad. I had put you up on this pedestal as the perfect man. You were the one who knew what to say when it needed to be said. You loved me like no other man ever has. You provided for us. You taught us about Jesus and loved me, even when I acted out in broken ways."

"I'm so sorry, Boo Boo," Cam said.

"Please. Let me finish, dad."

"Okay."

"When I was a little girl you were the one who gave me hope and you were the one who pointed me in the right direction. You were my rock and then, then you were gone. But not only gone, it was like your life was smashed into a million pieces and if I ever wanted a little part of you back— I didn't know where to go to find you anymore. The rug was just yanked out from beneath me. You killed me, dad."

"I'm so sorry, Jenna."

"Well it turned out that I was basing so much of myself on you and I needed to find out who I really was. I needed to grieve the death of my old life and learn how to walk with my own legs— apart from you."

Cam was looking at the woman before him and was beyond proud. Here she was, confronting the one who had damaged her the most and doing it with calmness and maturity. His guilt also pressed against him, calling him to retreat into his forest of regret again.

"It has taken me so many years," She fought against more tears and a cracking voice. "It has taken me years, and countless hours in counseling to get over this. Hell, I couldn't even call you dad until I finally was able to forgive you. Do you know what I called you? Him. I referred to you as, him, the entire time."

"You've forgiven me?" Cam thought he had heard her say those three magic words.

"Well, after years of burying it, I found out my unwillingness to forgive was hurting me, not you. And I wanted to hurt you for so long. I wanted to make you pay for what you did. Some days I tried to rip you to pieces. But that isn't my job or my right. I'm not any better than you. I had to learn my own sin was just as ugly as yours. I had to figure out that I needed Jesus, which is different from saying a sinner's prayer to get into heaven or away from something painful. I had to see my own desperation, dad. Then from that place, I had to choose to love you.

"Huh?"

"Dad, I choose to love you."

Cam was undone. Spilling his emotions out all over his mechanical bed, unable to control his sobs. Jamie and Jenna grabbed for him to comfort their father as they cried along with him over all the painful losses they had endured.

Cam cleared his throat. Many minutes, and a growing pile of tissues later. his mouth was dry, and he reached for his cup with the straw and sipped.

"After I did what I did," he paused, choking back more emotion.

"After I did what I did, the only thing I could think of doing was running away. In the running, I thought I could keep my darkness from hurting you further. I thought the thing I was hiding from was evil. He was hunting me— trying to finish me off once and for all. But that wasn't the truth. Abba was hunting me down with his love and forgiveness, but I could only see my shame. I could only see how I had killed you and your mom when I lit your world on fire. I could only see me. I'm so, sorry."

"Dad, the Lord had to teach me so many things during those years," Jamie said. "I wasn't ready to listen. I didn't want to hear it at first. I thought you'd come back to your senses and see the damage you had done. As a matter of fact, I convinced myself you would see the error of your ways and run back to Jesus like you taught us to do, not further away from him. I think it was Uncle K, who said that sin wasn't logical, which is true from the human perspective. I needed to see how God's redeeming grace isn't logical either. I had to re-learn a thousand times that only God is sovereign, and if he pulls his hand away from any of us, we'd be undone. Believe it or not, all of this pain has led me to worship him more and it's changed me. I chose to love you, too."

Cam had spent years wondering if his kids would overcome his sin. He knew he had destroyed them, killed them in his fire. He was most ashamed that he had not cared enough about them to stop himself from setting it. Now, God had allowed him to see how he had used his pain and sin to miraculously grow all of them closer to himself. It had been hell to live through, he would never recommend running away from God to anyone, but God is more significant than any human failure. His love pursues us through our rebellion.

* Aftermath *

In the aftermath of his daughter's visit, Cam still wanted Sheryl to move him outdoors as often as possible. To him, it now felt the bird's songs were sweeter, the sun's rays were less harsh, and the blue sky's blue was more inviting than ever before.

His parents came to visit several times over those final weeks. They felt a growing dread and powerlessness hound them, which they had to fight off before every visit. They would pray on the trip up and out in Cam's driveway before entering his home. Marty would find his way out to the mailbox and retrieve the letters inside for his incapacitated son.

On this particular visit, there were a couple of bills and a handwritten letter with a Munising, Michigan postmark. He showed Mags as they met on the front porch. Mags had been picking off some of the dead petunia flowers to let more grow in their place. They both knew what was in the letter and were sad for Cam.

"We're here!" Mags announced when coming in through the front door.

"Come in, come in!" Sheryl said in a loud enough voice that both Marty and Mags assumed Cam was already awake.

"How's my Cameron today?"

"Hey mom," Cam said.

Both Marty and Mags saw how much Cam had physically gone down-hill. His yellowed eyes and teeth, along with the deep circles around his eyes, signaled that death was settling in and drawing close.

"I got your mail," Marty said, trying to be upbeat, and laid it on Cam's belly, then squeezed Cam's hand.

"I'm afraid one of those holds some difficult news," Mags said, gesturing toward the mail and leaning in to kiss him.

"Oh?"

"It's got a Munising post mark."

Cam found the pale yellow envelope and pressed a finger into the corner, tearing the paper. He flipped it over to try to read the return address. It was only a street number and city, but he knew where it had come from.

"Mr. Cam,

I wanted to be the first to inform you that my dad has passed away. I wish I could have brought you the news in person and driven you to the memorial service, but I knew that wasn't possible. His heart finally gave out, and he went peacefully to be with Jesus.

My father loved you, Cam, and I am so glad he had such a good friend as you were to him for all these years. He always remembered you with a particular fondness. I found him several times looking at and touching the carved table board— which hangs on his bedroom wall like it does on yours.

I may move it out to the pavilion, so it can bless other wanderers on their long journey home.

Thank you, Mr. Cam.

May God bless you.

All my love and peace,

Miss-T."

It would be the last he would hear from her. As the impact of the news washed over Cam, something settled inside him. He looked at the board hanging on the wall, the one his friend had given him. It had been adorned with his original pair of boots with the heel cut out of one. Curtis had tied the laces together and hung them by the same nail on his last visit.

Cam could not see the instantaneous disassembly of the Oasis— as a supernatural hand put all the molecules of wood back where they belonged, except the one board hanging on Cam's wall. As it turns out, the "leave no trace" practice of the hiking community also applies to the work of angels. The final board from Butter's Oasis would serve another purpose for a few more days.

* The Beginning *

"Mom."

"Mom." The eight-year-old boy was pulling on his mother's sleeve while she talked with someone else.

"Cameron Martin, you're being rude." She was not happy, but the other woman told her she was sorry for her loss, hugged her, and walked away into another part of the funeral home.

"I'm sorry," the boy said.

"What do you need?"

"I was wondering if you could go up front with me?"

"Up front?"

"You know, to see Grandpa."

"We can go see Grandpa's body, if you want."

Jenna excused herself from the line of people waiting to see her and offered their condolences. She knew her son needed closure and wanted to ensure she paid attention to his needs and not just her own need to grieve.

"Why does Grandpa have a board with carvings in with him?" He asked and pointed.

"It was very special to him."

"What are all the names on it?"

"There are a few different people's names carved into it."

"Like who?"

"Both of my uncles are carved into it right here," She pointed to Uncle K and Uncle Curtis' engravings.

"These three are from Mr Butter, your Grandpa's best friend and that's his daughter, Tonya."

"Yeah I met her today. She's nice."

"So what else do you want to know, Mr?

"What about the rest of the names?"

"Well, they were all from the man you are named after."

The boy pointed to the empty body beside the board inside the casket and asked the question with his eyes.

"Yes. All of those names were part of my dad." Tears gathered in her eyes as young Cameron read through the names, and she played with his thick brown hair.

The funeral was quirky as funerals go— exactly as Cam would want it. A rock band played modern worship songs for the first half, with Jenna leading the singing. Then Curtis gave a message— he said his brother would have given if he could, even ending with an altar call and the sinner's prayer.

Tonya finished up the remembering ceremony at the graveside interment by reading the entire old poem, which ends with:

"Halts by me that footfall;

Is my gloom, after all,

Shade of His hand, outstretched caressingly?

"Ah, fondest, blindest, weakest,

I am He Whom thou seekest!

Thou dravest love from thee, who dravest Me."

* Begin Again *

Cam rested above his body the second he drew his final breath. In a blink of an eye, he left his brothers, sister, daughters, and others standing around his expired shell and stepping into a different kind of light. It was a seamless exit from the old world into the new.

A fog lifted from his eyes when he took his first step, and the brilliance enveloped him. His new existence was brimming with life and colors and sounds. He was surrounded by creatures of every imaginable kind. Even more than he could imagine, and the new life wasn't just outside of him, it was permeating through him and with him.

"It's overwhelming at first," came the familiar voice behind him.

Cam spun and blinked at the image in front of him. It was not human, but he was not afraid either.

"You've come a long way, old friend."

"Butter?"

"You have called me that for so many years," he said

They embraced, and Cam noticed the vast wings. Then Cam held him at arm's length to get a better look at him.

"I am a "Sent One," Butter said.

"What?"

"I was sent in service of you and the King."

"I sent him," said another voice from Cam's right. He recognized the voice right away and turned to see Jesus.

"My Lord and My God!" Cam said as he fell at Jesus' feet with his face in the dirt. His face bent low, Cam noticed that even the ground smelled good up here. He cried with spontaneity while filling with holy glee.

"I sent him to you, when you needed me," Jesus said.

"Thank you. Thank you for loving me." Cam looked up.

"I thought we could go for a walk, a hike, as you call it," Jesus said.

"A hike?"

"Yeah. Just the three of us."

"All three of us?" Cam stood with his goofy smile beaming.

"Yes. It will be like old times," Jesus said and pointed to three loaded backpacks leaning against a small flowering tree.

Cam noticed something on Jesus' hand.

"You want to know what's on my hand, don't you?"

"Yes. I do."

Jesus smiled and opened his palm to reveal a curious scar above his grotesque nail hole.

The scar was a written word, and the word was "Cameron '21."

The End

Thanknowledgments

I would like to acknowledge my thankfulness for people who have changed my life and directly impacted this book.

God. For your grace, mercy, and forgiveness found in your Son, Jesus Christ and empowered by your Holy Spirit.

Jeff. For your life, heart, faith, love, struggles, and redemption.

Parents. For always practicing a humble self-sacrificial love.

Connie. Your constant love, support, and freedom for me to be creative.

Larry Giroux. Your love for God, your family, the Body of Christ, for me, and for words. In that order.

Mark Coon. Your selfless service to absolutely everyone around you.

Greg May. Decades of professional service to your community and blessing me with your firefighting acumen.

Bruce Dancy. Your love of God, family, country, and all things firearms.

Beta Readers. Kristin. Thomas. Joan. Bob. Mark. Brian. Dean. Your contribution of your precious time and energy have been a tremendous encouragement!

Joy Neal Kidney. You have blessed and encouraged me so much!

Tracy Jones. Finding my hidden flaws is your specialty! I am so blessed.

Nancy Kuykendall. You have believed in me and blessed me when many have not.

Epilogue

Allegory Blossoms

When we were young, we didn't get along all that well. My brother Jeff was four-and-a-half years older than I was. He lived in an older world than I did, plus we had many different interests. Some of the things he liked I found to be outright weird.

As we aged, we became closer. We worked on cars together and even tried starting an auto repair business that went bust with the slightest life change.

After marriage, him in '79 and me in '81, we vacationed together and shared more in common. When he went to Bible College, I followed him a couple years later. We started an outreach to poor families in Warren, Michigan, that is still serving emergency food to desperate families.

Jeff and I had many late-night theological discussions over the years. He became a Minister for Outreach, and a couple years later, I began my ministry as an MYE (Minister of Youth and Education).

Our churches changed over the years. Seven years into ministry, Jeff planted a church that met in a school. Several years later, I began a church designed to reach out to people in their twenties called The Quest.

Jeff was a guest speaker for me a couple times over the years. Once, he drove his Harley down the center aisle to begin his talk. I spoke and taught at his church and during some of his youth group outings. My wife and I are Godparents to his youngest daughter. Jeff and his family supported us through my darkest days— giving time and treasure to keep my family afloat.

Jeff became a brewmaster, taking classes in Chicago, Illinois, and Munich, Germany, to hone his skills. He eventually left the full-time ministry to pursue ministering to people in and around a brewery in Frankenmuth, Michigan. The folks loved him and began calling him the "Brew Pastor."

During a significant life crisis, Jeff moved into my house several years later and lived with my wife and me for five months. During the winter months, we spent a lot of time together. He went to church and an accountability group with me. We spent many late nights talking about life.

Winter turned to spring, and I began working long hours doing concrete, leaving Jeff to his own devices during the daytime. He was mired in stinking thinking and kept undermining his own effort to find freedom. I could not get him to see where I was coming from— like he was blind to what he was doing.

The struggle he was involved with and refused to give up led me to ask him to leave. I felt used and confused as he had manipulated living in my house to hide his motives. That situation bothered me for years. I had also been working with people struggling with addictions for several years. The men I sat with in those groups for six months at a time (every Monday night) couldn't naturally see their own blind spots either.

Was it because they didn't want to? Was it they were being stopped from seeing the truth? Was it their own choice? Or was something bigger going on? This decade-long search has led me to this book.

When we turn away from God to pursue our own agenda, what does He do? What does his love look like? Does God stop wooing us to himself and turn away?

This struggle was the soil from which the idea seeds for this allegory were planted and took root. Another puzzle piece was the old poem, The Hound of Heaven, by Francis Thompson.

Thompson was a strung-out opiate addict on the streets of London who was pursued by God. A relentless pursuit ensued. In the end, Thompson penned one of the best poems in the history of Christianity, describing how God woos us to himself, even when it feels impossible or when we have run to the opposite side of the world.

I believe God pursues us even when we run. We may not feel this chase or expect it, or see it. Even when we experience God's pursuit as vile or evil, he seeks us. He has not given up on you. He's running after you, even now.

The story that flowed from my life experiences contains part of my brother's story, but it is not him. So many situations were changed and morphed. This allegory is not a memoir to him. Stories from his life, my life, and the lives of the people I have served over the years are melted together.

My desire was to alert the running souls that they haven't run too far from the loving arms of their Savior. Another person was on my mind as I wrote; those left in confusion when someone they love melts down and succumbs to the lies of the enemy or the ways of this world. I explored this story to give them hope. I wrote this tale to reassure myself the ones I love who don't currently follow Jesus are not out of his reach. Neither is yours.

Ultimately, Jeff succumbed to his stage four colon cancer after a twenty-seven-month fight. It was a great privileged to pray over his body as he took his final breath. He was 62.

I have wrestled with this book in so many ways. I still cry every time I read it because I miss him. He turned out to be a big cheerleader in my life. When he read my first book before it was published a couple weeks before he passed away (it was our maternal grandparent's story), he let out an enthusiastic expletive from his hospice bed in his living room. It was just like Jeff.

Throughout this process, I prayed that his life would be honored and Jesus would be praised. I know if he can save a wretch like me that no one is beyond his grace.

Much peace, fellow traveler.

Craig Matthews

2023

After thought:

People struggling with addictions and blind spots need help. The Companion Workbook to my novel "The Stars in the Sidewalk" is designed to offer those struggling with that kind of genuine help.

Watch for its release at www.craigmatthewsmedia.com

The Stars in the Sidewalk— My Demons Don't Die Easy is available at bookstores everywhere.

The Stars in the Sidewalk is a story of Lawrence, an everyday working guy, who gets triggered by a tragedy on the job site and is forced to face his many issues he had buried in deep in his past. Ronnie is a young boy who is thrown back into the foster care system and is intrigued when a concrete crew shows up at his new foster home to put in a pool. Ronnie grows close to the guys over the course of the project. The concrete being poured is special and designed with hundreds of small stones that look ordinary during the day, but glow a bright blue at night, looking like stars.

Tragedy strikes the worksite, and no one knows who is to blame. Is it the foster parents, the construction crew, young Ronnie, or the bully next door? Perhaps, something far more nefarious is at work. The tragedy sends Lawrence spiraling back to Angie, his beautiful counselor, after a four year hiatus. It also puts him back on the road to dealing with the issues he has kept buried since childhood. The negative patterns he thought he had killed had been active in keeping him a prisoner. He was convinced he was controlling them, but their influence was leaking a destructive power into his life. Demons don't die easy. Could he break their stranglehold at this critical point, or would he retreat back into his cave of addiction for another twenty years?

Addiction is a powerful force, and its tentacles can build impregnable fortress that are impossible to break out of in our own strength. Your demons don't die easy. Lawrence had given his life to Christ many years before this event, but would God continue his silent routine in these areas of his life, or finally move? Could Lawrence 'will' his way out of this trap if God wouldn't help, or was he stuck?

Poem

The Hound of Heaven

by Francis Thompson 1890

"I fled Him, down the nights and down the days;
I fled Him, down the arches of the years;
I fled Him, down the labyrinthine ways
Of my own mind; and in the mist of tears
I hid from Him, and under running laughter.
Up vistaed hopes I sped;
And shot, precipitated,
Adown Titanic glooms of chasmed fears,
From those strong Feet that followed, followed after.
But with unhurrying chase,
And unperturbèd pace,
Deliberate speed, majestic instancy,
They beat— and a Voice beat
More instant than the Feet—
"All things betray thee, who betrayest Me."
I pleaded, outlaw-wise,
By many a hearted casement, curtained red,

Trellised with intertwining charities
(For, though I knew His love Who followed,
Yet was I sore adread
Lest having Him, I must have naught beside);
But if one little casement parted wide,
The gust of His approach would clash it to.
Fear wist not to evade, as Love wist to pursue.
Across the margent of the world I fled,
And troubled the gold gateways of the stars,
Smiting for shelter on their clanged bars;
Fretted to dulcet jars
And silvern chatter the pale ports o' the moon.
I said to dawn, Be sudden; to eve, Be soon;
With thy young skyey blossoms heap me over
From this tremendous Lover!
Float thy vague veil about me, lest He see!
I tempted all His servitors, but to find
My own betrayal in their constancy,
In faith to Him their fickleness to me,
Their traitorous trueness, and their loyal deceit.
To all swift things for swiftness did I sue;
Clung to the whistling mane of every wind.
But whether they swept, smoothly fleet,
The long savannahs of the blue;
Or whether, Thunder-driven,
They clanged his chariot 'thwart a heaven
Plashy with flying lightnings round the spurn o' their feet—

Still with unhurrying chase,
And unperturbèd pace,
Deliberate speed, majestic instancy,
Came on the following Feet,
And a Voice above their beat—
"Naught shelters thee, who wilt not shelter Me."
I sought no more that after which I strayed
In face of man or maid;
But still within the little children's eyes
Seems something, something that replies;
They at least are for me, surely for me!
I turned me to them very wistfully;
But, just as their young eyes grew sudden fair
With dawning answers there,
Their angel plucked them from me by the hair.
"Come then, ye other children, Nature's — share
With me," said I, "your delicate fellowship;
Let me greet you lip to lip,
Let me twine with you caresses,
Wantoning
With our Lady-Mother's vagrant tresses'
Banqueting
With her in her wind-walled palace,
Underneath her azured daïs,
Quaffing, as your taintless way is,
From a chalice
Lucent-weeping out of the dayspring."

So it was done;
I in their delicate fellowship was one—
Drew the bolt of Nature's secrecies.
I knew all the swift importings
On the wilful face of skies;
I knew how the clouds arise
Spumèd of the wild sea-snortings;
All that's born or dies
Rose and drooped with— made them shapers
Of mine own moods, or wailful or divine—
With them joyed and was bereaven.
I was heavy with the even,
When she lit her glimmering tapers
Round the day's dead sanctities.
I laughed in the morning's eyes.
I triumphed and I saddened with all weather,
Heaven and I wept together,
And its sweet tears were salt with mortal mine;
Against the red throb of its sunset-heart
I laid my own to beat,
And share commingling heat;
But not by that, by that, was eased my human smart.
In vain my tears were wet on Heaven's gray cheek.
For ah! we know not what each other says,
These things and I; in sound *I* speak—
Their sound is but their stir, they speak by silences.
Nature, poor stepdame, cannot slake my drouth;

Let her, if she would owe me,
Drop yon blue bosom-veil of sky, and show me
The breasts of her tenderness;
Never did any milk of hers once bless
My thirsting mouth.
Nigh and nigh draws the chase,
With unperturbèd pace,
Deliberate speed, majestic instancy;
And past those noisèd Feet
A voice comes yet more fleet—
"Lo naught contents thee, who content'st not Me."
Naked I wait Thy love's uplifted stroke!
My harness piece by piece Thou hast hewn from me,
And smitten me to my knee;
I am defenseless utterly.
I slept, methinks, and woke,
And, slowly gazing, find me stripped in sleep.
In the rash lustihead of my young powers,
I shook the pillaring hours
And pulled my life upon me; grimed with smears,
I stand amid the dust o' the mounded years—
My mangled youth lies dead beneath the heap.
My days have crackled and gone up in smoke,
Have puffed and burst as sun-starts on a stream.
Yea, faileth now even dream
The dreamer, and the lute the lutanist;
Even the linked fantasies, in whose blossomy twist

I swung the earth a trinket at my wrist,
Are yielding; cords of all too weak account
For earth with heavy griefs so overplussed.
Ah! is Thy love indeed
A weed, albeit amaranthine weed,
Suffering no flowers except its own to mount?
Ah! Must— Designer infinite!—
Ah! must Thou char the wood ere Thou canst limn with it?
My freshness spent its wavering shower i' the dust;
And now my heart is a broken fount,
Wherein tear-drippings stagnate, spilt down ever
From the dank thoughts that shiver
Upon the sighful branches of my mind.
Such is; what is to be?
The pulp so bitter, how shall taste the rind?
I dimly guess what Time in mist confounds;
Yet ever and anon a trumpet sounds
From the hid battlements of Eternity;
Those shaken mists a space unsettle, then
Round the half-glimpsed turrets slowly wash again.
But not ere him who summoneth
I first have seen, enwound
With blooming robes, purpureal, cypress-crowned;
His name I know, and what his trumpet saith.
Whether man's heart or life it be which yields
Thee harvest, must Thy harvest fields
Be dunged with rotten death?

Now of that long pursuit
Comes on at hand the bruit;
That Voice is round me like a bursting sea:
"And is thy earth so marred,
Shattered in shard on shard?
Lo, all things fly thee, for thou fliest Me!
Strange, piteous, futile thing,
Wherefore should any set thee love apart?
Seeing none but I makes much of naught," He said,
"And human love needs human meriting,
How hast thou merited—
Of all man's clotted clay rhe dingiest clot?
Alack, thou knowest not
How little worthy of any love thou art!
Whom wilt thou find to love ignoble thee
Save Me, save only Me?
All which I took from thee I did but take,
Not for thy harms.
But just that thou might'st seek it in my arms.
All which thy child's mistake
Fancies as lost, I have stored for the at home;
Rise, clasp My hand, and come!"
Halts by me that footfall;
Is my gloom, after all,
Shade of His hand, outstretched caressingly?
"Ah, fondest, blindest, weakest,
I am He Whom thou seekest!

Thou dravest love from thee, who dravest Me."
Francis Thompson (1859-1907).
This Poem remains in the Public Domain.

328